Malice

An Agent Jade Monroe FBI Crime Thriller
Book 5

C. M. Sutter

AUTHOR'S NOTE

ABOUT THE AUTHOR

C.M. Sutter is a crime fiction writer who resides in the Midwest, although she is originally from California.

She is a member of numerous writers' organizations, including Fiction for All, Fiction Factor, and Writers etc.

In addition to writing, she enjoys spending time with her family and dog. She is an art enthusiast and loves to create handmade objects. Gardening, hiking, bicycling, and traveling are a few of her favorite pastimes. Be the first to be notified of new releases and promotions at: http://cmsutter.com.

C.M. Sutter
http://cmsutter.com/

Malice:
An Agent Jade Monroe FBI Crime Thriller, Book 5

Omaha's finest are baffled and the city is on edge following a rash of brutal murders of women, all killed in similar fashion. Local law enforcement believe a misogynistic killer is in their midst.

With little to go on, the central police department requests assistance from the Serial Crimes Unit of the FBI. Agents Jade Monroe and J.T. Harper are tasked to fly to Omaha and lend a hand.

Without any leads, the investigation stalls until a chance meeting between Jade and a stranger with memorable blue eyes turns the entire case on its ear. With the killer quickly losing patience, the investigation takes a turn for the worse. Not only are more of the city's ladies being targeted, but now Jade Monroe is on the killer's radar too.

Stay abreast of each new book release by signing up for my VIP e-mail list at:
http://cmsutter.com/newsletter/

Find more books in the Jade Monroe Series here:
http://cmsutter.com/available-books/

Chapter 1

Ed Tanner turned the knob on the truck's radio and silenced the Monday news report. Movement at the front door across the street had just caught his attention. His body stiffened involuntarily as he peered out the driver's side window with his hand cupped against his face to shield his identity. The family of four that had arrived thirty minutes earlier had driven away, but the Realtor remained inside.

Come on. What's the holdup? Quit your jibber-jabbering.

He continued to watch the door. Ed was surprisingly calm for someone about to commit a heinous crime, yet he was itching to get started. The door finally opened a second time, and a friendly looking exchange of words passed between the homeowner and the Realtor. The handshake sealed it, and the Realtor was finally leaving. He followed the sidewalk to his vehicle then turned back and waved as he climbed into his car.

Ed grasped the door handle of his banged-up truck. He watched the Realtor back out of the homeowner's driveway and leave the neighborhood, and he was dying to get started.

He waited an extra minute to be sure. He craned his neck left out of the truck window, then right, then left again. It was midday—a quiet time—and nobody was out and about or keeping tabs on their neighbors. No joggers, no dog walkers, and no prying eyes.

Ed flicked his wrist and checked the time—1:45. The rusty hinges creaked as he gave the driver's door a hard shove and stepped out of his truck. He jogged across the two-lane street to the sidewalk of the home with a clean, well-kept façade. It had to look pristine—it was on the market. The early October breeze caused the For Sale sign to sway slightly as it hung from the post in the yard. The sight of it fueled the fire building inside of Ed.

He looked both ways down that quiet street one last time before knocking. The coast was clear, and his mind was made up. There was no turning back. He slipped the fitted work gloves over his fingers and waited. The sound of approaching footsteps caused his ears to perk. He cocked his head toward the door and listened. It had to be a blitz attack. There wasn't time for words or, in her case, screams for help.

The surprised expression on her face gave Ed an adrenaline rush. It took only a second for her to realize she'd made a mistake, and it wasn't the Realtor returning because of something left behind. Now with the door pulled open widely, she stared at a stranger wearing gloves and a sinister glint in his eyes. She tried to slam the door, but he was halfway in, so closing it was impossible.

With a fierce thrust of both hands, Ed launched her backward and watched as she slid across the marble foyer and hit the wall with a thud. The woman scrambled to get her feet under her as Ed quickly closed the door and turned the dead bolt.

His voice was deep and slow. Each word was deliberate and clear. "There's nowhere for you to go. You can't outrun or outwit me, and I'm far stronger than you, but I will promise you one thing."

Her fingers gripped the carpet as she scooted backward into the living room. Her terror-filled eyes darted left and right. "Who are you, and why are you here? What do you want with me?"

"Why I'm here isn't your concern, and this isn't about you."

"Then what do you want? Do you promise not to hurt me?"

Ed took two steps toward her then reached for something at his side. The afternoon sun crept in through the half-opened blinds at the patio doors and caught the steel just right. The blade glistened in the rays when he pulled the knife out of its leather sheath.

She tried to scramble again, but he caught her by the right ankle. The knife sliced through her Achilles tendon. Blood pumped out with each beat of her heart. She screamed out her pain as she stood to run.

Ed smirked his response. "Sorry, but this isn't your lucky day. The only promise you'll get from me is today you're going to die."

The woman stumbled frantically through the house, coating the walls with bloody handprints. Ed followed her down the hallway to the master bedroom, where she tried to slam the door, but his foot blocked her efforts.

"You aren't going to come out of this alive, so just accept your fate."

Ed pushed the door forward against her body, and her blood-soaked feet slipped on the carpet as she lost precious ground. With a final shoulder blow, the door flew open, and her fate was sealed. She swung the nightstand lamp wildly in front of her. The sudden crack to Ed's forehead caught him off guard. Blood ran down the outer edge of his eyebrow and sent him into a rage.

"Now you're going to feel every slice, you stupid bitch." In seconds, he was on her and pushed her down on the bed. She thrashed with every ounce of strength left in her body, but she was no match for the stranger who had her pinned flat with his knees. He silenced her screams with his gloved left hand and met her frantic eyes with his own. Blood from his wound dripped in her face. Ed drew back the knife and, with a violent thrust, plunged it into her throat over and over again.

Chapter 2

The Realtor stood in the driveway and watched for the couple to arrive. It was Wednesday, and this was the first house of three he would show the newly married couple that day. When their blue Kia sedan turned the corner and headed his way on Prentice Street, Bob Flannery waved to get their attention. The husband pulled in and parked alongside Bob's car.

"Hey, guys, good to see you again," Bob said. The couple exited the car, and he shook hands with them. "You're going to love this place. It's in pristine condition, and according to the listing agent, the owner is very motivated to sell. She's moving out-of-state to be closer to her family."

Josh and Ann Grant took in the home's façade, the landscape, and the surrounding street as they stood next to the Realtor.

"The partially wooded lot gives the property a quiet, almost private feel, yet it isn't totally secluded," Ann said as she admired the yard.

"Wait until you see the inside. It's to die for. Shall we?" Bob led the way to the front door, where he entered the code on the lockbox and popped it open. He pulled out the key, slipped it into the keyhole, and turned the knob. The door remained locked.

He let out a quiet chuckle. "Sorry. The homeowner must have forgotten and locked the dead bolt by mistake. Give me one more second, please." He pulled the key out of the doorknob and slid it into the dead bolt then gave it a turn. "Here we go. After you." Bob pushed the door open wide, and the couple stepped over the threshold.

"What the hell?" Bob took in the sight ahead of them. Signs of a violent struggle were more than apparent. Shoe scuffs covered the white marble floor, telling them that somebody had scrambled across the entryway. Dried blood coated the floor and streaked the carpet. A side table had been toppled over, and the contents of a flowerpot were strewn across the living room. The houseplant, now wilted, lay among clumps of potting soil that had been ground into the once white rug.

"Oh my God, what happened here?" Ann Grant clenched her husband's forearm as she craned her neck around the corner to the right, where the kitchen was located. "And what's that smell?"

Bob ushered the couple back into the foyer, where they huddled together near the door. "Folks, please stay right here. Josh, call 9-1-1 while I check the rest of the house. This could be bad." Bob cupped his hand against the left side of his mouth and called out to the homeowner by name but got no response. He noticed more flies than would usually be seen in a well-kept home—especially that house. He had shown the property several times, and it was always clean and odor free. Having watched plenty of *CSI*-type TV shows, Bob knew what those flies meant.

Damn blowflies.

From the blood-streaked carpet, he knew where the crime scene led. He crept apprehensively down the hallway toward the bedrooms. Two doors were open, and the last was closed. With his back against the wall as he inched closer, Bob peeked around each open door to find nothing out of place. The only room left was the master at the end of the hall—the one behind the closed door where most of the blood was located. Bob reached for the knob.

Josh yelled out to Bob when he clicked off the call. "The police are on their way, and they said we should wait outside."

Bob released his grip on the doorknob, took in a deep breath, and stepped away from the room. He retreated to the foyer and mindfully stepped around the blood as he walked. "Let's sit on the porch bench and wait for the police. I really didn't want to look in that room, anyway." He tipped his head toward the front door.

Within minutes, an Omaha Police Department cruiser turned in to the driveway and parked behind Bob's vehicle. A fortyish looking man in relatively fit shape grabbed the top of the car door as he opened it and pulled himself out of the driver's seat. A second officer, who appeared to be of the same general age, exited the car from the passenger side.

"Did somebody here call in suspicious activity?" the first officer asked.

"That was me," Josh said as he extended his hand.

The name *Sgt. P. Franklin* was engraved on the pin attached to the officer's shirt pocket. "And you are?" Sergeant Franklin pulled his notepad and a pen from the car door pocket and lifted his mirrored sunglasses to the top of his forehead.

"My name is Josh Grant, and this is my wife, Ann. We met up with Bob Flannery, our Realtor, to tour this house. It looks like a violent attack happened in the foyer area."

Bob took over and explained the details. "I checked the first two bedrooms and didn't see anything out of the ordinary. That's as far as I got. The last door at the end of the hall is closed, so I can't tell you anything about that room, but there's a lot of blood leading down the hallway. We went back outside after Josh called 9-1-1."

"Did you touch anything, Mr. Flannery?" the second officer, a Sgt. D. Lyles, asked.

"Only the lockbox, the key, and the front door. Oh, and the master bedroom doorknob. Sorry about that."

Sergeant Franklin spoke up. "Okay, I want all of you to remain outside, but don't leave the premises. I have to clear the house, and then we'll talk." His radio squawked as he slipped on a pair of latex gloves. He reached the front door, spoke a few words with Sgt. Lyles and Dispatch, then pushed the door open. Lyles circled around to the backyard.

Sergeant Franklin—the *P* stood for Paul—took note of his surroundings as he entered the home. Even the initial signs told him nothing good had taken place there. He pulled out his sidearm from the shoulder holster, peeked around the right corner, and saw an empty kitchen. A jiggle of the patio door handle confirmed it was locked from the inside—nothing amiss there and no broken glass. Paul turned left at the hallway and followed the blood trail. The two open doors Bob had mentioned were directly ahead on his right. He swatted at the flies buzzing near his face as he inched toward the first room. The house reeked of death. The rusty odor of blood and decaying flesh was pungent— a dead body lay somewhere in that home.

From the quantity of blood ground into the carpet in front of that last door, Paul was certain he knew where the attack had ended, yet each room needed to be cleared. As he crept down the hallway, a quick glance into the first two bedrooms told him those spaces hadn't been entered. He pulled open the linen closet and bathroom door too then moved on. Finally, that last bedroom behind the closed door stood in front of him. With his head cocked and his ear against the door, he listened for sounds on the other side but heard nothing. Paul took in a deep, slow breath through his mouth and turned the doorknob with his left hand. He held the Glock 22 in his right.

With his body pressed against the hallway wall, he looked in through the narrow two-inch space between the door hinges and the framework. Blood stained the carpet next to the bed, and spatters covered the wall behind the headboard. A woman's bloody leg extended over the side of the bed, and a shoe suspended from her foot looked ready to drop. Sergeant Franklin covered his nose with the back of his hand and pushed the door open with the barrel of the gun. He took in the full scene of what had happened as he slowly scanned the room.

Cautiously, he approached the bed and took note of the bloodstained areas on the carpet. He'd watch his step to avoid disturbing any important evidence. Forensics might be lucky enough to come up with a shoeprint from blood transfer. Paul clicked his radio and called his partner, Don. "Hey, buddy, we've got a bad one in here. See anything unusual outside?"

"Not yet, but there's a small shed at the back I still have to clear."

"Okay, I'll make the call." Paul clicked the button and silenced his radio. With his body craned forward over her, he gave the woman a long thorough look. A wide pool of crimson blood, which appeared to be nearly dry, covered most of the quilt beneath her. She lay centered on the bed with her legs and arms splayed out, and her wide-open eyes wore a glaze of white film. Her mouth hung open as if she'd died while screaming out for help. Lividity was evident on the underside of her body and at her extremities. She had been lying there for a while, and the disgusting blowflies had made themselves at home on her corpse. A violent battle had taken place in that room, and from all appearances, she fought for her life right there on that bed.

She's been dead for at least a day or two.

Paul stepped back and checked the closet, beneath the bed, and the master bath. The screen on the bedroom window showed no signs of forced entry or exit.

With his radio engaged, he called the precinct for backup. "We need officers out here at the address on Prentice Street. Send some patrol units to set up barricades too. We have a female DB, and by the looks of her body and the room, there was definitely a fight to the finish. Get the coroner and forensic team out here right away." Sergeant Franklin clicked off and closed the door behind him. He'd leave that part of the investigation alone until the ME and forensic team arrived. He returned to the front of the house and cleared the family room, office, and garage. The homeowner's car—parked inside the two-car garage—was cold to the touch when he put the back of his hand on the hood. That vehicle hadn't been used by anyone recently.

Chapter 3

"What have we got, Sergeant Franklin?" Joe Torres opened the door of the medical examiner's van and stepped off the running board. He shielded his eyes from the sun glaring down on the cement driveway.

Paul made the introductions between the county ME and the Realtor, who stood to his right, and the shaken couple standing several feet away. He summarized what he saw in the master bedroom then excused himself when the forensic team headed for the front door.

Before entering the house, Paul called out to his partner, who had just returned from clearing the property's perimeter and the backyard shed. "Hey, Don, would you mind finding a slice of shade and taking their official statements while I walk the forensic team through the house?"

"Sure thing. Folks, right over here, please."

Paul waited on the porch as the ME and the forensic team of three covered their hands and feet before entering the house. "I've already done the initial sweep of the premises and found nothing other than here at the foyer, where the assault likely began, the path through the hallway, where it appears she'd tried to flee, and the master bedroom. Blood-smeared handprints cover both sides of the hallway wall."

Todd Mills, a member of the forensic team, added his opinion. "That in itself is odd if the victim was running for their life. Normally they'd head in a straight line for the safest area."

Paul nodded. "I think her body will explain that to you. Right this way. The homeowner met her death in the master bedroom. It's a gruesome scene, that's for sure."

The ME spoke up as they followed through the hallway with blue booties covering their feet. "She's obviously been dead a while. The presence of these damn blowflies and the odor—"

"I came to the same conclusion, Joe." Paul pointed at the master bedroom and stepped out of the way. "She's in there."

At Paul's back, heavy footsteps were coming quickly down the hallway. He glanced over his shoulder. Captain Kip Hardy was wearing a scowl and heading toward him.

Paul pushed off the doorframe of the linen closet, unfolded his arms, and stood up straight. "Cap."

"What the hell is going on here? A vicious murder in this storybook neighborhood? That's unheard of." Captain Hardy passed by Paul and entered the bedroom as he yanked a pair of gloves out of his pants pocket and slipped them over his sausage-sized fingers. "Holy shit." He stared at the woman's mutilated body lying on the bed then turned back to Paul. "Who is she? What's her story?"

"We haven't gotten that far, sir. The call came in only thirty minutes ago."

Hardy raked his fingers through his gray-tipped hair. "Get her name from that Realtor outside. Is she married, single, divorced, or in a bad relationship? Have Lyles pull up her name on the cruiser's computer and see if she has a jacket. Find out if there's ever been a police call to this house or a restraining order filed at this residence and, if so, against whom. Let's get the ball rolling." He twirled his index finger then pointed in the direction of the front door. Paul disappeared down the hallway. "What's her body telling you, Joe?"

The ME stepped away from the body momentarily and joined Captain Hardy near the master bath doorway. "I'll know more once I get her on the table, but under initial exam, I'd say she's been deceased for several days. The lividity showing on her underside tells me she was here, on this bed, and in this position when she died. Her rigor has almost subsided, which normally takes between thirty-six and forty-eight hours. Then of course, there's the smell of decomposition too."

Joe and Captain Hardy returned to the body. Joe pointed at the knife wounds. "Looking closely, you can see the maggots inside the injured areas. I'd venture to say they're in the second stages of development, meaning around two days in. She has a large number of stab wounds, primarily to the throat area. Take that however you'd like, but we both know that knife wounds are usually personal and indicate rage toward the victim. Your investigation will lead you in the right direction, just keep that in mind."

Captain Hardy sighed as he stared down at the woman's body. "Yeah, I know. What I need to find out now is what she did to piss off somebody that much and who committed the crime."

Paul reentered the bedroom as the captain was walking out. "I don't have much, boss, other than her name, age, and how long she's lived here." He looked down at his notes. "Her name is Sarah Cummings, she's thirty-seven years old, and she's lived at this address for nine years. She's squeaky clean, no priors, and unfortunately her husband was killed in a car accident last spring. Maybe that's why the house is for sale."

"Yeah, maybe." Hardy scratched his chin and let out a puff of air.

"We have no record of her ever filing a restraining order against anyone, and there's never been a police call to this residence."

"Okay, find out who her next of kin is and if there are children involved. Gather the officers out front and get them started on a neighborhood knock and talk. Interview everyone on both sides of this street, a block in each direction, as well as the street that runs behind these homes. A backyard neighbor may have seen someone walking through the yards without realizing that it was our suspect. I'm heading back to the station to do more digging, and I want an update call"—he checked his watch—"by five o'clock. Cut those people loose but get me that Realtor's card and the written statements that Lyles took. I want to review everything myself. You and Lyles are on point for the day. Andrews and Tyler are working another case, but I'll update them when I get back to the station. Make sure you two stay here until the house is sealed by Forensics."

"You've got it, Cap."

With the statements and Realtor's business card pressed into his pants pocket, Captain Hardy climbed into his cruiser and sped away.

Back at his desk twenty minutes later, and with a fresh cup of stale coffee, Kip Hardy began reviewing the statements provided by the Grants and Bob Flannery. He rubbed his furrowed brow as he read. Nothing seemed out of the ordinary except that a violent murder had taken place at that clean-cut thirty-seven-year-old woman's house in a no-crime neighborhood.

"What was going on in your life, Sarah Cummings, and who had it out for you?"

He tapped the Realtor's card against his desk then noticed that Bob Flannery worked for Citywide Realty, not the company on the For Sale sign. Hardy pressed the number four button on his desk phone.

"This is Detective Andrews. How may I help you?"

"Fred, it's Hardy. I need your input. Got a minute?"

"Sure, Cap, I'll be right there. Need a coffee?"

"Nah, don't bother. I already have a cup. It's gray and tastes like shit."

"Perfect. I'll grab myself one and see you in two minutes."

Chapter 4

A knock sounded on his office door, and Captain Hardy called out, "Come on in, Fred. Have a seat and explain to me how the real estate industry works."

"Going to start moonlighting?" The padded vinyl chair seat let out a gush of air when Fred planted himself on it.

Hardy smirked. "Wish I had that kind of time. Nah, you must know something about it, though. How long has Lisa been a Realtor?"

"It's going on fourteen years, and she still loves it. What do you need to know?"

"It's related to a case that came in this morning. Dead homeowner found by the Realtor who was about to show her house."

Fred groaned. "I'm guessing it wasn't from natural causes. That's the part that worries me about Lisa's job. You just never know who's going to show up to tour a house."

Kip slid Bob Flannery's card across his desk to Fred. "How does it work? He's employed at Citywide Realty, but the sign outside the house is from Scenic View Realty."

"Yeah, MLS is why. Any agency can show the house, not just the listing company. More Realtors involved means more potential people in the buyer's pool."

Kip grimaced after swallowing a gulp of his cold, stale coffee. "Damn that's bad. Anyway, what does MLS stand for again?"

"Multiple Listing Service, and it's a very effective selling tool. The greater Omaha area probably has fifty or more real estate companies listed online and in the yellow pages. The buyer's agent already has their client's wish list and can zero in on exactly what they're looking for in a home. Houses sell faster using MLS than when a homeowner puts a sign in their front yard. They just don't have enough resources at their disposal to sell it themselves."

"In other words, any agency or broker can show a house that's listed with MLS?"

"Exactly, but why would a real estate agent kill a homeowner? That's ass-backward. Selling houses is how the Realtor earns their commission, not by murdering the homeowner."

"I know. I'm just wondering how many Realtors you and Tyler are going to have to interview who showed the house on Prentice Street. I'm going to need names of every potential buyer who did a walk-through of that home. Maybe instead of killing a Realtor, the psycho went back and killed the homeowner."

Fred shook his head. "I think you're barking up the wrong tree, sir. As far as I know, the homeowners leave the premises when the houses are shown. That's why Realtors sometimes find themselves in sticky situations. They're in the house alone with who-knows-who."

"Family pictures placed throughout the house could tell the potential buyer who lives there."

Fred rubbed his chin. "True enough. Lisa says they encourage staging homes or putting away personal items, though."

Hardy pushed back his chair and stood then cocked his head toward the door. "Come on. Let's hit the vending machine and buy some decent coffee. We need to update Tyler on this case. I have a feeling we'll be working overtime tonight."

An hour later and with Brad Tyler on board, Hardy was interrupted by his ringing phone as he made calls to real estate agencies in Omaha and the surrounding suburbs. The captain glanced at the time on his wristwatch—5:00.

"Take a five-minute break, guys. This has to be Franklin with an update." The captain picked up the phone and placed it in the crook of his neck while he gathered a pen and a blank sheet of paper. "Hello, Paul. Tell me something useful."

"We're striking a big fat zero, Cap. We've conducted interviews with the residents up and down both sides of the street as well as the homes that run along the backyards. Nobody saw or remembered hearing anything unusual in the last few days. The neighbors on either side and across the street from Sarah's home said they don't pay much attention anymore. They're used to seeing people come and go because the house is on the market. I did find out where she worked, though."

Hardy lifted his pen. "Go ahead. I'm writing it down."

"She worked three days a week as a children's storyteller at the Millard library."

"You're kidding, right?"

"Sorry, but no. Sarah was an upstanding citizen and well liked, according to the neighbors."

"Damn it. I have a feeling this is going to be a tough case to crack. Any word on the next of kin and where they're located?"

"Looks like most of the husband's family is here in Nebraska," Paul said.

"And Sarah's?" The captain scribbled notes as Paul spoke.

"That took a little longer to track. We needed to find records of her maiden name first, which was Fleming. Apparently, she's from upstate New York, where she was born and raised. Her family hasn't been contacted yet. I thought I'd let you decide who would handle that, especially since Tyler and Andrews will end up as the lead investigators."

"Yeah, I'll take on that responsibility. Meanwhile, I'll get Tyler and Andrews to find out more on Scenic View Realty. It may be a privately owned company. Either way, whoever initially interviewed Sarah Cummings and walked the house before listing it might have more personal information about her intentions to sell the home. Has Forensics left yet?"

"They're wrapping up now and sealing the house. I thought you ought to know the latest, though."

Hardy leaned back in his chair and let out a long sigh.

Whatever Paul was about to say wouldn't be what he wanted to hear. "Go ahead and tell me."

"The press is here with the TV vans. They want to know what happened."

"Shit. That didn't take long. One of the neighbors probably leaked the information. You know the drill—ongoing investigation, yada, yada, yada. All they need to know is basic information, nothing else."

"Absolutely, Cap,"

"Okay, pack it up. Send Patrol back to their duties and gather all the statements from the knock and talks. I want to look them over. We're putting in overtime tonight, and that includes you and Lyles. Meet us in the conference room when you get back." Hardy clicked off the call as Tyler and Andrews returned. The captain jerked his chin toward the door while he gathered his notes, several pens, and cell phone. "This office isn't big enough for all of us. Let's work in the conference room." He turned his attention to Detective Tyler. "Brad, I want you to find out who owns Scenic View Realty and get them and the listing agent in here."

"You got it, sir."

Hardy addressed Fred as they walked the hallway. "Locate the nearest family members on the husband's side. They need to be interviewed tonight."

Fred nodded. "Do you think Lisa would be any help to us with her real estate knowledge?"

"Probably, but she's a civilian, and we aren't getting her involved. This may be a personal issue someone had against

Sarah Cummings that had nothing to do with her house being for sale. Maybe a disgruntled coworker had a problem with her."

"Where was she employed?" Brad asked.

"Would you believe at the Millard library? We'll learn more when Paul and Don get here with the statements from the neighbors, but we can't go off in a hundred different directions. Tonight, we'll focus on the husband's family and the people from Scenic View Realty and see where that leads us."

Chapter 5

Captain Hardy glanced at the clock to his right—6:00 p.m. It was time to make that inevitable call, first to the nearest family members of Sarah's deceased husband then to her own family in New York later.

Sergeants Lyles and Franklin had arrived at the station a half hour earlier. Two detectives, two sergeants, and a handful of officers gathered in the conference room and waited for the captain's return. He had stepped back into his office to make that heartbreaking call to the parents of Daniel Cummings.

The door opened twenty minutes later, and a hush overtook the conference room. The group of men looked at Hardy and checked his expression. Law enforcement personnel never got used to being the bearers of bad news.

The captain raked his hand through his hair and let out a long groan. "That was tough, especially since the Cummings family lost their own son just six months ago. I went ahead and called Sarah's folks too. They have the right to know sooner rather than later, but I didn't give them the

23

morbid details over the phone, only that she was deceased. They're catching the first flight in the morning. Fred, you're in charge of the in-laws interview. They'll be here in a half hour."

"Sure thing, boss. I'll have Dana text me when they arrive."

Hardy nodded and continued talking while Fred stepped out to tell Dana Branco, the desk sergeant, who he was expecting and when. "Okay, people, I'm hoping for a solid lead tonight. Go through every statement twice and see if a common name pops up in any of them. I want to know every friend and coworker that was in Sarah's inner circle. Lyles and Franklin, get to the Millard library and start interviewing her coworkers and supervisor. If they've left for the day, get their phone numbers and addresses and start banging on doors." Hardy turned to Brad. "What's going on with Scenic View Realty?"

"It's a privately owned real estate company, sir. The owner is a local man named—" Brad flipped the page in his notepad—"William David Stewart."

"Did you talk to him?"

"I have, and he's on his way in. He sounded a bit perturbed."

Hardy smirked. "Really, in what way?"

"Like we were interrupting his evening."

"Tough shit. A woman has been brutally murdered, and I'm sure we're going to inconvenience a lot of people. What about the listing agent who did the initial interview and walked the house?"

"He's coming in with Mr. Stewart. They should arrive any minute."

"Good. I want everyone else to keep working on getting names from the Realtors who showed Sarah's house."

Fred returned to the conference room and took his seat. "Cap, do you want to sit in on the interview with the Cummings family?"

"Yeah, I think I should."

A faint buzz sounded, and everyone looked toward Brad as he pulled out his cell phone from his pocket. He read the text aloud. "Dana says Mr. Stewart and Mr. Nolan, the listing agent, have arrived." Brad pushed back his chair and stood then headed toward the door. "Where do you want me to conduct the interview, sir?"

"Take them into that empty office near the lunchroom. Make sure you have your recorder along."

"Got it." Brad left the conference room and turned right at the hallway.

Hardy slapped his hands together. "Okay, let's get busy. Fred, we'll interview Mr. and Mrs. Cummings in my office." He tipped his wristwatch toward him. "They should be here soon. I'm heading back to my office to compile a list of questions. Bring them in when they arrive."

Fred nodded. "Will do."

Chapter 6

He pushed the cat away with the side of his leg. "Quit bothering me. I'm busy." Ed's index finger maneuvered the roller wheel on the computer's mouse as he viewed the listings of homes for sale. Four new ones had been added that day. "Here we go. This one is only a few miles away. I'll be back in time to watch a murder mystery on TV." Ed entered the address into the proper slot on the PeopleSeeker website that he had paid an overpriced monthly subscription fee to use. The homeowner's name, age, and phone number popped up.

A husband and wife, huh?

Ed gave that some thought. He'd never taken on two people at once, but since they were older, he was sure he could manage them both. He'd take the Taser.

Looks like this is your unlucky day, Bob and Gloria King. Says you're sixty-six and sixty-three years old. Downsizing, are ya? Now you don't have to worry about it. This should be a cakewalk.

The sheet listing the name of every Realtor who worked

for that agency lay to his right. It sat on the makeshift desk he had assembled from plywood and two used end tables from Goodwill. He tapped the names as he mulled over his choices.

I feel like being Chad Nolan tonight. Nice name if I do say so myself.

Ed dialed the number and waited as the phone rang at the King residence.

"Hello."

"Mrs. King?"

"Yes, this is she."

"Good evening, ma'am. This is Real Estate Agent Chad Nolan. I'm the agent in charge of double-checking everything on the real estate papers before it's considered a legal document. During my review of the home listing paperwork, I found an area where your and your husband's signatures were missing. It's imperative that we get your names on the contract so I can make the listing legal. If not, I'll have to pull it from the MLS until that's done. To avoid inconveniencing you folks, I can stop by in, say, fifteen minutes and get those signatures from you. It won't take but a minute of your time, and then we'll be all set."

"Of course, it isn't a problem at all. We're just sitting here in front of the TV, anyway. I'll turn on the porch light for you."

"Wonderful. Then I'll see you soon." Ed hung up, gathered the tools he'd need to render the husband and wife senseless, and placed them on the bench seat of his truck. Before climbing in, he pushed aside the stacked tires in the one-car garage and opened the small utility closet. A grin lit his face when he felt the shape of the sheathed knife on the back shelf. With that and several homemade garrotes in his hand, he climbed into the truck and turned the key. "Shit. I can't show up in a T-shirt and jeans." He killed the ignition then went back into the house and down the hall.

Five minutes later, and with a final look in the mirror, he nodded at his reflection and confirmed his attire was fine. Ed grabbed a pair of gloves and a stack of printer paper to use as a prop, climbed into the truck, and left. The deed would be complete in no time, and he'd be back at the cottage to relax in front of the television with a cold beer.

He turned down the street where the elderly couple lived. The sun had long set, and the families in that older neighborhood had likely drawn their curtains hours earlier. Ed turned in to the driveway, thankful that the only visible light was at the porch and most assuredly intended for him. The street in front of the house and driveway remained in the shadows. Ed double-checked the Taser's location—right sport coat pocket. The garrotes and gloves filled the left pocket. The knife sheath, attached to his belt, was hidden from view. With a final smoothing of his coat and several neck cracks from side to side, he was ready for whoever answered the door.

Sidelights, that's nice. That heads-up will tell me who to expect.

Ed rang the doorbell and waited. The sound of heavy shoes approaching told him Mr. King would be greeting him. There was no need to glance through the glass. One last feel in his right pocket gave him a sense of confidence.

The Taser would be ready when he was. He'd take Mr. King by surprise once he welcomed Ed through the door and closed it at their backs. Ed would make nice for a minute then zap the old man when his back was turned. The missus wouldn't pose a problem as long as she was taken off guard and away from a phone.

"Come on into the kitchen, Mr. Nolan." Bob King led the way, giving Ed ample opportunity to hit him in the back, but Ed needed to see where the wife was first.

He nodded and smiled a thank-you. "This won't take long, but I do need both of your signatures."

"Sure thing, Mr. Nolan." Bob called out to his wife in the family room, where she had been working diligently on a crossword puzzle. "Gloria, come in here. You have to sign these documents too."

"Hold on, I have to fill in this word before I forget it."

Bob shook his head and grinned. "She's hooked on crossword puzzles."

It took but a second for Ed to size up the woman when she rounded the corner. She was like a lamb heading to the slaughter. Her hands were empty, Bob was facing her, and neither had a clue. It was time to act. Gloria's smile turned to a look of confusion when she heard the electric buzz. Bob jerked forward, his knees buckled, and he hit the floor. A contorted, pained expression covered his face, and a deep grunt sounded from his chest.

"Oh my God, honey, what happened?" Gloria sprang to Bob's side then caught a glimpse of the Taser in Ed's hand. "What—"

"You're next, Gloria."

The kitchen chair fell to the floor as the fearful, screaming woman backed into it. Ed needed to silence her and quick, before a neighbor heard her cries for help. He pounced on her. She was zapped in the chest, and the impact of the Taser knocked her against the wall. Ed worked fast to keep them subdued before either regained consciousness. With the gloves stretched over his fingers, he grabbed a handful of napkins off the kitchen counter and jammed them into each of their mouths. He used the garrotes, knotted tightly around their necks, to keep their oxygen levels to a minimum. The couple would be able to take only shallow breaths. He would save the knife for last—it was his killing tool of choice. With the couple secure on the tiled floor, Ed turned the handle, leaned over the sink, and guzzled icy water from the kitchen faucet. He wiped his mouth with the back of his hand. "Now, where were we?"

Ed knelt over Bob, who was coming around. He watched as Bob's eyelids flickered, then opened, and panic took over his face. He began to flail.

"I wouldn't recommend that. It's hard enough for you to breathe the way it is, isn't it? You'll die within a minute or so if you don't relax."

A moan caused Bob to carefully turn his head to the right. Gloria lay several feet away in the same predicament.

Ed chuckled. "Aren't you two a sight? Check it out, Bob. Gloria is waking up. This should be good."

The woman's eyes bulged with fear. Tears rolled off her

cheeks and pooled in her ears. She frantically pulled at the garrote.

"Okay, enough is enough. Geez, you're bloodying your own neck." Ed tipped his wrist to check the time. "I don't want to miss my favorite TV show, so let's get started." He pulled out the twelve-inch bowie knife from the sheath and looked it over with admiration. He taunted the couple while he thumbed the razor-sharp blade. Without a second of hesitation, Ed plunged the knife into Bob's gut then turned and twisted the handle. Bob lurched forward then fell back. Several hard slams into Bob's chest buried the blade all the way to the staghorn handle. One final twist of the knife confirmed the man was dead.

Ed turned to Gloria, who was trying to stand. "Going somewhere?" He pulled back his arm and, with a quick forward thrust, caught her in the throat with the blade. Several more deep stabs almost took her head off. She slumped against the wall, and her head fell to her chest. Gloria slid to the floor and landed in a sitting position. Blood covered the tan tiles and followed the grout lines like water in canals. Ed studied the scene closely. Both husband and wife wore garrotes tightly secured around their necks, although Gloria's was well hidden within the devastation at her throat. Blood spots dotted the whites of their eyes, and their faces already showed a hint of blue. Their open mouths revealed the napkins jammed deep inside. Ed slowly scanned the area. He had walked only into the foyer and kitchen, but he needed to make sure nothing was left behind.

Yep, looks good. I'm out of here.

He pocketed everything he had brought inside, turned the outer doorknob with his sleeve, and made a clean, quiet exit.

Chapter 7

"Is this going to take long?" William Stewart was agitated as he plopped down on the large leather chair in that vacant office.

Brad pointed his finger and wiggled it at the other side of the desk where two guest chairs were located. "Let's start out on the right foot, shall we? You're on that side of the desk, and I get the leather chair. I'm conducting the interview, got it?"

William sneered. "Why are we here, anyway?" He rounded the desk and took a seat on one of the two uncomfortable looking chairs.

"You have somewhere better to be, Mr. Stewart, or are you just nervous around law enforcement?" Brad turned to Chad Nolan. "And how about you? Are you going to make it, or will you have a meltdown too?"

Chad rubbed his brow. "I'm good, just wondering why we were called in, that's all."

"You are the listing agent for the home at 439 Prentice Street, correct?"

"That's correct."

"And you, Mr. Stewart, own the agency?"

"Of course I do, but it's a corporation, not an agency, and you already know that or I wouldn't be here."

Brad chuckled. "Humph, you're a smart guy. Were either of you aware that the homeowner of that residence was murdered and found in the house earlier today by another Realtor?"

With his head lowered and his fist against his mouth, Mr. Stewart mumbled something under his breath.

"What was that? Care to share?" Brad leaned forward against the desk.

"I saw something on the local news and recognized the address, that's all. I've never met the woman, but yes, it is unfortunate. That still doesn't explain why I'm here."

"Or me," Chad piped in.

"You're here to tell me more about Sarah Cummings. I'm going to turn on this recorder and tape our conversation. I want to know everything from the moment she called your office and set up the appointment to have Scenic View Realty list her house."

William cocked his head toward Chad. "I may own the company, but you're the listing agent. It looks like you have the floor."

Brad pulled out his notepad and a pen then clicked on the recorder. "It's seven o'clock on the evening of October fourth. Go ahead, Mr. Nolan, and tell me everything you remember from the initial phone call with Sarah Cummings."

Chad let out a long sigh, pressed his palms against his temples, and began. "She called about four weeks ago, so every detail of our conversation isn't fresh in my mind."

Brad nodded.

"She said she was looking to sell her home before it got too cold outside. She mentioned knowing that the market slows down in winter, especially during the holidays. She wanted a quick sale and was very motivated."

"Then what?"

"Then I made an appointment to view the home and explain our procedure. I—"

William interrupted. "Why do I have to be here? I don't know anything about Chad's interaction with that woman."

Brad leaned forward and clicked off the recorder. "Because you own the company. Have you pissed off somebody recently?"

William snickered. "Doubt it. Everyone loves me. I don't have a single enemy."

Brad took in a slow breath. The man was wearing on his nerves. "Stay still and keep quiet. You'll get your turn to talk when this interview is over." Brad pressed Record again and gave Chad a nod.

"Like I said, I set up an appointment for the next day to walk through her home. She seemed anxious to get started."

"As if she feared something or someone?"

"Nah, I didn't get that impression. Just that she wanted to move on. I understood more the next day."

"Go on."

"The house was in great shape, three bedrooms, two and a half baths, a bookcase-walled library, and—"

Brad clicked off the recorder again. "Mr. Nolan, I'm not

trying to buy the house. I want to hear about the interaction you had with Sarah Cummings. Just tell me everything you remember about that." With his finger about to press the record button again, Brad was interrupted by William's ringing phone. "Seriously?"

"Give me one minute. I'm an important businessman, you know. People seem to need me at all hours." With his phone cupped in his hand, he answered it. "What's up, honey?"

Brad rolled his eyes and groaned.

"What? Are you shitting me? Yes, I know which house you mean. It was just listed this morning. Okay, I'm on my way."

"What's going on, Mr. Stewart?" Brad pushed back his chair. The side of the conversation he'd just heard indicated that something bad had taken place.

Captain Hardy burst through the door. He pointed at William, who had just stood up. "Neither of you are going anywhere just yet. Brad, I need a word with you in the hallway."

Brad rounded the desk, walked out, and closed the door behind him. "What's going on, boss?"

"Another murder. Patrol is taping off the neighborhood as we speak. More units, the ME, and Forensics are on their way."

Brad tipped his head toward the closed door. "Let me guess. The house is for sale, and the listing agency is Scenic View Realty."

"You nailed it, and we've got to roll. I have the Cummings

family interview covered with Jones for now, and Dixon can keep an eye on those two."

"Just a heads-up, boss. Mr. Stewart already got a call about the murder. I'm guessing it was from his wife."

Hardy groaned. "I don't need him muddying the waters. I'll have Dixon pull their phones."

Two cruisers with lights engaged entered the neighborhood ten minutes later. In the lead, Hardy's vehicle snugged up against the curb near the yellow crime scene tape. The other cruiser fell in behind his. What appeared to be a normally quiet, modest neighborhood of middle-class homes was now lit up with red and blue flashing lights atop the patrol cars that blocked the street. The ME and forensic vans sat side by side in the homeowner's driveway.

Hardy exited his vehicle and approached a patrol officer standing in front of the crime scene tape. He nodded a hello. "What have we got in there, Mike?" Hardy jerked his chin toward the well-lit house.

Andrews and Tyler climbed out of the second cruiser and crossed the street to join the captain.

"I've been told it's a pretty horrific scene, Captain, although I haven't been inside the residence myself. They're trying to preserve evidence, you know, and keep the foot traffic to a minimum."

"Absolutely. Older husband and wife?"

"That's the word from the house. Both have multiple stab wounds and garrotes around their necks."

"Garrotes? What the hell is going on this week? What's the crime rate in this neighborhood?"

"Not much of any as far as I know, and I've never been called out here. The neighborhood consists of older folks and middle-class bungalows. I don't understand it, boss."

"Well, neither do I, but I intend to and damn quick." Hardy gave the officer a pat on the shoulder. "Keep your eyes peeled, Mike."

"I will, sir."

Hardy, Andrews, and Tyler entered the home to find the crime scene spread out in the kitchen, only ten feet beyond the foyer. Finding a clean spot on the tan-colored tile floor would take effort.

Constant clicking came from the camera held by Tony Myers, one of the forensic technicians. Stan Fleet, the forensic department head, gave Hardy a nod. "Quite a scene, Captain. My initial take is that the perp was allowed into the home. There aren't signs of forced entry at any doorway. The foyer is undisturbed, meaning the attack didn't happen until the couple and the killer were in the kitchen. It seems like all was well until the blitz attack took place where the bodies lay."

"Nobody is going to allow someone to put a garrote around their neck without a fight. They had to have been subdued."

"Good point, Captain, and they were." Joe Torres looked over his left shoulder at Hardy standing behind him. "I found evidence of Taser burns on both victims. The husband had burns on his back, and the wife had burns on her chest. That's telling me the husband went down first, hence, a blitz attack from the back to knock him out momentarily."

Hardy added. "Right, and the wife got it in the front as she entered the kitchen. That's why her body is closer to the family room."

"Exactly, sir."

"TOD, Joe?" Brad asked.

"Thirty minutes ago, give or take a few."

Hardy let out a long whistle. "Their bodies aren't even cold yet. The bastard could be hiding in the brush, watching this scene unfold in front of him."

"Boss, do you want me to get a few units out searching on foot?" Andrews asked.

"No, but they should be banging on every door on this block." Hardy waved him on. "Get them started."

"Yes, sir." Andrews headed for the front door.

Hardy approached one of the first officers at the scene. "Who called it in?"

"A woman who lives three doors down. According to her statement, she was driving home from dinner with friends and noticed that the front door was ajar. She said normally she wouldn't have seen anything at all, but tonight the porch light was on. She stopped, got out, and went up to the house to see if everything was all right." He pointed toward the couple. "That's how she found them."

Hardy rubbed his chin. "So normally the porch light isn't on. That means they were definitely expecting someone. Our job is to find out who. Come on, guys. Let's go back to the station and work through this. Somehow, some way, there's a connection between these folks and Sarah Cummings." Hardy's cell rang as they were about to leave. He dug in his pants pocket and pulled it out. "Lyles, did you learn anything at the library?"

Don chuckled. "That was funny, sir."

Silence filled the other end of the phone line.

"Sorry, boss. Anyway, yes, we may have a lead. Paul and I are headed back to the station. We were told a Liz Manthis, one of Sarah's coworkers, wasn't too fond of her, and they argued often. Several library employees actually heard threats from Liz aimed at Sarah."

"Go pick her up for questioning. I want to have a word with her myself. There's been another murder."

Chapter 8

"Kind of late for your phone to be ringing, isn't it?" Amber jumped off the couch and retrieved it from the breakfast bar.

"Huh? What about my phone?"

Spaz hissed his disgust at the interruption. He had been comfortably sleeping on Amber's lap.

I sat up, rubbed my eyes, and reached for the cell phone in Amber's outstretched hand. "My throat feels like sandpaper. I was snoring, wasn't I?"

"Yeah, like a freight train."

I grabbed the nearest pair of reading glasses and put them on.

Amber smirked. "Those are mine."

"I don't care, at least I can see through them." I squinted at the screen. "Oh no, it's Spelling. I hope it isn't bad news." I gave the wall clock over the kitchen table a quick check— 10:07 p.m. After a quick gulp of warm beer from the half-empty glass on the coffee table, I answered the call. "Evening, boss. Is everything okay?"

"Sorry for the late hour, Jade, but I have a confidential question for you that I don't want to discuss tomorrow morning in front of the group."

I felt a temporary sense of relief even though I had no idea what was coming next. "Sure, go ahead."

"Do you, as his partner, feel that J.T. is ready to go back out in the field?"

I took in a deep breath and thought carefully before answering. "Physically or mentally?"

"Both. Cam has filled J.T.'s shoes for the last six weeks, but it's hard on his family life. He was also injured in that fiasco with Carden Vetcher."

"I know, boss, and Maria as well. As far as running, jumping, or climbing if need be, I'd say maybe not quite yet. Those Pirelli goons did a number on him. On a day-to-day basis, without that extra physical effort, yeah, sure. The doctor has already cleared him for normal activity."

"And mentally?"

I finished the last two swallows of beer while I pondered that question. "Boss, J.T. is a strong, level-headed agent. He knows what this job entails."

"He also saw his former partner tortured and murdered right in front of his eyes, not to mention the physical and mental anguish Julie went through. J.T. carries a lot of guilt even though he tries to hide it."

"Counseling has helped both J.T. and Julie. I believe he's ready to get back out there, sir. I know he hates sitting behind a desk all day, and he feels bad that Cam has taken over his out-of-town responsibilities for the last six weeks."

"So, if a situation occurred and your life depended on J.T., do you think he's up for the challenge?"

"If we were running for our lives, we'd depend on our weapons to get us through. Anything else, absolutely. I trust J.T. one hundred percent."

"Good answer, Monroe. That's exactly what I wanted to hear. I just received a call from Captain Kip Hardy of the Omaha Central Police Department. He's an old friend of mine who's asked for our assistance. There have been three similar murders this week, two being just tonight. They need this nipped in the bud before another killing takes place. You and J.T. are heading to Nebraska tomorrow. I'll update everyone during our morning meeting. Get some sleep, Jade, and thanks."

"Thank you, sir. Good night."

As I lay in bed a half hour later, I was filled with both hope and worry. J.T. was chomping at the bit to get back in the field, yet would those nightmares he endured after seeing Curt's murder and Julie's abuse come back with a vengeance? I let out a deep sigh.

I guess time will tell.

I reached for the switch on the table lamp and turned it off. With a few punches of my pillow to fluff it, I closed my eyes and said a prayer for J.T.

I woke to what felt like a frown on my face. I squinted toward the window. A sliver of sun found an opportunity to pierce a laser ray right between my eyes. I sat up in bed and groaned. The blackout curtains weren't completely closed, and the rising sun took full advantage of the opening.

"Damn it, I could have slept for seven more minutes."

With the blankets tossed back, I grudgingly climbed out of bed and knotted my robe belt around my waist. I stumbled down the hallway to start the coffee then realized Amber had set the auto-start feature last night. A full pot of piping hot coffee waited in the carafe in front of me.

"Bless you, Amber, and bless the person who invented coffee." I reached for my favorite cup, a chipped one, from the cabinet above the dishwasher.

"Talking to yourself?" Amber chuckled when she reached the kitchen and grabbed her own favorite cup from the cabinet.

"Isn't coffee amazing?" I took a seat at the breakfast bar to enjoy a leisurely cup of the brew before I began my frenzied routine to get ready for work and actually make it there on time. Traffic into the Milwaukee suburbs was always unpredictable.

I finished the first round of coffee and poured a second cup to take into the bathroom with me.

"Have time for breakfast?"

"I'm good with a couple of raisin English muffins."

"Okay, just yell when you want me to pop them into the toaster."

I stopped and hugged Amber before I headed down the hallway. "I love you, girl."

"And I love you. Now get showered before you're late for work."

"Yes, Mom."

I gobbled down my muffins twenty-five minutes later

after finger styling my damp hair. It would dry during my drive to Glendale.

"Good luck in Omaha, Jade, and text me when you have a chance."

"I will, hon. Gotta brush my teeth and hit the road."

"Okay, I'm leaving now. Talk to you later, and be safe."

"Always."

Amber kissed Spaz and headed out the door.

After a thirty minute drive, I reached our satellite office at 7:52—eight minutes early. I grinned as I rounded the back to our parking area until I noticed that J.T.'s car wasn't in his slot. He usually arrived at work before me since his commute was a short ten minutes. My heart began to race until I heard the familiar chugging sound of him driving in second gear but going only ten miles per hour. I turned to see his new V8 six-speed Camaro stalling out. I laughed when he coasted into his parking spot and killed the engine.

"What's the problem? Do you need more lessons?"

He climbed out of the low-slung seat and gave me a frown. "I don't know how I ever let you talk me into buying this hot rod."

"Because a four-cylinder base model Corolla is so much cooler?"

"This car is a lot of work, especially in heavy traffic. I-43 is like a parking lot."

"Accident?"

J.T. shrugged. "Maybe. All I know is that my knees are throbbing."

I felt an instant twinge of regret. I razzed J.T. so much

about getting a manly car after the Corolla burned in that warehouse fire that I gave no thought to the low seat or the clutch and his injured body. With his knees still healing from the constant abuse he endured from the Pirelli brothers, I realized now that a sports car with a manual transmission was the wrong choice. Manuals were a lot of fun but also a lot of work, especially in stop-and-go traffic. In hindsight, I knew he'd agreed to buy the Camaro only to get me off his back.

"J.T., I'm sorry."

He raised his brows. "You should be." He grinned. "About what?"

"The car. I feel terrible. You've never complained about your knees hurting before."

"Nah, don't sweat it. I'll learn how to drive that beast sooner or later. Some days my knees hurt more than others. It comes and goes."

I hoped whatever our task was going to be in Omaha wouldn't involve overexertion on J.T.'s part. His broken jaw was healed, and the wires were removed only four days ago. His physical therapy sessions had gone from twice a week to three times a month, yet now I was second-guessing the overly confident conversation I had with Spelling last night. I wondered if J.T. was truly ready.

"What's with the face?"

"Who, me?" I gave him a side-eye glance.

J.T. slid his ID badge through the slot and pulled the back door open after hearing the click.

"Yeah, you. You're wearing a weird look."

"Hogwash. I just worry about your well-being, that's all."

J.T. grinned again. "Thanks for caring, partner."

We followed the hallway to the conference room, where our usual morning update awaited us. That morning would be slightly different since I already knew J.T. and I were heading out as soon as the meeting wrapped up.

"Good morning, agents."

We responded as we pulled out our usual pad of paper and pens. Spelling gave me a few extra seconds of eye contact before he began.

"A request for our assistance came in last night."

"That's odd," Val said. "Who calls an FBI satellite office at night, and who would have answered?"

"Well, the call would have been kicked back to the downtown office, but this was a call to my cell phone. A personal friend, Captain Kip Hardy of the Omaha Central Police Department, asked for our help." Spelling waited until each of us stopped writing and returned our focus to him. "It appears that there have been three very similar murders just this week. Two of the deaths were a retired husband and wife and the other was a widowed woman who lived alone. They haven't gotten the ME's reports back yet, but they think the woman was murdered on Monday. She was discovered on Wednesday."

"Just yesterday?" Maria asked.

"That's correct, and the husband and wife were murdered last night. Several people have been interviewed and let go. There were no eyewitnesses, weapons, or unidentified prints found in either case. Normally we wouldn't be called in so quickly, but the fact that all three victims had nearly identical stab wounds and were murdered in their homes leads the PD to believe they have a serial killer roaming the streets of Omaha."

"Any personal connection between the victims?" J.T. asked.

"Not at first glance. Like I said, these are very new cases, but Captain Hardy doesn't want to wait around for more murders to take place before asking for our assistance. One other thing, in both cases the homes were for sale by the same realty company."

"That's a new one and maybe something we can work with," Cam said. "When do we leave?"

I shot a quick glance at Spelling then returned my attention to the notes I had taken.

"Jade and J.T. are leaving after the meeting. If anyone has concerns with that, speak up now."

The room fell silent.

J.T. jerked his head toward me and grinned. I returned the smile.

Cam leaned back in his chair and let out a relieved sigh. "It's about damn time."

Chapter 9

I drove to our hangar at the airport. It was the least I could do. I was horrified to realize that J.T. actually hated his Camaro.

The flight from Milwaukee to Omaha would be an easy hour and a half. We got comfortable as the plane took to the sky, yet J.T. seemed quieter than I would have expected. "You're happy to be back in the field, aren't you?"

"Sure I am. That's saying Spelling is confident that I'm good to go."

"And are you? Confident, I mean?"

J.T. stared out the window as if deep in thought. I looked out too. Farm fields dotted the landscape in rich October tones of yellow, brown, and green.

"J.T.?"

"Curt's brother lives in Omaha, you know. Maybe I should stop in and see how he's doing."

"That would be nice if there's time." I reached across the table that separated us and covered J.T.'s hand with my own. "Curt's death wasn't your fault. There was nothing

49

you could have done to change what happened."

J.T. frowned and turned his head to the window again. "Isn't that our job, Jade, as FBI agents, to change things and stop the bad guys from killing people? What about justice?"

"Carden Vetcher and the Pirelli brothers won't see freedom for quite some time. Isn't that a form of justice?"

"Sure, but not enough. Try telling Curt's mother and brother that being locked up in prison is justice." J.T. groaned and pressed his temples. "I'm so sorry, Jade. You know all this firsthand. I completely forgot about your dad while I sat here and wallowed in guilt."

I unfastened my seat belt and stood. "Want something to drink?" I needed to regroup and think of a different topic of conversation before we both started to cry.

"Yeah, a soda is fine, thanks."

I grabbed two out of the jet's mini fridge and took my seat. "Come on, enough sad sacks. Let's brainstorm this new case even though we don't have much information."

We landed at Eppley Airfield without incident at eleven o'clock. The central police department was a short five and a half miles away. We deplaned on the tarmac and entered the building on the lower level.

"Pick out the most comfortable rental car you can think of because that's the one we're getting."

J.T. gave me a smirk. "Humph. That's the best idea you've had in six weeks."

I punched his arm. "Smart-ass."

We viewed the available vehicles from the list behind the counter.

"Look, they have Corollas." J.T. elbowed me.

"They have Camaros and Mustangs too, wise guy."

"Yeah, I'll pass on both of them. How about the Explorer?"

"Sure, it's a Ford."

J.T. climbed in behind the wheel and grinned. "Man, I forgot what having room felt like." He tilted the seat back a smidge, adjusted the mirrors, and pulled out of the rental lot. "Lead the way, copilot."

We reached the central police station on South Fifteenth Street twenty minutes later and grabbed a parking spot near the front of the nondescript concrete building.

J.T. tipped his head toward the glass-walled entrance. "Let's make our introductions and go from there. If they have another place for us to park, I'll come out and move the car later."

"Sure thing."

J.T. held the front door open as I passed through. He followed at my back. A long counter with a thick Plexiglas wall separated us from the people behind it. Three uniformed officers sat on the other side. A large box built into the counter enabled items to be passed back and forth between visitors and them.

"Can I help you folks?"

I noticed the name tag worn by a middle-aged officer who approached the window separating us. T. Hillman gave us a quick smile.

"Yes, thank you. We're here from the FBI's Serial Crimes Unit to see Captain Hardy."

"Credentials, please."

We dropped our badges in the box, and he pulled it toward him.

He compared the images on our badges to our faces. I felt like a monkey in the zoo even though we had gone through that same process many times before. He placed our badges back in the box and slid it to us. "Have a seat, agents. I'll see if the captain is available. There's a refreshment stand at your back in the visitors' lounge. Make yourselves comfortable." Officer Hillman disappeared around a door on his side of the counter.

I filled a plastic cup with water and took a seat. J.T. flipped through a car magazine while we waited.

Officer Hillman returned to the counter and called to us through the intercom. "Captain Hardy is watching an interview in observation room one. He said you're welcome to sit in on it if you'd like. It's related to the case you're here for."

I gave J.T. a nod. "Sure thing. Lead the way."

We followed Officer Hillman down several corridors until we saw the signs for observation rooms one through four. We stopped in front of the first door.

"Here you go, agents. The captain is inside."

We thanked Officer Hillman, and he turned back the way we came from. I gave the door several knocks, and a deep voice on the other side said to come in. J.T. and I entered the standard-sized observation room that held three chairs, one of them occupied by a stocky man with a hint of gray in his hair. I guessed him to be in his fifties. He reached forward, silenced the intercom, stood to introduce himself, and extended his hand.

"Captain Kip Hardy here. Nice to meet you, Agents—"

"Monroe and Harper, respectively, sir."

He chuckled. "Please, you outrank me. No need for formalities. I just appreciate Phil allowing you agents to come to our assistance so quickly. I know it's a bit unusual, but three victims have met their deaths in the last four days. That's highly unusual, even for a city our size."

It sounded strange to hear SSA Spelling being referred to as Phil. "You must know SSA Spelling well," I said.

"Sure do. We went to college together in Madison. He was a year ahead of me in school but took time off after graduation to sow his wild oats before joining the police academy. We did that together too, but eventually, after being on the Milwaukee police force for two years, I was offered a nice position in Omaha. We each found our own place in life—mine here as the police captain and Phil as a Supervisory Special Agent with the FBI." Captain Hardy let out a long whistle and shook his head. "If you would have known him then"—he chuckled again—"who would have thought?"

J.T. gave Hardy a quick grin then tipped his head toward the mirror. "Officer Hillman said this interview is related to the case at hand?"

Hardy blew out a puff of air. "Yeah, evidence at the murdered couple's house leads us to believe this man is somehow involved." The captain pointed at the empty chairs. "Have a seat, agents."

"Thank you, s—" I caught myself before saying *sir*.

"Cap will do, Agent Monroe."

"Then please call me Jade."

He nodded and pointed through the glass. "That's Detective Fred Andrews interrogating Chad Nolan. Chad is a real estate agent at Scenic View Realty. I had him and the owner of the company here just last night for an interview."

"Why Chad Nolan in particular?" J.T. asked.

"He was the listing agent for the home of the first victim. We brought him in to see if there was any information he could give us about the conversation he had with the woman on the day he toured her home."

"So why is he here again?"

"Several of our detectives went back to the King home this morning to search for anything that could give this case a pulse. We had nothing to go on at that point and wondered if there was a connection of some kind with the first victim, Sarah Cummings, and the couple, Bob and Gloria King. Wouldn't you know, Detective Andrews found a name written down on the edge of a newspaper crossword puzzle." Hardy jerked his head to his right. "It was his."

"That is interesting. What does he have to say about it?"

"He swears he's never shown that couple's house or had a phone conversation with them. The listing agent on the King home was Gary Gibson."

"So, the police think that particular real estate company is somehow linked to the murders?" J.T. asked.

Captain Hardy rubbed his forehead. "I'll be honest, agents, we're at a loss. It could be totally coincidental that both houses were for sale by the same company. There weren't any witnesses or a motive of any kind that we've found in either case. The first victim was squeaky clean, and so was the couple from last night. We did knock and talks throughout both neighborhoods and came up empty. Nobody saw or heard anything unusual. Sergeants Lyles and Franklin interviewed coworkers from the library where Sarah Cummings worked. One woman in particular was reported to dislike Sarah. She was overheard making threats."

My curiosity was piqued. "Then what?"

Hardy shook his head. "We hauled her in last night. Sounded like the typical argument between coworkers, spouting off with no real intentions of anything. The conflict was about work hours, so we cut her loose."

"Okay, we need to have a better handle on this. Everything seems a bit unorganized at the moment. How about a meeting with your crew when the interview with Chad Nolan is over?" I suggested.

"That sounds really good, Jade. Thanks."

We got comfortable as Hardy clicked on the intercom. With our notepads and pens in hand, we listened to what Chad Nolan had to say.

"Maybe Gary wasn't doing a good job for them. You said my name was written on a newspaper. Someone in the house could have jotted it down after seeing our real estate ad."

"It's possible."

I turned my head toward Hardy. "The man has a point. Let's get Gary Gibson in here too."

Chapter 10

"I'm telling you, sir, something isn't right. Jackie doesn't just leave her house with all of the groceries sitting on the kitchen counter. I saw the mess through the patio doors. I'm worried sick that something may have happened to her."

The sergeant at the Southeast Omaha precinct took notes while the young lady sat alongside his desk. "Miss, it's been how long?"

Tara Lamar stared at her lap and wrung her hands. "Only a few hours, but we were supposed to have lunch together, and when she didn't show up or answer her phone, I drove to her house."

"And you found what?"

"The door locked. I rang the bell a million times and called her phone. I didn't hear it ring inside the house, so I started looking through windows. That's when I saw the groceries on the countertop. The ice cream had melted and was seeping through the grocery bag to the floor. Jackie wouldn't do something that weird. She's a clean freak, and you never know when somebody is going to make an appointment to see her house."

"And this clean freak is how old?"

"Twenty-seven. I know, she's old enough to do as she likes, but I've called everyone in our circle of friends, and nobody has spoken to her since ten thirty."

"But her car was gone, correct?

"Yes, that's correct."

"Miss Lamar, we can't file an official missing persons report yet since your friend hasn't been gone long enough. Finish filling out this paperwork, and if she's still unaccounted for by tomorrow, come back and we'll initiate a formal investigation. It's all we can do at this point. Keep trying to reach her, though, and call me tomorrow either way." Sergeant Bateman slid his card across the desk to her. "There's my name and my desk phone number. Keep me posted."

"Thank you. I will."

Sergeant Bateman watched from the window as the young woman left the building and disappeared into the parking lot. He hoped she'd find her friend safe and sound.

Chapter 11

Lunchtime was over, and the officers, sergeants, and detectives filed back into the building and gathered in the large conference room on the third floor. Fourteen of us sat around the walnut veneered table. J.T., Captain Hardy, and I sat at the far end, facing the group.

"Okay, guys, let's quiet down. I need everyone's attention. These recent murders are very disturbing and far from what we consider normal for our community. With that said, and nothing to go on yet, I called in the assistance of the FBI." Hardy made the introductions between the group and us.

Murmurs sounded in the room. "Why the FBI, and why so soon? We've barely had time to get this investigation under way, sir."

I sensed a hint of resentment in Sergeant Lyles's voice. I understood how he felt and had dealt with many police forces in the past who thought we were stepping on their toes. "Cap, if I may?"

"Go ahead, Jade."

"First, I'd like to say it's nice to meet everyone, and I hope with our joint efforts we can nip this killer in the bud. We don't want the death toll to climb, and that's why the captain called us in. Three murders committed by the same person labels him or her a serial killer. My partner and I are from the Serial Crimes Unit of the FBI, and our job is to apprehend serial killers and bring them to justice. Before I was in the FBI, only a short year ago, I was a sergeant at the sheriff's office in the town I live in." I gave Lyles a nod to ease his insecurity toward us. "I've been on both sides of the situation you men are facing now. We aren't here to step on any toes, and believe me, I've felt the same way you guys do now. But I've also been snubbed by local police because they didn't want to share the case. Keep in mind, no case we're brought in on is about us or the police force requesting our help. It's about the innocent victims and getting the bad guy off the street. We're on the same team." I gave the room a minute to digest what I'd said, then Lyles spoke up.

"Do you mind if we call you Jade and J.T.?"

"We don't mind at all. So, shall we begin?"

Hardy cracked his knuckles then passed out sheets of printer paper to everyone. He slid a box of pens down the center of the table.

"We're having a test?" Franklin asked half-jokingly.

"Nope, but we need to be better organized so we can solve this case. I want everyone who had any involvement in the calls about these murders, beginning with Sarah Cummings, to write down what role they played, who they spoke with, and what the outcome was."

"That's already documented," Franklin said as he turned toward me.

J.T. took over. "Believe it or not, not every detail ends up in police reports. Officers get interrupted during interviews, witness accounts may not be written down exactly as they were spoken, everyone is too frazzled, or the scene is too hectic at that moment for reports to be accurate. The best thing you can rely on is your memory of events. What you write can be compared to the police report you filed. I've often seen discrepancies."

Franklin smirked. "So this is a test?"

"It's a good self-check but also a way for us to make sure nothing was overlooked before we proceed. We're in this together, Sergeant Franklin."

Hardy spoke up. "Take thirty minutes to write down what you remember and then we'll start brainstorming and create a plan of action."

Hardy's cell phone rang, and he stepped out to the hallway to answer it. I watched as he paced ten feet in one direction, turned, and paced the same distance back. He looked anxious. The call was short, then he dropped his phone into his front pants pocket. He rapped on the glass wall and waved J.T. and me toward him.

"Excuse us, guys." We pushed back our chairs and exited the room to join the captain in the hallway.

"What's up, Cap?" J.T. asked.

"That was the desk sergeant downstairs. Apparently Mr. and Mrs. Fleming, the parents of Sarah Cummings, just arrived from Albany, New York. They're waiting for me to tell them what happened to their only child."

"How much do they know?"

Hardy wrinkled his brow and answered with a sigh. "Only that she's deceased. I didn't want them to hear the gruesome details over the phone. Even now, they'll only be told what is necessary."

"I agree. Come on. We'll join you."

J.T. tapped my arm. "Go ahead, Jade. I'll get the ball rolling with the officers in the conference room."

"Thanks, partner." I walked with the captain to the bank of elevators around the corner. We stood in front of the closed doors and waited. The distinct sound of jingling change came from the captain's front left pocket, where his hand was buried.

Nervous energy.

The bell dinged, and the light above the door showed the elevator was coming to a stop on the third floor. We entered and rode down two more levels. When she saw us come toward the reception counter, Dana pointed at the visitors' lounge. Mr. and Mrs. Fleming were waiting behind the closed door.

"Are you ready, and how do you want to tell them?" I asked before we stepped into the room.

"I'll say she was the victim of a home invasion and the perpetrator killed her. I don't want to tell them that she wasn't discovered for two days and had multiple stab wounds covering her body. That image will—"

"I understand, and I'll handle that part, Cap. Come on, they're waiting for an explanation." I turned the knob and pulled the door open. Mr. and Mrs. Fleming stood when they saw us enter. We approached the couple with outstretched hands.

Captain Hardy took the lead. "Mr. and Mrs. Fleming, I'm Captain Kip Hardy, the person who spoke with you on the phone last night, and this is Agent Jade Monroe of the FBI. We're so sorry for your loss."

"What happened to Sarah, and why is the FBI involved?" Mrs. Fleming's voice cracked when she spoke. Her swollen red eyes told me she had spent the previous night crying.

"Let's sit, shall we? We'll tell you everything we can." Cap gave me a look of relief. I'm sure he realized I was wording my sentences as carefully as I could while still being truthful.

"Isn't it unusual for an FBI agent to be investigating the death of an everyday civilian? Sarah didn't have a criminal background, and she's never done anything illegal," Mr. Fleming said. "What's really going on here?"

Captain Hardy spoke up. "There have been several suspicious home invasions this week resulting in the death of the homeowners, Sarah being one of them. Agent Monroe's direct supervisor in the FBI is a close friend of mine, and I asked for their assistance. At this point, we don't have any clues."

Mrs. Fleming cupped her face in her hands and broke down. I rose from the chair I had been sitting on and took a seat next to her then put my arm around her shoulder.

"Are you saying our Sarah was murdered?"

The captain stared into the anguished eyes of Sarah's

father. "Yes, sir, I'm afraid that's exactly what I'm saying."

"How is that possible? She lived in a safe, family-oriented neighborhood. The house was for sale, and she was anxious to move home to be near family. Daniel's death took a serious toll on her health and well-being. Her decision to sell and move back to Albany was the right one. She needed a new start, and we were excited for her, so what went wrong?" Mr. Fleming pulled a white handkerchief out of his jacket pocket and wiped his eyes.

"Sir, Sarah didn't do anything to cause this. Our best guess is that it was a random attack, but to gather as much information as we can, do either of you know anyone who would have a reason to harm her?"

Mrs. Fleming blew her nose into the tissue she had pulled from her purse. "Of course not. Sarah was a wonderful person. She and Daniel had a loving marriage. They even spoke of starting a family."

Silence filled the room for a minute. I was sure the parents were trying to absorb what we had just told them.

Mr. Fleming blew out a long, slow breath before speaking. "How did she die, and where is her body?"

Cap folded his hands in his lap. "She's at the morgue with the ME, sir, and she was killed with a knife."

Mrs. Fleming squeezed her husband's hand tightly. "We need to see our daughter."

"Of course, ma'am, and I'll set that up with the ME. If you'll excuse me for just a moment, I'll give him a call." Captain Hardy stepped out of the room, and I was left alone with the distraught couple.

I rose, went to the water fountain, and filled two plastic cups. I handed them to the couple. "Is there anything I can do for you, Mr. and Mrs. Fleming?"

"Yes, find the person who killed our daughter."

Hardy returned moments later and told the Flemings that the ME could see them at two o'clock. "The morgue and coroner's office is only a few blocks from here on Farnam Street. It's one forty-five now."

Mr. Fleming stood. "Then we should go, Linda. Please keep us posted with the investigation, Captain Hardy and Agent Monroe."

I nodded. "We definitely will, sir."

Chapter 12

We returned to the conference room, where it appeared that everyone was working together like a cohesive unit. I was thankful for that, and it would make our job much easier. At the back of the room, words written in red marker filled a whiteboard. Along with the dates, locations of the homes where victims were found, and manner of death, four names were bullet pointed. Chad Nolan, William Stewart, Gary Gibson, and Sarah's coworker, Liz Manthis, were listed on the board. Three of the four people had been interviewed and released.

"I think Chad Nolan should remain a person of interest," Hardy said. "He has no explanation for his name showing up on the newspaper next to the crossword puzzle Mrs. King was working on. It seems especially odd since he said he's never met them in his life. Even with that lame excuse, he still raises a red flag with me."

I nodded. "We'll have to see that newspaper. I assume it's in evidence. If there isn't an ad for Scenic View Realty within the pages, then I agree with Cap. Chad Nolan would definitely need another interview. Has anyone dug deeper into Mr. Nolan's personal life? See if he's married, and if he is, interview the wife too. Everyone has secrets in their home and skeletons in their closet. We need to weed through that information and determine if anything is relevant to these homicides."

Hardy pointed at the board where J.T. stood. "Make a note of that. We'll bring Sarah's coworker and Gary Gibson in too."

"How far did you get with names from the Realtors?" I took a seat, grabbed a pen, and slid a sheet of paper toward me. I jotted notes as I thought.

"Not far enough." Kyle Dixon, one of the officers assigned to make calls to the real estate companies, spoke up. "After news of the second murder came in, we were reassigned to other tasks."

I tapped my pen against the table. "We'll check every possibility, but I don't want anyone to get tunnel vision here. These murders may be the act of a random killer who has nothing to do with the real estate business. Maybe the killer is an opportunist and saw the For Sale signs. He may have thought the houses were empty and wanted to squat in them. Or maybe he wanted to rob them and accidentally came upon the homeowner. Without leads, we don't have anything to base our theories on."

"None of the victims' neighbors had any information?" J.T. asked.

"Nope," Lyles said. "The only person who had an actual statement to give us was Beth Sloane, the woman who called in the King murders."

"And how did that come about again?" I asked.

"She told us the porch light is never on at their house. She said she was actually happy to see it lit up when she passed by in her car, thinking they had company, until she noticed the front door ajar. That's when she stopped to see if everything was okay."

"So the light being on indicated that the Kings were expecting a visitor, not the MO of someone who would sneak in and rob the house." Hardy said.

"True enough. Let's bring Beth Sloane in for a more thorough interview." J.T. added her name to the list.

"What about surrounding counties?" I asked. "Has anything like this happened elsewhere in Nebraska lately? Do all of the police stations share information?"

Sergeant Franklin answered. "Only if it ends up on the news and it rings a bell. Sarah's death got some initial coverage, but since we have nothing to give to the press, they're kind of sitting on the sidelines. Now the murders of Bob and Gloria King? That will definitely start tongues wagging. The serial killer news sensation is about to begin."

J.T. rubbed his forehead. "That's just great. The press is actually more of a hindrance than a help. All they do is instill fear in the community so their ratings go up." He refocused his attention on the group. "Okay, what about the neighborhoods where Sarah Cummings and the Kings lived? Are they normally crime-free, safe areas?"

Detective Andrews answered for everyone. "Absolutely, and as a matter of fact, other than a dog-barking nuisance call, we haven't gone to either neighborhood in over a year."

J.T. brought up Daniel Cummings, Sarah's husband. "His death wasn't at all suspicious?"

"Not according to the police report at the scene of the accident. He was hit by a drunk driver. Wrong place at the right time, nothing more," Hardy said.

"His parents were interviewed last night, correct?" I asked.

Officer Jones responded. "Yes, by me. Their son's death was an untimely and unfortunate accident, and to the best of their knowledge, neither Daniel nor Sarah had enemies. They got along well with the neighbors and each other. They said Sarah was devastated when Daniel died."

"Life insurance policies?" J.T. asked.

Hardy spoke up. "Yes, we checked that out, and no new policies were issued recently for either of them. They both had standard life insurance—nothing overly substantial."

"And neither of them were involved in affairs?"

"Not to our knowledge, Jade." Hardy jerked his chin at Lyles. "How thoroughly was Sarah's house gone through this morning?"

Don shrugged. "Maybe not thoroughly enough, boss."

"Get Forensics on the phone and see if they have a reason to go back inside. If not, I want Dixon, Jones, and whoever isn't busy right now to head over there. I want that house gone through from top to bottom. Look for a connection to the Kings or anything that looks wonky, whether it was from Sarah or her husband. Agents, what do you suggest next?"

"Let J.T. and me have a crack at those people listed on the whiteboard."

Chapter 13

He slammed the door of the rented cottage so hard it almost shattered the two window panes built into the top panel. The cat bolted for the bedroom. Ed paced back and forth through the living room with his fists jammed into his pockets.

"I can't believe that stupid bitch. I have every right to see my kids. Who the hell does she think she is, anyway? Just her voice sets me off. It's like fingernails on a chalkboard. Who died and made her boss?" Ed thought about the words he'd just spewed and snickered. "Oh yeah, three people died, but there's more to come. I'll ruin her life one way or another."

With all his ranting, Ed had forgotten about the woman tied up in the corner. He grabbed the remote and clicked on the TV. Their eyes met for a second, then she quickly looked down.

"Ha! I forgot about you. I guess you aren't very important, are you?" Ed turned off the television and crossed the room. He pulled over a small stool and placed it within a few feet of her. He took a seat and stared into her eyes. "What's your name again?"

"Jackie."

"Oh yeah, and why is your house for sale, Jackie?"

"No particular reason. I'm hoping to make some money on it, that's all. If this is about money, I can give you everything I have if you'll just let me go."

Ed stood and paced again. "Your abduction has nothing to do with money. It's about righting wrongs. I haven't decided how you'll come into play."

"But why me?" Tears streamed down her cheeks.

"Why you? Because I felt like it, that's why. I have personal reasons too, but you have to admit you *were* an easy target and stupid like most women. I've been watching you for a few days, and you aren't the most cautious person. Who takes groceries into their house and doesn't close the front door between trips to the car?"

"I don't know, everyone?"

Ed slapped her across the face. "Wrong answer, idiot, and now look where you are. You're tied up in some pissed-off psycho's cottage in the middle of nowhere. You're as stupid as my ex-wife. You even look like her." Ed fixated on her hair and began stroking it.

Jackie winced as tears streamed down her cheeks. "What are you going to do with me? I'm sure my friends are wondering where I'm at. They've probably called the police."

"Don't worry. I've covered my tracks. Nobody is going to find you unless I want them to."

"But we took my car. Your vehicle must be somewhere near my house."

Ed chuckled as he walked to the refrigerator and cracked open a beer. He guzzled half the bottle without taking a breath then wiped his mouth and approached Jackie again. He leaned in, only inches from her face. "Are you a criminologist?"

"No."

"Then shut the hell up. I've already said I know what I'm doing." Ed dropped down on the sofa and turned on the TV again. With the remote in hand, he channel surfed until he came to the four o'clock local news. Seven commercials in a row wasted five precious minutes of his time. Ed wanted to hear the latest. He got up, grabbed another beer, and placed it on the coffee table. Finally, the news and the anchorman returned to the screen.

"Aah, here we go. What do you have to tell us today, Mr. Newsman?"

The anchorman sitting at the news desk shuffled papers and began. "Breaking news of a double homicide has just reached our station."

Ed leaned forward, his elbows on his knees, and his eyes filled with interest. "Tell it like it is, newsman."

"Information just released from our news team on the street tells us police had Greenhaven Street at Wilson and all the way to Normandy Avenue blocked off last night from what appears to be a double homicide. A retired couple, their names not yet released to the public, was found brutally murdered inside their home on Greenhaven Street.

Violent crime is unheard of in that quiet, unassuming neighborhood, and the locals are on edge. Captain Kip Hardy of the Central Police Station downtown has agreed to set up a tip line. Please call the 800 number at the bottom of the screen if you have any information regarding this or the homicide on Prentice Street that occurred earlier in the week. Omaha wants to know, can this be the work of the same perpetrator, and do we have a serial killer roaming our city? Stay tuned as more information comes in."

Ed slapped his knee. "That was a damn good broadcast if I do say so myself." He jerked his head at the sound coming from the corner of the room. "What's going on over there? Are you bawling?"

"Was that broadcast about you?" Jackie's eyes gave away her fear, and her body visibly shook.

Ed laughed. "Don't you worry your pretty little head about it. As long as I'm not pissed off, you'll be fine. I haven't decided what to do with you yet."

Chapter 14

"So who do you want, Gary Gibson or Liz Manthis?"

"Are they both here?" J.T. asked.

"Yeah. According to Don, Manthis is in box one, and Gibson's in box three." I bit into my turkey club and jammed a handful of salty chips into my mouth. J.T. and I had a spare ten minutes to grab our supper of vending machine food. It was already after six.

"Take your time eating, Jade, or you'll be complaining of indigestion in an hour. Those people are on our time, not vice versa. They can sit and stew for a while."

I leaned back in the cafeteria-style chair and took a deep breath. "You're right. It would be nice to enjoy my food now and then, even if it is a vending machine sandwich." I gulped my iced tea and took another bite.

J.T. stared at his beef stew suspiciously. He gave it a few stirs with his spoon, held the can under his nose, and sniffed.

"What the hell are you doing?" I chuckled.

"Just checking."

"For?"

"Whatever could go wrong, but I guess it's safe. It doesn't smell rotten."

"You're a weirdo, Harper."

"Maybe, but I'm a healthy weirdo."

I gave J.T. a smile. I was glad he was healthy, and so far, he seemed happy to be back in the field.

J.T. chowed down his beef stew and wiped his mouth. "I'll take the girl, and you can have the guy. Opposites attract, you know."

"Like I said, you're a—"

"Yeah, yeah, I know. Come on. Let's see what they have to say."

We parted ways at box one. "Have fun with Liz. Put on the charm, and maybe she'll tell you more about the disagreements she had with Sarah than what she told Lyles and Franklin."

J.T. smirked. "Jealous?"

"Not on your life. I get Gary Gibson, and it's his first interview. No sloppy seconds here, partner." I winked then continued on to box number three. "Talk to you later."

I watched Mr. Gibson for five minutes through the one-way glass in the observation room. He sat and fidgeted, then stood, circled the table, and sat again.

I wonder why you're so nervous, Mr. Gibson. Let's find out.

With two short raps on the door, I entered the room and introduced myself to Gary Gibson, the listing agent for the King house. I stuck out my hand and shook his. It was wet and limp. I tried to hide my disgust. "Mr. Gibson, do you know why you're here?"

"No, not really, but I imagine it has something to do with Mr. and Mrs. King."

"So you know about their murders?"

Gary's left eye began to twitch. "It was on TV, ma'am."

I stared at him. His eye twitch was distracting. "It was on TV, but their names weren't mentioned in that news segment."

"They showed a quick shot of the house. I'm the listing broker, so I recognized it immediately, and they are an elderly couple."

"Okay, anyway, I'm not here to bust your chops, but I do want you to tell me everything you can about them."

"Agent Monroe, I didn't know them personally. I only put their house up for sale."

"I understand." I stood and rounded the table. "Would you like a water?" Gary had begun to perspire profusely.

"Yes, I'd appreciate that."

"Okay, I'll be right back." I needed to get to the bottom of things. Logically, Gary had no reason to be that nervous. I stepped out of the room and called Hardy.

"Captain Hardy here."

"Hey, Cap, it's Jade. I don't know the guys in your tech department, so I'm calling you."

"What do you need?"

"I'm interviewing Gary Gibson, and he's unusually nervous. I want to know if he has a police record. Can you help me out with that?"

"Sure thing. I'll call you back in five."

I walked the hallway to the cafeteria and dropped all my

change into the vending machine. With two bottles of water in hand, I returned to interrogation room number three. "Here you go." I took my seat and cracked the top off my bottle. Gary did the same and guzzled half of it without stopping to breathe. "Is something wrong?"

"No." He wiped his forehead with the back of his hand.

My cell vibrated in my pocket, and I pulled it out. Cap was calling me back. "Excuse me for a second." I stepped into the hallway and answered the call. "What do you have, Cap?"

"Would you believe twenty unpaid parking tickets? It adds up to a couple hundred bucks in fines, but that's it."

I chuckled. "Damn, that guy needs a sedative. Okay, thanks." I returned to the room and took my seat. "Shall we begin?"

"What do you want to know?"

"Everything from the first minute you spoke to either of them."

Gary went over the details as I wrote. "I had an initial meeting with them to view the house and take notes. After I toured the home last week, I told them I'd get the comps together, set a sales price, then they could sign the contract. As soon as the photographer took the pictures, the house would be listed and a sign would go in the yard. The property went on the market only yesterday."

I cut Gary loose thirty minutes later but not before I reminded him to pay his parking tickets. He seemed relieved to be leaving and promised to send in a payment the next day. I walked him out then took a seat in the lobby and reviewed his comments again. He didn't have anything to say that would help the case. According to what Gary remembered, Mr. and Mrs. King wanted to downsize, possibly to a condo, and live closer to their daughter and her family in St. Louis. That was as much personal information as he got out of them. Most of their appointment was spent going over the sales procedure.

I saw J.T. heading my way with Liz Manthis. He thanked her and showed her out.

"How'd it go with Liz?" I grinned.

He plopped down next to me. "That was a bust. She gave me the same story she gave Lyles and Franklin. She and Sarah had been coworkers for five years. They didn't click, just a personality thing it sounded like. Liz seems to be a hothead and spouted off about not getting enough overtime on several occasions. Sounds like the library favored Sarah."

"Maybe because she was a calmer employee?"

J.T. nodded. "Probably. What are we missing, Jade? There doesn't seem to be any connection between the victims. The only thing found was Chad Nolan's name written on a piece of newspaper at the King's house."

"Oh yeah"—I cocked my head—"let's go find the evidence room and have a look at that newspaper."

Chapter 15

Ed became agitated again as he thought of his ex-wife. His hatred for her consumed him.

She's not getting away with this.

He stepped outside and dialed the number from his prepaid phone and waited as it rang on her end. His cell, placed on the railing, was set on speakerphone. She picked up on the fourth ring.

"Hello."

"You can't withhold my kids from me!" Ed stomped back and forth on the cottage's rickety porch as he shouted.

"I most certainly can. Ask the judge who granted me full custody. Did you somehow forget that you've been diagnosed with severe depression and off-the-charts anxiety? The kids are afraid of you, Ed, and I don't blame them. Your personality can turn on a dime. Why do you think we're divorced?"

"Because you're a cheating bitch!"

"Wrong. It's because you can't be trusted to take your medication, and you're unstable. You don't even live around here anymore, and as far as I know, you can't hold down a J-O-B. If you did, you'd be paying child support. You're obviously off the grid and have no money. How could you even afford a plane ticket? Please, just leave me the hell alone."

"You're the last person who needs—" The phone went dead as Ed was about to unleash his verbal wrath on the woman he had been married to for seven years. He swung the door open and pulled out the knife from its sheath as he stomped across the room toward the restrained woman. Jackie's screams bounced off the paneled walls as she wrenched at the ropes around her wrists and ankles. Ed's eyes—filled with craziness—told her what was to come. He pulled back the knife and plunged it into her throat. Gurgles sounded from her body, and blood bubbled out of the wound as he continued to attack until she stopped breathing.

Chapter 16

"Well, now we know Chad Nolan's theory was wrong." With my hands gloved, I carefully placed the newspaper on the small table just outside the evidence room. "Take a couple pictures of this side, then I'll flip it over. There isn't an ad for Scenic View Realty anywhere on either side."

"Got it. Go ahead and turn it to the back side."

I did, and J.T. snapped several more pictures. He leaned in closely to the crossword puzzle and the name written in the margins of the paper. He took two pictures of that as well. "I think we have what we need."

I placed the paper back in the evidence bag and gave it to the officer at the counter. "Thanks." I wrote down the time and signed my name. "Ready?"

"Yeah. Chad Nolan needs to be pulled in. At this point, he's our only person of interest. We also need the records from each real estate company that showed the King's house."

"I think the detectives have that information already. A lot of people are going to be interviewed before these cases are cracked. Has anyone contacted the daughter in St. Louis?"

"Not sure. Let's ask."

J.T. and I went back to the third floor and met up with the officers in the conference room.

Hardy looked up when we entered. "Anything?"

I smirked. "Chad needs to be brought in again. There's nothing on that newspaper that would give Mrs. King any reason to know his name."

Hardy turned to Detective Andrews. "Do we have the forensic photos of the King house yet?"

"They said they'd be finished cataloging them in an hour, boss. Then they're ours to go through."

"Do you remember how the family room was set up?"

"Sure. We're assuming it was Mrs. King's recliner where the newspaper was found. A pair of women's reading glasses sat on the side table, and a soap opera magazine was beside the newspaper. According to the crime scene and where the bodies were located, Mrs. King had just entered the kitchen from the family room. We believe it was Mr. King who let the perp in the door."

I spoke up. "What about a cell phone or a house phone?"

"There was a house phone on its base next to her recliner," Andrews said.

"Did anyone check incoming calls?" J.T. asked.

"Yes, Forensics did." Andrews pulled out his notepad and flipped the pages then frowned. "I don't have the information from the phone written down, but Tony Myers took pictures of the call log."

Hardy cocked his head. "We need to see everything right away. They can finish cataloging the photos later. Go find Stan and tell him we need those pictures sent to my email now, then stop by my office and grab my laptop."

"You got it, sir." Andrews rose and left the room.

Hardy's cell phone buzzed on the table. He picked it up and looked at the screen. "It's the ME." He clicked Talk and set the phone down. "Joe, I have you on speakerphone, and we have a full conference room. What are your findings?"

"Good evening, everyone. I'll begin with Sarah Cummings. I'd place her death on Monday, October second, in the early afternoon, likely before two o'clock. Her stomach contents hadn't been digested yet, meaning she had eaten an hour or so before her death. From what I can tell, the stomach contained salad, which leads me to think that was her lunch. I found seventeen stab wounds in all, with eleven of them located at her neck area. Once again, and generally speaking, murder by knife is a very personal way to kill someone. The perp is face-to-face with their victim. Her face wasn't covered, which indicates there was no remorse involved. There's a killer out there who is very pissed off at somebody. Strangely enough, the Kings were also murdered by knife, and the sizes of the wounds tell me it was the same weapon used in Sarah's death. Mr. and Mrs. King had recently finished dinner, and from their body temperature, we know they had died less than an hour before we arrived. Mr. King had four stab wounds to the abdomen and chest, and Mrs. King had six stab wounds, five to the throat and one to the chest. They both had Taser burns. Mr. King had burns on his back, which leads me to the conclusion that his was a blitz attack, and Mrs. King had burns to the chest, a head-on attack."

I cleared my throat. "Dr. Torres, this is FBI Agent Jade Monroe speaking. Is there any way to identify the type of knife used?"

"Yes, ma'am, to a degree. The depth and width of the wounds tells me the knife was large, yet there weren't any knives missing from the knife blocks at either house. I'm certain he brought the weapon with him and used it in both murders. That said, I'd guess it to be a type of bowie knife— long, wide, and sturdy."

I took a drink of water then jotted down Dr. Torres's findings.

"J.T. Harper here, sir. I'm curious about the throat wounds found in both women yet none in Mr. King. Could that be representative of something?"

"It's very possible. Like I said before, knife wounds are personal. Either this killer had something against both women, he's a misogynist, or he's transferring his rage for a particular woman to these ladies."

Hardy ground his fingertips into his temples. "Okay, Doc, thanks. That's a lot to digest. You've already signed off on Sarah's identification, correct?"

"Yes, her folks were here earlier and are very disappointed they can't make funeral arrangements yet. I don't think they understood the way murder investigations work."

Hardy sighed. "Unfortunately the bodies stay put, at least until we have some bona fide leads."

The call ended, and we dug in once more.

"We need to come up with a connection between Chad Nolan and both families. Any mutual friends, associates, or clubs they all belonged to? Did he owe money to either family? How about his wife? Did anyone check into her?" I looked from person to person.

"There is a wife, but she hasn't been interviewed yet."

Captain Hardy groaned. "Lyles and Franklin, go pick her up. If something weird is going on, I don't want to give them time to come up with matching alibis. We'll deal with Chad again after we talk to her."

Andrews returned to the conference room with Hardy's laptop tucked under his arm. "Stan said the photos should be in your in-box by the time you log in."

"Good. Let's see if anything at either home raises suspicion. We'll check the phone log at the King house first. What about Sarah's phone?"

"That was checked and cleared," Dixon said. "No unknown callers."

"All right, let's take a look." Hardy opened the email attachment where the photos were separated into files. A folder of pictures was marked *Sarah Cummings*, and the other folder was marked *Bob and Gloria King*. Hardy opened the King folder first and scrolled through the thumbnail-sized photos.

"There"—I pointed—"that looks like a telephone call log."

Hardy clicked on the picture and enlarged it to fit the screen. "Okay, it looks like the Kings had four incoming calls on Wednesday with the last one at six o'clock."

I wrote down the phone number on my sheet of paper. "Can Tech pull up this number right away?"

Hardy dialed the tech department from the conference room phone and covered the receiver for a second. "They can unless it's a burner phone. Hey, Leon, it's Hardy. We need you to put a rush on this phone number. Yeah, are you ready?" Hardy read off the phone number to Leon Tripp, the tech department lead, and told him to call the conference room the second he had something. "Okay, what's next?" Hardy glanced at the wall clock. "In one hour I'm cutting everyone loose. Nobody is any good if they're exhausted. We'll resume with fresh eyes in the morning." The phone on the table against the wall rang. It was Lyles. Hardy pushed the speakerphone button. "What have you got, Lyles?"

"Mrs. Nolan, that's what."

"Take her to box one and make sure you tape the interview. We're waiting for information from the tech department right now." Hardy hung up.

J.T. stood. "Anyone up for coffee? I need to call SSA Spelling, anyway, and update him."

The nodding heads told me a full pot was in order. "I'll go along and start a twelve-cupper." I joined J.T. in the cafeteria and started the coffee while he spoke to Spelling. I pulled out my notepad from my pants pocket and began creating a list of things to follow up on. Women stabbed in the neck, both homes for sale from the same realty company, no known connection between victims, and Chad Nolan.

J.T. looked over my shoulder. "What are you doing?"

I sighed. "Trying to figure this out."

"Do you mind?" J.T. reached for my notepad and read what I had written down. "The part about the women being stabbed in the neck sticks in my craw, pardon the pun. Find the woman hater and we might have our killer."

"Maybe Chad Nolan's wife can shed some light. What if they don't get along, he's sick of playing nice to homeowners, hates his job, is having a midlife crisis, or just snapped?"

"Let's drop off the coffee and check in on her interview."

J.T. and I returned to the conference room. I carried a cup of coffee in each hand, and J.T. carried the carafe, a stack of cardboard coffee cups, and a pocketful of powdered creamer and sugar packets.

"Anything from Tech?" I looked at Hardy as we entered the room and dropped off the coffee fixings.

"No luck. It's a burner phone. The only thing we can document is the time the call came in—6:07 p.m. last night."

Chapter 17

After a few sips of my coffee, I took a seat, inhaled a deep breath, and focused on the interview Lyles and Franklin were conducting with Kayla Nolan. J.T. turned the intercom's volume knob to the right. I placed my cup on the ledge of the one-way window and pulled out my notepad.

"The interview is being taped, Jade."

"I know, but I want to go over all of my notes back in the hotel room later. Do we even have hotel rooms booked?"

"I don't think so, but I'll Google to see what's in the area with decent ratings. If I'm lucky, I'll find something we can walk to."

I crossed my right leg over my left and rested my notepad on my lap. Kayla Nolan looked to be in her late thirties and a little rough around the edges. My opinion of her likely came from the overly processed, platinum-blond hair and thick black eyeliner. We listened as the interview continued.

"How well do you and your husband get along, Mrs. Nolan?" Franklin asked.

"Wow, you don't mince words, do you, officer?"

"It's Sergeant Franklin, ma'am, and no, we don't have the time or the inclination to beat around the bush."

"What did Chad do now?"

"As opposed to what?"

She snapped her gum and went silent.

"How long have you been married?" Lyles asked.

"Seven years."

"Kids?"

"Three under six."

"Three? That has to get hectic," Paul said. "I'd go bonkers."

She smirked. "He does every day. Only the oldest kid is in school. Chad is always yelling at the other two." She caught herself and gave Franklin a suspicious look. "What is this about, anyway?"

"Is Chad away from the house a lot?"

"Duh, he has a job. What do you think?"

Don caught up with his notes. "Is he away more than he has to be, possibly?"

"I don't pay attention. I'm too busy with the kids."

"Where was he last night between six o'clock and seven thirty?"

She shrugged. "Not at home. I'd imagine showing a house, at least that's what he always says he's doing."

"So no problems on the home front? Nobody is stepping out?"

"I can only speak for myself, officer, and I don't have time for that nonsense."

"It's Sergeant—"

"Yeah, I know. Is there anything else?"

"Not at the moment. Where is Chad now?"

She stared at Franklin and blew a bubble with her gum. It snapped, and she stretched it between her pinched fingers then popped it back into her mouth. "I'm not his keeper." She stood, and Lyles walked her out.

I shook my head. "Wow, she covers her husband's ass pretty well."

"Yeah, but we can work around her avoidance in answering their questions. We'll check every house that's listed with Scenic View Realty and see if any had showings last night with Chad Nolan between six and seven o'clock."

J.T. and I returned to the conference room, where everyone was packing it up for the night. Hardy jerked his head toward us. "Call it a night, guys. We're all beat and heading home. Let's reconvene at eight a.m. Cracking this case will be a challenge with the lack of leads or evidence to go on."

J.T. let out a long yawn. "It'll get done. We'll make sure of it. Anyway, Kayla Nolan didn't give up her husband, but we'll follow up on Chad's whereabouts from last night when we get here tomorrow morning. The realty office is already closed for the night. Kayla thought he was showing a house, but that's easy enough to check out on their schedule of showings."

"Good enough. Good night, agents."

"Good night, Cap." I grabbed my purse and folder of notes and followed J.T. outside. "Did you find a hotel we can walk to?"

"Nah, the downtown ones are all full. There's a sports event going on. We'll have to drive, but I booked the Element Omaha Midtown Crossing. It isn't far away, and there are a number of restaurants within walking distance of it."

I let out a tired sigh. "I won't complain. A cold beer, hot shower, and a soft bed is all I need."

"No food?"

"Oh yeah, and food."

I called out the directions as J.T. drove. The hotel was less than ten minutes away via Douglas Street.

"Can we stop at that gas station for a minute?" I pointed at the QuikFuel station on the next block.

"Sure, what do you need?"

I felt my face blush before I stammered that the lottery was pretty high. I wanted to buy a ticket.

J.T. laughed. "I guess I should have known you were the gambling type. Hell, you gamble with your life nearly every day. It must be in your DNA." He pulled into the gas station, tucked the SUV alongside the air pump, and killed the engine.

I stepped out and tipped my head back in the door. "Want a ticket?"

"Sure, why not. Between the both of us, it might be our lucky day."

Inside, I waited in line at the gas station's counter. Two

people stood ahead of me. The man prepaying for his gas seemed impatient and fumbled with his wallet. He kept looking out the window. The woman behind him held a box of doughnuts and two candy bars. I realized as I stared at her goodies that I was hungrier than I had thought. When I reached the counter to buy the lottery tickets, a plastic card lying on the floor caught my attention. I knelt and picked it up, and it belonged to the man who had been fumbling with his wallet. "Oh dear, that man dropped his license. Which pump is he at?"

The clerk reached for the license. "I'll take it."

"I don't think so." I jiggled my badge that hung from the lanyard around my neck and held it in front of the sketchy looking character. He pulled back his hand and told me the man's pump number. With the lottery tickets tucked away in my purse, I walked out and headed for pump number seven. The man had just finished filling up his clunker and had placed the gas hose back on the pump.

"Excuse me, sir." I held up his license and waved it to get his attention. "You dropped this on the floor when you were paying for your gas."

A quick frown crossed his brow as he stared at me with bright blue, suspicious looking eyes. "You could get valuable information off of someone's driver's license. What's your angle, lady? Want a reward or something?"

I chuckled. "Hardly. Maybe it's because I'm an FBI agent. Anyway, here you go. Try to be more careful next time."

"FBI, huh? Working on some high-profile case, are ya?"

"Well, I hope it doesn't lead to that, but anyway, have a

nice night." I handed him his license and my card. "Here you go, just in case you ever need our help." I turned and headed to the Explorer. Through the passenger side window, I saw J.T. laughing as I got closer. "What's your problem?" I climbed in and closed the door then pulled the seat belt over my chest and snapped it.

"Trying to pick up a date? I thought you'd at least go after someone with a high-performance sports car instead of that rust bucket."

"You're funnier than you look, smart-ass. The man dropped his driver's license near the counter. Luckily it was me that found it, you know, the honest FBI agent, rather than some random criminal with bad intentions."

"So you didn't make a date? Did you at least get his name in case you reconsider?"

I slugged J.T. in the arm. "Very funny and no, I didn't make a date. He seemed kind of sketchy, but he did have pretty eyes." I played along with J.T.'s foolishness.

"And pray tell, Agent Monroe, what do you consider pretty eyes?"

"You know, big and blue, but he wasn't my type. He looked sort of ragged."

"You didn't even ask his name in case you change your mind later?"

"No, but I did glance at it on his license. His name is Ed Tanner."

"Ed Tanner, huh? You don't look like an Ed type of gal."

"Whatever, dork. Can we get to the hotel now and check in? I'm starving."

"You've decided you're hungry after all?"

"Yeah, blame it on the woman in line ahead of me. She had two candy bars and a box of doughnuts in her hand. Come to think of it, I should have bought a candy bar. I'm Jonesing for chocolate."

J.T. smirked as he turned right out of the gas station. "Then we better make sure you have dessert."

Chapter 18

Ed pounded the steering wheel with his fists.

Son of a bitch, that was a careless mistake. Now that FBI woman knows my name, that is, if she actually looked at anything other than my picture.

He watched until the SUV she had climbed into drove away to make sure they weren't going in the same direction he was. The person behind the wheel clicked the blinker and pulled out into traffic.

Good, they turned right.

Ed took a deep breath to clear his head, started the truck, and shifted into first gear. He craned his neck over his right shoulder. Jackie's body, wrapped in a heavy tarp, lay in the bed of the truck just five feet behind him. With a deep groan, he pulled out of the gas station and turned left.

Now I have to come up with a plan B. I can't dump this body where I stashed her car. If anyone gives a description of my truck near any of the crime scenes, it will ring a bell with that damn FBI agent.

Making sure to drive the speed limit and come to a

complete stop at every stop sign, Ed drove north until he was out of the city limits. He knew the perfect place to dump Jackie where she would never be found. Her car would be located sooner or later, but there was no way it could be tied to the knife-wielding killer at large.

Ed took that thirty-minute drive to a rural area he remembered going to as a child. Once a month, on a lazy Sunday afternoon, his father would take him fishing to that little-known lake. It was a time in his life he always cherished and the most enjoyable thing he remembered doing with his dad. Years had passed since he was there last, but if the area looked anything like he remembered, it would be the perfect place to dispose of Jackie's body.

He turned left on Cypress Creek Drive and continued on for two miles then turned right on Yocum Street. Ed clicked on his high beams to avoid debris and potholes in the barely maintained roadway. The dark night and absence of street lights made it nearly impossible to find the dirt lane that led to the lake. He slowed to a crawl. He felt he was close.

There it is.

Ed stopped the truck, shifted in reverse, and backed up twenty feet. He leaned to his right, rolled down the passenger side window, and peered out. Although somewhat overgrown, the one-lane gravel path was definitely the one that led to the lake.

Good, nobody has messed with the area. It looks the same as it did years ago. It's time to get comfortable in your new home, Jackie. I'm sure the animals will enjoy your company.

Ed turned the wheel to the right and began the half-mile-long drive down memory lane. It ended, if his recollection was correct, at a wider area where several vehicles could park. Even with the car's high beams on, the path was dark, overgrown, and eerie. He'd park, pull her out of the back, and drag her into the thick brush that surrounded the lake. She'd never be found. With a pair of gloves and a flashlight always stashed under the driver's seat, Ed was good to go. Finally at the end of the road, he turned the truck around so it faced outward. He killed the engine and climbed out. The squeaky door creaked when he opened it, sending the nocturnal animals into high alert. The woods came alive with their calls sending shivers up Ed's spine.

Hurry up and get the hell out of here.

Ed reached the back of the truck and opened the tailgate. He felt the shape of her feet under the tarp and gave them a tug. She slid across the truck bed without resistance as he pulled, then a dull thud sounded when her body hit the ground.

"This is such bullshit." Ed spewed the words as he dragged the corpse over branches and tree roots far into the dense thicket. He stopped, pulled the flashlight out of his pocket, and checked his surroundings. Jackie's body couldn't be seen from the lake or the parking area. Ed slipped on his gloves, untied the tarp, and rolled her out. With the black plastic sheeting balled up under his arm, he bushwhacked his way back to the truck and climbed in. He'd find a dumpster somewhere far from the cottage and dispose of the blood-stained tarp.

Chapter 19

I leaned back in my chair and rubbed my belly for emphasis. "That dinner was delicious. Thanks for suggesting Italian. The carbs should help me fall asleep."

J.T. wiped his mouth with the cloth napkin and chuckled. "Does anything, other than a hammer to the head, help you fall asleep?"

I smirked. "Yeah, I know. Only guys have that luxury of drifting off anytime, anywhere. Girls? We think too much."

"And I know what you're thinking about, Agent Monroe."

"Really?" I played along. "I thought Kate was the psychic one in our group of friends. Okay, tell me, Agent Man, what am I thinking about?"

"Ed Tanner."

I burst out laughing, not expecting J.T.'s response. "You're a sick puppy, you know that? Come on. Pay the bill. I need some shut-eye." I pushed back my chair and stood then threw a ten on the table.

J.T. followed me to the counter with the check in hand and paid for dinner, then we walked the two blocks back to the hotel. At my door, J.T. looked at his watch. "It's ten o'clock. If you turn off the gerbil wheel right away, you'll get a decent night's sleep."

I nodded. "I'll try. What time are you going to bang on my door?"

"Six forty-five. That will give us time to hit a drive-through on our way to the station."

"Sounds good. Night, J.T."

"Night, Jade."

Inside my room, I sat at the table and sent a good night text to Amber before silencing my phone. I retreated to the bathroom for a hot, relaxing shower. My phone, notes, and brain, would be put away for the night. Tomorrow would come soon enough, and I just hoped for sleep.

I barely remembered going to bed last night, but now it was morning, and my phone alarm buzzed in my head. I reached for it and swiped the screen to silence the annoying tone. I ground my palms into my eyes and realized I felt somewhat refreshed. I had nearly seven hours of sleep. Another shower, this time to wash my hair, would revive me and get my day started on the right foot.

Right on time, a knock sounded at my door. It was six forty-five, and if a finger blocked the peephole, I could be certain it was J.T. I peered through and saw only darkness but heard chuckling from the other side of the door. I swung it open. "You're so immature."

"And you wouldn't expect any less of me. Ready to hit the ground running?"

"Sure am after we grab breakfast."

We found a drive-through restaurant that didn't have eight cars in line ahead of us. Our day was starting out right, and hopefully it would continue that way. With our coffees in the cup holders and our breakfast sandwiches in hand, we ate as we made our way to the police station.

I paged through my notes with my free hand. "I'm anxious to find out if there were any house showings Wednesday night and if they were with Chad Nolan."

"We'll know as soon as Scenic View Realty opens."

"That's right. Their office doesn't open until nine o'clock, but we can interview the King's daughter while we wait. According to Hardy, she and her husband left St. Louis yesterday afternoon, and it's a six-and-a-half-hour drive. Hopefully they made it here okay and got a little sleep too."

J.T. took a sip of his coffee and placed it back in the cup holder. "They'd have to stay in a hotel. The house is still sealed as a crime scene. I doubt if it's even been cleaned up."

"Yeah, they don't need to see that. Sarah Cummings's house is still sealed too. I'm sure her parents will have to get in before they go back to New York. Somebody needs to check into that."

J.T. pointed at my notepad. "Write that down. On a positive note, I didn't get any urgent texts or calls during the night about another murder."

"Me either, which leads me to believe there could be a personal reason he went after the Kings and Sarah Cummings. Maybe he's done."

"We can only hope." J.T. pulled into the parking lot

where he was assigned a space yesterday and killed the engine. He placed the parking permit where it would be visible through the windshield, then we grabbed our coffees and food wrappers and exited the Explorer. With an underhand toss, I made the ten-foot distance into the outside garbage can with the balled-up wrappers.

J.T. shrugged. "Is there anything you aren't good at?"

I gave him a wink. "I'll never tell."

We said hello to the desk sergeant and the officers at the front counter, signed in, and headed to the elevator. We entered the first set of doors that opened, and J.T. pressed the button for the third floor. Voices from the conference room echoed down the hallway as we exited the elevator. Our workday was about to begin.

Inside the conference room sat Hardy, the detectives, and the sergeants. A stranger sat to the left of the captain.

"Agents Monroe and Harper, this is Dr. Samantha Collins. Sam is an old family friend and a forensic psychiatrist. She's agreed to give us her input on why both Sarah Cummings and Gloria King were stabbed repeatedly in the throat, yet Mr. King wasn't. There could be a significant reason, at least in the killer's eyes, why he did that," Cap said.

I walked over and shook her hand, then J.T. did the same. Back at the opposite side of the table, we took the two empty seats across from her. I was happy to have face-to-face communication with the psychiatrist, and I was more than anxious to hear what could be a fascinating theory.

"Everyone good to go?" Hardy asked as he met each of our eyes.

The shuffling of paper and pens, then momentary silence, told Dr. Collins we were ready to take notes.

"Good morning, everyone. Like Captain Hardy said, we're old friends and occasionally run cases past each other. He gave me a call last night, I will admit, at a late hour"—she gave him a grin—"but chances were he couldn't sleep. I find myself in that same situation often."

I whispered *amen* under my breath.

"Cap allowed me to review the police and medical examiner's reports on both cases, and I do believe there is a specific reason for the killer's modus operandi. Using a knife as a murder weapon can be interpreted several ways. Yes, in some cases, but not all, it is thought to be a very personal way to commit a murder. That logic comes from the fact that the killer is in the same proximity as the victim—eye to eye, so to speak. A gunshot, on the other hand, creates distance between the shooter and the victim—no personal contact." Dr. Collins took a drink of water from her cup and continued. "Other reasons could be that a knife is easily concealed, is quiet, there aren't any bullet casings to pick up at the scene, it can't be traced to the registered owner like a gun, but most importantly, a knife instills more fear in the victim than a firearm."

"Really?" Lyles said.

"Indeed. A knife represents a slow, painful death. The victim can imagine torture and intense pain with a knife, where more commonly, with a gun, they are shot and die immediately. A knife also shows a certain amount of power the killer has over his victim."

I made eye contact with Dr. Collins and tipped my head.

"Agent Monroe?"

"Wouldn't that be far more dangerous for the killer as well when dealing with someone, a man in this case, who could be of equal size and strength?"

"Sure, but Mr. King is presumably older than the killer and, don't forget, was attacked from behind with a Taser. The killer needed to disable him in order to be that close to the man. In a woman-only scenario, he could likely overpower them easily."

J.T. nodded. "All of that makes perfect sense, but what's your take on the throat wounds to the women?"

"Usually something that specific holds meaning to the killer. I don't believe he's a misogynist—that's too broad—but I do think there's somebody in particular, a woman, of course, that he hates. The act of repeatedly stabbing somebody in the throat tells me he's trying to shut her up, or cut her off, so to speak. Her voice irritates him, her words anger him, and he wants to silence her permanently. In my profession, we call that transference, transferring his hate for this woman, somebody he can't access, to a different woman, somebody he can."

"Wow!" Everyone looked my way. I was sure I'd spoken too loudly.

"Jade, did that ring a bell with a particular person?" Hardy asked.

"Sorry for my overzealous outburst, and no, Cap, not yet. So the man has a wife, girlfriend, mother, sister, neighbor, or even a coworker that he hates?"

The doctor agreed with my conclusion. "It's a good possibility. I'd start with the most controlling person in a man's life, and that would be a mother or a wife."

"What about the fact that both homes were for sale with the same real estate company?" Andrews asked.

"I'm not certain that's relevant to the case. A person anxious to sell their home may have a moment of bad judgment and allow a stranger inside to look at it. Anybody can prowl the internet or newspaper at homes for sale."

"And the fact that it's the same company in both cases doesn't necessarily raise a flag?" Hardy asked. He raked his hands through his hair, and his expression told me we might be wasting our time with the real estate connection.

"I believe Scenic View Realty is the largest real estate company in the state. Is that correct?"

Hardy looked at Andrews and waited for his response. "Yes, it is, actually, with the company my wife works at as the second largest."

"Then there are more homes for sale with Scenic View than any other company. It's probably a matter of convenience and quantity, an easy choice for the perpetrator."

Hardy leaned back and stared at the ceiling. "Okay, I think we need to go back to the drawing board. Thanks so much, Sam. I'll walk you out."

We thanked the doctor, gave her our cards, and took a five-minute break. J.T. and I headed to the cafeteria to plug change into the vending machine. We both needed coffee.

"I'm still going to follow up on Chad Nolan," I said as we walked back to the conference room.

J.T. tipped his wrist. "It's after nine o'clock. The office is open. Use the desk phone once everyone is seated back in the conference room. I'm sure the entire group wants to hear if Chad was showing a house Wednesday night or not."

"Good plan." Once we returned to our seats, I looked up the phone number for Scenic View Realty. I rattled off the number as J.T. tapped the buttons on the desk phone and set it to speakerphone.

A friendly voice answered on the third ring. "Scenic View Realty, Kathryn Price speaking. How may I direct your call?"

"Hello, Kathryn. My name is Agent Jade Monroe with the FBI. I need to speak with the person who schedules home showings."

"Oh my word. Um, each Realtor schedules their own showings, ma'am."

"Well, there must be some type of board that lists all of the showings by day and time for the entire company, otherwise there could be overlap and confusion."

"Yes, ma'am, there *is* that."

"And do you have eyes on that board right now?" I looked at the group and smiled.

"I do."

"Wonderful. Now I need to know if anyone showed the home on Greenhaven Street between six and seven o'clock on Wednesday evening."

"Oh, that house? I'm so sorry to hear about the unfortunate—"

"Kathryn? Can you just check the board, please?"

"Yes, certainly. Give me one second."

I was put on hold, and we listened to smooth jazz for thirty seconds. A click sounded, and Kathryn was back on the line.

"Agent Monroe?"

"Yes."

"None of our associates' names show up for that time on Wednesday. The only appointment scheduled at that home on Wednesday with our company was at two thirty with Darren Grimes. Of course, other agencies may have shown the home throughout the day."

"Thank you, Kathryn. That's all I needed to know."

J.T. disconnected the call. "That was a bust. Looks like Chad Nolan is off the hook."

"Boss?"

Hardy turned to Andrews. "Yeah, Fred, what's on your mind?"

"I know you didn't want to involve Lisa, but with a few taps of her computer keys, she can access the MLS database with her log-in password and see if any real estate company had an appointment at the King house at that time. It would sure speed up this process."

Hardy sighed and jerked his head toward the hallway. "Go on, and I don't know anything about it."

"Thank you, sir." Andrews left the room and headed down the hall.

"If nobody at any company showed the house Wednesday night, then I'd suggest we close the real estate agent or buyer theory and look for some other connection."

Hardy tipped his head toward Lyles. "Have any reliable leads come in?"

"Plenty of leads, but none have panned out, sir."

Andrews returned a few minutes later. "Lisa said no showings came up on the MLS for that time slot."

"And the MLS listing database is one hundred percent accurate?"

"Yes, sir, I'm afraid it is."

Chapter 20

"We need to hit the streets and widen our parameters. Looks like we've been barking up the wrong tree for the last couple of days, and important leads may have gone cold. Pan out and go three blocks in every direction of both houses. Look at grocery store receipts and see where they shopped. Talk to the hair salon people and the personnel at the nearest hardware store to the King house. There's a chance Mr. King may have recently done repairs to spruce up the house before selling it. Go through the checkbooks and credit card statements at both homes. Find out what their favorite restaurants were and where they went to the movies. I want to know everything they did and everyone Sarah Cummings and the Kings came in contact with over the last month. Let's go, and someone interview Beth Sloane again, and this time tape it."

Dana peeked through the open door as everyone filed out. "Captain Hardy, Mr. and Mrs. King's daughter and son-in-law are here."

"Damn, I forgot they were coming in. Have them wait

in the visitors' lounge downstairs."

"We'll handle that interview if you have something else you need to do."

"Nah"—Hardy stood—"thanks, Jade, but we should do this together."

I noticed the anxiety on Hardy's face as we rode the elevator down to the first floor. "Cap, do you need a minute before we go in?"

"I'm a tough old codger, even though it doesn't always seem that way. I'll get through this, but it's hard when you have nothing of value to tell the next of kin. 'Sorry, ma'am, but some nutcase killed your parents, and we can't figure out who or why they did this.' It isn't good enough. Then there's the press. They want headlines, and the TV news stations want something salacious to put on the air about the killer."

"What we do isn't easy, especially when we have to be the bearer of bad news. Sarah Cummings and the Kings were about as different as they come. There's no common link between them that we've found yet. Let's tell the daughter the truth. It's the only thing we have, and it's always the best way to go."

"You're right, Jade." Hardy breathed in deeply. "What are their names?"

J.T. pulled out his notepad from the inner pocket of his sports jacket. He flipped the pages until he found the entry. "It's Jeremy and Diane Larson." He opened the door to the visitors' lounge, and we entered behind Hardy.

"Mr. and Mrs. Larson, I'm Captain Kip Hardy, and

these are Agents Monroe and Harper of the FBI."

We shook their hands and offered our condolences.

At the far end of the room was a table that would give us plenty of privacy. "Let's have a seat at the table, shall we?" I walked with the distraught daughter, and the men walked ahead of us.

After we took our seats, J.T. led the conversation. "There's no easy way to say this, Diane, but your mom and dad were brutally murdered. I'll spare you the details, but I'll be the first to admit, we're at a loss. We have nobody with a motive and no leads. We need your help. Can you think of anyone who had a beef with your folks?"

"Dad spoke of the neighbor two doors down. His dog always ran loose, tore up Mom's flower bed, and did his business in their yard. Dad called animal control on the guy several times. They had plenty of shouting matches, but that isn't quite a motive for murder."

I wrote as she talked. "Do you know the man's name?"

"Honestly, I don't remember, but I am sure Dad said it was the house two doors south of him."

Hardy made a note of that. "I'll check with animal control. Anything else?"

Diane wiped her eyes. "It depends on how serious of a situation you mean."

"At this point, we're checking all leads, ma'am," the captain said.

"Mom mentioned having to tell the grocery store manager about the bag boy. I guess she complained to him constantly about being careless with her produce. He'd put the gallon of milk on the tomatoes, that sort of thing. She finally called the manager, and the kid was fired. She found out during their phone conversation that she wasn't the only person who complained about him. Other than that, I can't think of anything. That in itself seems way too petty."

"You never know what sets people off. Do you know what store that was or the bag boy's name?"

Diane rubbed her forehead. "She shopped at Giant's Market and has for years. I would imagine it happened there."

Hardy nodded.

Jeremy spoke up. "How do we go about taking care of things here? We drove past the house, and there's crime scene tape all around it."

"Yes, the entire property is cordoned off," Hardy said. "I'll admit, it's going to take time to go through the house. At this point, anything can be a clue. The coroner will need you to identify the deceased, but it may be a week or two before we can release their bodies to you."

The couple stood to leave with the directions to the coroner's office in hand. Diane turned to me. "Agent Monroe, do you think they suffered?"

I put my hand on her shoulder. "I don't think so, Diane." I handed her my card, and she tucked it into her purse. "Please, if you think of anything else, we're only a phone call away."

"Okay, thank you."

Hardy escorted the couple to the lobby.

J.T. raised his brows. "What was that you said thirty

minutes ago about telling the truth?"

"Seriously? There's a time for the truth, and that wasn't it. Come on. We're going to wrap up things with Chad Nolan so we can officially eliminate him as a person of interest."

"Where are we going?"

"To Scenic View Realty." I stopped in the hallway just before the elevators. "We should wait for Cap and tell him what we're doing. After the final interview with Chad, we can track down that kid from the grocery store."

Hardy rounded the corner. "Well, they're on their way to the coroner's office. It's got to be devastating to lose both your parents at the same time."

"I'm sure it is. We're going to do some footwork, Cap. First, we'll finish up with Chad then check out the bag boy and his whereabouts for Wednesday night."

"Sounds good, Jade, and I'll find out what I can about the neighbor with the dog."

J.T. pressed the elevator button for Hardy, and the doors parted. "We'll be back after lunch."

Minutes later in the car, I chuckled as J.T. drove.

He cocked his head at me. "What's so funny?"

"It's nothing, only my inner visual of how it's going to look when two FBI agents enter Scenic View Realty and announce they want to talk to Chad Nolan. He may be innocent of murder, but there's something hinky under way on his home front. It doesn't seem like he and Kayla get along very well, and remember when she said, 'What did Chad do now?' How are we supposed to interpret that?"

"I guess we'll find out soon enough. He doesn't have a police record on file, so it has to be personal."

J.T. found a parking spot at the end of the block on Lilac Street. The real estate office was four doors away.

"A surprise visit is the best way to go. I hope he's still there and not out showing a property," I said.

J.T. checked his watch. "It's still pretty early to be showing houses. They've only been open for an hour."

We reached the building that was attached on both sides to other retail stores. Cute green-and-white striped awnings accented the windows on the front façade, likely because that side of the street faced the morning sun. We walked up the three steps, and J.T. pulled open the glass door. A buzzer sounded even though all of the Realtors' desks were in that main room. Kathryn, the gatekeeper and receptionist, sat nearest the door. The name plate on the desk gave her identity away.

"Hello, may I help you?"

I scanned the room and immediately saw Chad at his desk two rows back. He hadn't actually met us since we were behind the glass wall in the observation room during his interrogation. I assumed from his behavior as we stood there that he thought we were a husband and wife interested in buying a home or selling our own. Several customers sat alongside the desks of other Realtors.

"Hello, Kathryn. I'm FBI Agent Jade Monroe." I flashed my badge at her then tucked it back under my blouse. "We spoke earlier."

She stood and smoothed her dress then leaned forward

and whispered to me. "I thought our phone call took care of things." Her eyes darted from desk to desk.

I smiled. "Not entirely. We need to speak with Chad Nolan." I turned and looked directly at him. His face went white.

Chad pushed back his chair and stood. Every eye in the room was on him. "What is this about? Why do you want to speak with me? I've already given—"

J.T. interrupted. "Wouldn't you rather speak privately, Mr. Nolan?"

Chad jerked his head toward a closed door behind him. "Yeah, back here in our records room will do."

We followed him into the long narrow room. It had a small table and one chair, but nobody sat.

"We know you were interviewed several times, but we have a few questions of our own. I'm sure you're aware that an interview was conducted with Kayla too by the police department."

"Yeah, and I'm still wondering why. How many times do we need to be dragged in? And now the FBI comes to my workplace. This is harassment."

I grinned. "You have no idea what harassment is, Mr. Nolan, and you were considered a person of interest. The police and FBI can interview you as often as we feel necessary until you're cleared."

He smirked. "And when is that going to be?"

J.T. spoke up. "Where were you Wednesday night between six and seven?"

"At home with my family."

We stared him down. The silence seemed to make him uncomfortable. Chad pulled at the tight shirt collar and tie around his neck.

"Choking on something or just hanging yourself?" I smiled at him then at J.T. "Maybe he needs that chair after all. He's looking kind of faint."

"I agree. We might be here for a while."

"Okay, fine. I wasn't at home, but I'm sure you already know that."

"Don't waste our time saying you were showing a house, either. We've checked that angle too."

Chad plopped down in the chair and let out a deep groan. "I have a girlfriend, all right? We were together at her apartment Wednesday night until nine o'clock."

"What's her name, address, and phone number?" I asked.

"Come on!"

"Do we look like we're kidding?" J.T. said. "The lies you dish out to your wife are on you. Now give us your girlfriend's name, address, and phone number."

He rattled off the information and her name—LeAnn. "Are we done now?"

"Hardly. Stay put."

I dialed the number Chad had given us, and a female voice answered right away. I told her who I was and that we were conducting interviews with people about the recent murders. I said she was welcome to come down to the precinct for a formal interview or she could answer a few questions over the phone.

"But why me?"

"It's because your name came up in an interview with someone else. So would you mind telling me where you were Wednesday night between six and seven p.m.?"

"Oh, sure, I was having dinner at my mom's house."

"Okay, that should do it, but we may have to confirm that information. Thank you." I clicked off. "Now the fun part begins."

J.T. stuck out his hand to Chad.

"What?"

"Give me your phone."

"Why should I do that?"

"You'll see."

Seconds later, Chad's phone rang. J.T. laughed when he saw the name on the screen. The number was LeAnn's, but the name showed Ralph Farcy. "You couldn't do better than Ralph?"

Chad buried his face in his hands, and J.T. let the call go to voicemail. We waited a minute before playing the message on speakerphone.

LeAnn was angry and frazzled. She said Chad needed to call her right away because the FBI had just contacted her. She had made up a lie to cover Chad's ass for Wednesday night, and now he owed her one.

"Wow, now you have two women pissed at you. Good luck with that," J.T. said.

"Yeah, thanks. Am I in the clear now?"

I tipped my head toward the door. "Sure, with us, but you're on your own with the wife and girlfriend."

We left the building and headed back to the Explorer. As I sat in the passenger seat, I crossed Chad's name off my list.

"Okay, now to track down that grocery store kid." I Googled Giant's Market in Omaha, and the address popped up. We would interview the manager to get the name and address for the fired bag boy.

Chapter 21

Our interview with Mr. Reynolds, the manager at Giant's Market, proved to be a dead end. He explained that the young man in question, Bradley O'Conner, was indeed fired due to bad performance but shortly afterward had moved to Denver.

"You can check with the kid's mom to be sure, but he said he was going to quit anyway to go live with his dad. Maybe that's why he didn't do his best to keep his job. His final paycheck was sent to that Denver address."

We took down his mother's name and phone number and made the call. She confirmed that Bradley had moved to Colorado a month earlier and hadn't returned to Omaha.

I checked the time on the dashboard. "Let's head back and see if anyone has a lead to follow up on. I don't mind my lunch coming from a vending machine."

We walked into the precinct fifteen minutes later and found Hardy eating a sandwich at his desk. He nodded for us to come in.

"Have a seat, agents. I'll be done here in a minute. What's the word with Nolan?"

"He was visiting his girlfriend Wednesday night. It's what we suspected from the lack of concern Kayla showed for him."

"Yeah, and the kid?"

"Dead end," J.T. said. "He moved to Denver after he was fired and hasn't returned to Omaha since. The mother confirmed it."

"How about the nasty neighbor and his dog?" I asked.

Hardy wiped his mouth, took a sip of coffee, and answered. "Bad blood between them for a while, nothing more. He and his wife were visiting friends in Arizona until yesterday. He showed me the airline receipt and the crumbled-up boarding passes he dug out of the garbage can. He said, in hindsight, he feels awful to have let the rift about his dog ruin their friendship. He took the blame for everything."

As we were about to get up, Hardy's desk phone rang.

I pointed at the door. "We're going to hit the vending machines, Cap. We'll give you some privacy."

J.T. and I left Hardy's office, and I closed the door behind me. In the cafeteria, with a club sandwich, a bag of chips, and a soda, I took a seat across from J.T., who had a matching meal.

"I hope something pops soon. If there aren't any leads coming in, Spelling might reassign us somewhere else."

J.T. nodded with a mouthful of sandwich.

"Since both houses were in a quiet, residential neighborhood, nobody had any security cameras. So we're out of luck there."

J.T. finally swallowed. "I have an idea, even though it's far-fetched."

"Anything would sound good about now." I leaned forward and waited.

Hardy burst into the cafeteria. "Agents, I need you in my office now!"

I jumped up. "Oh shit, did I speak too soon?"

I tossed our plastic containers and napkins in the wastebasket as we left the cafeteria. "What's going on, Cap?"

"You aren't going to believe this, and it's the fastest way I could think of to get an official statement. I have Skype open on my desktop computer, and there's a young lady sitting at the desk of Sergeant Bateman over at the southeast precinct."

"Okay?" I looked at J.T., whose eyebrows were already raised.

"Pull your chairs over here and have a seat, agents."

We did as Hardy instructed and saw a young lady and Sergeant Bateman sitting side by side at his desk.

Hardy introduced everyone, and instinctively, I pulled out my notepad from my pants pocket.

"Okay, Len, the floor is yours," Hardy said.

Sergeant Bateman told us how the young lady to his left, Tara Lamar, came to him yesterday fearing something had happened to her friend, Jackie Stern. Jackie hadn't shown up for their lunch date, and after driving to her house to check on her, Tara peered through the patio doors and saw several bags of groceries left on the kitchen counter. Jackie hadn't answered any calls or texts by the time Tara arrived at the precinct, which was several hours later.

I wrote as fast as I could.

Sergeant Bateman went on to tell her that he couldn't file a missing persons report after only a few hours but said for Tara to contact him if Jackie hadn't been located after twenty-four hours.

Bateman pointed at the distraught young lady at his side. Her eyes were swollen and red "She called my desk today since her friend still hadn't been located. I told her to come in to file a report. Meanwhile, I sent an officer to the missing girl's home to conduct a wellness check. That's when I got the call."

"What call?"

"From my officer, who said that through the windows, the house looked normal. He did see the bags of groceries on the counter like Tara described yesterday. They were still sitting in the same place. He didn't notice anyone inside, there was no purse on the counter, and the driveway was empty. For all intents and purposes, nothing looked out of place. That's when my officer saw the For Sale sign."

"Shit. Not Scenic View Realty again."

"Bingo, Agent Monroe. Shall we breach the house?"

"Meet us there. We need that address, and don't enter the premises until we arrive." I looked at Hardy. "Do you use the same crime lab throughout the county?"

"Sure do. I'll let Stan know we need them at the scene."

Chapter 22

With his siren blaring and lights flashing, Hardy led the way. By following his cruiser down the surface streets, we reached the address on the southeast side of the city in twenty-five minutes. Luckily, he knew all the shortcuts. As we were leaving, the police scanner squawked out an alert about a three-car pileup on the freeway that was blocking traffic. Patrol units and EMTs were on their way, and the freeway would look like a parking lot before long. I was thankful we were following somebody who knew a different route to the house.

We pulled up to the curb behind Hardy and got out. The unassuming single-story white house was now a possible crime scene. Squad cars lined both sides of the street, and crime scene tape sealed the area around the house.

I recognized the face of the man that we had spoken with on Skype. Sergeant Bateman stood against the handrail that led up three steps to the front door. Hardy, J.T., and I reached him and the officer who'd conducted the wellness check. We shook their hands.

"Any evidence of foul play along the perimeter of the property?" Hardy asked.

"We haven't checked or touched anything yet, Captain. My superior said to follow your instructions to the letter. He's stuck at a fundraising event that he's committed to."

"Understood, and Agents Monroe and Harper are calling out the instructions. Do whatever they say," Hardy said.

"Yes, sir."

J.T. pointed at the back of the house. "Get several men back there and start walking a grid. Mark anything that looks out of place. Officer, did you look through every window when you did the wellness check?"

"Yes, sir, and I didn't see any movement. I also called out to the homeowner, and nobody answered."

"Okay, let's get inside and see what we have." Seven of us gathered at the front door. "Everyone who's going in the house needs to glove up before entering." J.T. waited until we were ready. He turned the knob—the door didn't budge. He nodded, and we backed up several feet. The officer with the ram approached and pushed the door in.

We entered slowly and made sure to watch our every step. Stan Fleet, the forensic lead, and two of his team members waited until we cleared the house for their own safety. When we called out to them, they entered.

Stan studied the scene in the kitchen. "There was likely some sort of struggle right here. Not only are the groceries still on the counter, but several canned goods have fallen to the floor. That tells me someone possibly entered the house as she was bringing in the groceries. The perp may have hid in the coat closet by the door then took her by surprise." He pointed at the floor. "That's evident by the cans of vegetables strewn about. Either she didn't think of locking the door behind her when she brought in the last bag of groceries or the person had already entered the house without her knowledge. Because there wasn't a huge struggle, knocked-over furniture and the like, I'm guessing he zapped her with the Taser just like he did Mr. and Mrs. King. She didn't have time to react." Stan pulled the soggy carton of ice cream out of the wet bag. "We have a half gallon of ice cream here." He placed it in the sink and removed the lid. "Every bit of it is liquid, and nearly all of it has seeped out. The friend reported her to you about twenty-four hours ago, Sergeant Bateman?"

"That's correct."

"She's probably been missing for nearly thirty hours."

"How about a grocery receipt in the bags?" I asked. "They're time stamped."

Stan checked each bag. "No luck. She probably stuck the receipt in her wallet after she paid. At least that's what my wife does."

"Hang on here," J.T. said. "The grocery bags are marked with Shop and Save's logo." He jerked his head at Hardy. "Get somebody to that store and pull up the videotapes from yesterday between eight a.m. and two p.m."

Hardy called out to a nearby officer. "Did you hear that?"

"Yes, sir."

"Okay, get another officer to join you and report directly to me when you know something." He handed the officer a small framed picture of Tara and Jackie that sat on a bookshelf. "Take this with you. That has to be Jackie, according to Tara's description of her."

Stan entered the living room and clicked on the TV. "Programs taped but none watched from nine a.m. yesterday until now." He pointed at the phone on the end table. "That's odd, for a twenty-seven-year-old to have a house phone."

I added, "Probably came with the all-in-one package. The light is flashing." I checked the screen, and it showed thirteen messages, beginning at ten forty-five yesterday.

Sergeant Bateman nodded. "That looks about right. Tara Lamar said she and all their mutual friends tried calling Jackie. I'm sure as a last resort they called the house phone too."

I pressed the message button as we stood around the phone. One by one, friends asked where she was and said to call them. Everyone was worried about her.

"What kind of vehicle does she drive?" I waited as Bateman looked up that information.

"She drives a 2015 burnt-orange-colored Ford Fiesta."

"Got a plate number?"

"No, ma'am, but I'll get our tech department to pull that up."

I returned to the kitchen. "No cell phone, keys, or purse. Would an attacker worry about taking those items with him?"

J.T. answered. "Sure, if everything was in the purse. She parked, killed the ignition, dropped her cell in the purse, and unlocked the front door. She may have jammed the keys in her pocket as she entered the house. She set her purse on the kitchen counter and went back outside to grab the first bag of groceries. It's easier for a perp to grab one item if everything you need, including her wallet, was inside."

"Yeah, that's a valid point. So they left together in her car. Either he had a weapon pointed at her and she drove or she was out cold and he was behind the wheel. Get some officers to photograph every vehicle on this street that isn't issued to law enforcement or parked in a driveway. Make sure they photograph the plate numbers too. Start a knock and talk throughout the neighborhood. These houses are close together. Somebody had to have seen something."

"You've got to be kidding," Hardy said as we stepped outside. He pointed at the end of the street to several TV station vans that were approaching. He kicked a rock and yelled to the officers who stood at the police tape. "Cordon off the whole block. I don't need these busybodies interfering with our investigation. For God's sake, we've only been here for thirty minutes."

I shielded my eyes and looked down the street. "Police scanners, Cap. They're a double-edged sword."

Hardy nodded. "Yeah, yeah, I know."

"Sir, we've pushed back the TV crews, but they've put their telephoto lenses on their cameras."

Hardy turned and looked at the For Sale sign. "Damn it, there's nothing to block that sign from their cameras, either. I'm sure the news is going to have a field day with this. It's the third killing in a week and all at houses for sale with Scenic View Realty. I hate to sound morbid, but the other real estate companies are probably loving this. Squelch the competition."

Bateman hung up his cell and crossed the lawn to where we stood. "We have her plate number, Agent Monroe."

"Okay, get a BOLO out for her car right away." I jerked my head toward J.T. and found a shade tree to stand under. He followed me.

"What's up, partner?"

"I doubt if Forensics is going to find any useful evidence in the house. Other than with Sarah, the perp has stayed within the entry and kitchen areas."

"True, so what set her apart?"

"Maybe she was his first, and he realized after chasing her through the house that there could be a chance of DNA, prints, or some other evidence left behind. That could be why the Taser came into play with the Kings and now possibly with Jackie Stern. He wants to keep the crime scene as small as possible."

"I hate to admit it, but this guy isn't stupid."

"That's the scary part, J.T., and so far we have nothing. I know crimes go unsolved now and then. Maybe he's one of those friendly next-door neighbors that nobody would ever suspect." My eyes darted from house to house, where people stood on their porches, talking to officers. A lot of heads were shaking. "He could be anyone, even one of these neighbors. I can't figure out what we're missing."

"Don't blame yourself, Jade. Nobody else can figure this out, either. We only need one reliable lead to set everything in motion. Think of it like dominos—tip one and you tip them all. I'll be damned if I'm going to let this guy outsmart us."

"I'm glad you're so confident."

Additional officers had been called in. Some took pictures of vehicles, others looked to the ground for clues, and the rest were interviewing homeowners.

"What about the canine unit?"

J.T. shrugged. "Jackie's scent will end at the driveway. The dogs won't have anything beyond that."

"We can't sit back and wait for another person to go missing or be murdered. I have an idea!"

"Yeah? Spill it."

"We can stake out every house that's for sale with Scenic View Realty. The perp is bound to show up sooner or later."

"That sounds logical, Jade, except for the fact that they're the largest real estate company in the state. I doubt if we can spread any police force that thin. If he caught wind of it, he'd leave Omaha, move on to another town, and continue the killing."

"So if the victims aren't his real target, then who is?"

Chapter 23

Ed filled the bucket with hot sudsy water then dropped in a scrub brush and rag. He had to clean up the mess he had created yesterday when his fury at his ex-wife caused him to take out his anger on Jackie.

Wrong place, wrong time, Jackie. I would have grown tired of you, anyway. Women aren't my favorite people.

He carried the bucket to the corner of the living room, knelt down, and began scrubbing. The water quickly turned a crimson red. Chunks of bone and flesh bobbed up and down with each dip of his hand into the water. He flushed the contents down the toilet and filled the bucket again. After he'd made three refills, the floor looked as if nothing out of the ordinary had taken place in that room. Ed poured the last of the pink-tinted water into the toilet and gave it a final flush.

Bye-bye, Jackie. Nobody will ever know you stopped in for a visit.

Ed dried his hands and took a seat on the couch. The remote lay on the cushion next to him.

Let's see what's on the boob tube.

With the remote pointed at the television, Ed scrolled through the channels and found nothing that interested him.

Every station plays crap. Wait—what's this? Local breaking news, huh? Let's see what they have to say.

Ed's interest was piqued when he recognized the neighborhood. "Hey, that's Jackie's street."

The reporter stood outside the yellow-taped perimeter and pointed over his shoulder. "Police have this entire neighborhood cordoned off, and from the number of officers in the area, we're assuming something horrific has taken place. The taped-off perimeter was expanded even farther out as soon as our and all the other news vans were spotted. With the recent murders in Omaha, our team can't help but believe something of that caliber has taken place in this primarily older and quiet neighborhood. Sources in the area tell us that the county crime lab van arrived earlier and is parked in the driveway of the house where everyone has congregated. We have yet to see or hear of the coroner arriving. As of now, there's one defining similarity between this scene and the earlier murders in the area, and it's this."

The cameraman zoomed in on the For Sale sign that stood in the center of the yard.

Ed paused the TV. "Wait a minute." He pushed the back arrow on the remote then hit Play again. His finger hovered over the pause button until the perfect second. He hit the button. "Sure as shit, it's that FBI lady from the gas station standing there with all the cops." Ed pressed Play again, and the reporter continued.

"At this point in time, the For Sale sign behind me looks to be the only connection police seem to have. This is Lon Cabrera reporting live for Channel 4 Breaking News."

Ed slapped his knees and laughed. "Pretty soon this entire city is going to be frozen with fear. Everyone is going to be afraid to put their house up for sale. That FBI bitch is about to earn her fat paycheck. I think it's time to up the ante."

Chapter 24

Most of the officers had gathered back at the house. Three hours had gone by. Every car on the street had been photographed and every neighbor had been interviewed.

"I can't believe nobody noticed a damn thing." I pressed my palms against my temples in hopes that it would subdue my pounding headache. "Okay, listen up, guys. We need everyone who took photographs of the cars to send those pictures to the tech department at the central station. They can start checking into who owns the vehicles and if the owners have police records. We appreciate your help with this." I turned to Sergeant Bateman. "Did your men find anything unusual or questionable along the street, sidewalk, or on the property?"

"No, nothing, Agent Monroe."

"I figured as much. He's in and out quickly and leaves no evidence. J.T.?"

"Sure thing, Jade. Cap, have you heard back from the officers who went to the grocery store?"

Hardy looked at his watch. "Nope, but I'll take care of

that right now." He stepped away to a quieter spot to make the call.

I looked down the street and noticed that the news vans had left the area. "Okay, I think we can pull down the tape so the neighbors can come and go as they please, but we'll keep the house cordoned off. We need someone out here to nail plywood over the door."

J.T. tipped his chin at the officer standing next to him. "Take care of that, please, and stick around until the job is done."

"Yes, sir."

I leaned in next to J.T. "We need to take down that For Sale sign or this house is going to be the neighborhood sideshow. As a matter of fact, we should do that at all the crime scenes. No need to advertise where the murders took place."

"Good point, Jade. Officer Blake, make sure that gets done too."

An hour ago, Stan and his forensic team left and took the grocery bags along to dust for prints. I wasn't optimistic that they'd find anything since they hadn't at the other crime scenes. I was certain the perp was gloved at all times.

"How about heading back to the station where we can figure out what we do and don't have."

I heard a smirk behind us and turned to see Hardy approaching. "That'll be a short list, Jade."

"Get anything from the grocery store?" J.T. asked.

"Sure did. The officers said the videotape showed Jackie checking out at nine thirty-seven. The parking lot cam showed nothing amiss—nobody approached her. She put the groceries in her trunk, walked the cart to the cart corral, got in her car, and drove away. The last they saw of her, she was turning left out of the parking lot."

"There are cameras at most retail stores, though. We can follow her car."

Hardy furrowed his brows. "Sure, but only up to a point. The nearest camera to this older neighborhood is three miles away at the gas station on Hillside Street. This area is still undeveloped as far as retail and commercial establishments."

J.T. dipped his hand into his pocket and pulled out the keys for the Explorer. "Let's go back to the station. We need to come up with a plan of action. Somehow, some way, we have to stay a few steps ahead of this guy or we'll never catch him."

"Roger that, just follow me," Hardy said as he climbed into his cruiser and turned the key.

Back at the police station, we joined the captain in his office and dropped down in his guest chairs.

"You know this case may go unsolved, don't you, Cap? It isn't often that we have no evidence, no suspects, no motive, and no connection between the victims." I rubbed my temples again.

"Head still hurting?" J.T. asked.

"Yeah, I guess my brain is in overdrive." I pulled the tin of ibuprofen out of my purse and excused myself. "Gotta get some water. I'll be right back."

"I have water here. Stay put, Jade." Hardy reached into his desk drawer and pulled out three small bottles of water.

He slid two across his desk and cracked open the cap of his own.

"Thanks." I guzzled down four ibuprofen tablets with a gulp of water. "Anyway, back to our conversation. The victims aren't the connection, so that takes us back to Scenic View Realty. It's the only common link between any of them."

"Okay, so what does that actually mean, and why a real estate company?"

A knock sounded on Hardy's door, and Andrews popped in. "Just wanted to update you, sir. We have Beth Sloane in box one and Tara Lamar in box two. Beth is giving us as much information as she can remember about the night she discovered Mr. and Mrs. King on their kitchen floor. She may have passed someone walking down the sidewalk or driving out of the neighborhood. We're hoping she may have seen something that she doesn't even realize is important."

"Good idea. Try to jog her memory as much as you can. And Tara?"

"We need to know everything about Jackie that she can tell us. Apparently they've been best friends for years."

"Where's her family? Have they been notified yet?" J.T. asked.

"It's Bateman's jurisdiction, so we figured they would take care of that. At this point, all anyone knows is that she's missing. According to Tara, the parents are divorced and have been estranged from Jackie for years. They don't live in the area, and Tara doesn't know how to find them."

"Any siblings?"

"A brother in the service who is currently deployed overseas."

Hardy groaned. "Nothing is ever easy. Okay, tape both interviews. I'll review them later."

Andrews nodded. "You got it."

"Back to the real estate company," J.T. said. "Maybe we need to check into each agent personally and see if there's bad blood between them and someone else."

I shook my head. "But why kill innocent homeowners? That part of it doesn't make sense. We need to look at the bigger picture. Scenic View is a huge corporation, but maybe they're shady. They could be connected to the mob or doing underhanded transactions. They could be in cahoots with the banks, the home appraisers, or the inspectors and getting kickbacks from any of them. I'm not saying that's what's happening and I don't want to start a smear campaign, but we could be looking at this entirely backward." I jotted down some quick notes so I wouldn't forget. "Either somebody is trying to take down Scenic View Realty specifically or they want to stop all home sales in the metro Omaha area, one company at a time."

Chapter 25

Ed blended in with the crowd of people who stood twenty feet away from the King house. Candles, flowers, and cards filled the sidewalk. The house and property, still wrapped in yellow tape, was off limits to looky-loos.

Humph, the For Sale sign is gone. Afraid of bad publicity, are you? Let's see what's going on at poor Sarah's house.

The drive from one home to the other wasn't far. Ed arrived fifteen minutes later and walked the final block to find a similar scene in front of Sarah's house. A makeshift memorial honoring Sarah Cummings lined the sidewalk and extended into the grassy area in front of the street. Her yard, still taped off, was watched by a patrol unit that circled the neighborhood to make sure nobody trespassed on the property. Ed engaged in senseless chitchat with onlookers and snapped photos to fit in with everyone else. A TV crew setting up in front of a neighboring house caught his eye. He moved in closer to hear the broadcast.

"This is Tammy Hawn, Channel 9 News, reporting from the home of slain library employee Sarah Cummings.

The sidewalk along the house has been transformed into a memorial to pay respect to the woman who was senselessly killed Monday afternoon. To our knowledge, the police are still stumped by these recent murders. Ahead and to my right, the For Sale sign stood until the police department had it taken down just thirty minutes ago. Even without the sign, the location of this brutal murder can't be forgotten. Hundreds of people have come by to pay their respects with cards and flowers. The yellow crime scene tape, still present, is a constant reminder of the horror that took place at 439 Prentice Street. This is Tammy Hawn, Channel 9 News, signing off in front of the home of Sarah Cummings, whom we believe to be the first victim of the Scenic View Serial Killer."

The cameraman panned the crowd and zoomed in on the house and sidewalk before shutting down his equipment. Tammy Hawn handed her microphone off to an assistant. "Let's go. We need to get this piece ready to broadcast on the evening news."

Ed turned around and headed down the sidewalk with his fist covering his laughter. The nickname Tammy Hawn had come up with—Scenic View Serial Killer—was brilliant. He had seen and heard enough, and he had work to do. A new plan—the best one yet—bubbled up in his mind. It would definitely make law enforcement stand up and take notice. The city would panic, and the press would demand answers.

Chapter 27

It was dark by the time Ed put the finishing touches on the painted sign. He'd let it dry overnight, install the hooks tomorrow, then search for another home seller. His deeds would have to be done under cover of darkness from now on. Too many police had been patrolling the residential neighborhoods.

He pulled the string attached to the overhead bulb, and the shed went black. Only the light shining from the cottage's porch illuminated his way as he crossed the driveway to the front door. Inside the house, Ed woke up his laptop and clicked on Google Maps. He'd blindside a neighboring city while all eyes were watching Omaha.

Bellevue might work. The city is definitely large enough. Let's see how many houses are for sale in the area.

Ed entered the words *homes for sale in Bellevue, Nebraska* in the search bar and browsed the results.

"Perfect, there's plenty to choose from. Now to pick the next victim and make a real statement."

With the PeopleSeeker tab open, Ed typed in several

home addresses. He had time to be particular in choosing a victim. His next attack wouldn't take place until well after dark.

Chapter 28

William Stewart took a deep breath and cracked his neck from left to right. A glass of water sat on the table next to him, and he'd need it. He had a lot of explaining to do.

"Before you start, Mr. Stewart, I just want you to know everything you say is being recorded and videotaped," I said.

He nodded with a groan. "Whatever. I don't know what you expect to get from me."

"How about the truth?" Hardy said. "This isn't some kindergarten prank, Mr. Stewart. People are being murdered, and we need to put a stop to it. If you've participated in any wrongdoing and have been threatened because of it, we need to know right now."

"Who hasn't done less than legal things?" He looked at J.T.

"You're really looking at me? I'm an FBI agent, moron."

I had to hold my laughter.

"Fine, I've had gambling debts that I've borrowed against, but I swear, they've been paid off with over-the-top penalties attached. A year ago I began to invite big-time players to invest in real estate holdings I had assembled. The plan was to get people to invest their money in these holdings that I had bought for deeply discounted prices. I'd make improvements and then flip them for double the price that I'd paid. Everyone would make money."

"Yeah, people flip properties all the time. What was so different about yours?" J.T. asked.

"None of them really existed. All of the documents were fake. The pictures I sent the investors were random lots and homes that I didn't really buy. I had attorneys, bankers, inspectors, and title companies in my pocket, and they were getting big bucks to falsify the documents. I'd pay the oldest investors with the newest investors' money. Because they got great returns, they'd recommend my company to their friends, and the money pool grew exponentially."

"Is your middle name Bernie?"

He glared at me. "The problem is, I don't know who I pissed off the most. Anybody involved in my scheme could be doing this, or none of them. I'm only guessing."

"You've received threats, though, haven't you?" Hardy asked.

"No, and none of this has come to light publicly. I want to pay people back and keep my reputation intact. If my real estate business is ruined, I'd have to sell all of my other businesses to raise capital."

I shrugged. "It sucks to be you. Maybe you would rather go to prison? Ponzi schemes are a federal crime, you know. You'll probably serve time no matter what when this is all said and done."

J.T. pushed a piece of paper and a pen across the table. "Start writing down the names of people or companies that invested in your scheme. We want the largest investors first. Also, what's the name of your fake company?"

"Wipast Holdings."

"What the hell does that stand for?" J.T. asked.

"It's just an acronym, nothing more."

I got up and walked to the door. "I need to update Spelling."

J.T. pointed at the table as he and Hardy rose too. "Keep working on that list. We'll be back soon."

We headed to Hardy's office and met up with Andrews and Tyler in the hallway.

"Beth Sloane and Tara Lamar's interviews are done, and they've both gone home, sir," Andrews said.

"Did you learn any more than what was on their initial statements?"

"I'd have to compare them side by side. All Beth added was that the Kings were well liked and often got together with the neighbors in the clubhouse to play cards and board games. Most of those activities were held during the daytime hours. That's why she thought it odd that their porch light was on that night. They rarely went out or had people in after dark."

Hardy looked at Brad Tyler. "What about Tara?"

"She's a mess, but she said Jackie is tough. She's holding out for the best and praying that Jackie will be found alive. She didn't have anything new to add other than she and all of her friends would like to help in the foot search."

"Where are we on that?"

"It's in the preliminary stages, sir. We're setting up search grids from her house outward. It isn't like there are rural areas nearby, though. Jackie's house is in the middle of a residential neighborhood, but there's plenty of vacant land to the south. The perp could have taken her out of the immediate area, and probably did. We plan to search all retention ponds, parks, dumpsters, and empty houses in a five-mile radius. After that, I'm at a loss."

"Okay, keep us posted."

We entered Hardy's office and sat down.

"We can hold Stewart for the time being, right?" Hardy asked.

J.T. tapped his fingers on the desk. "He admitted to running a Ponzi scheme, so yes. That kind of scam takes time to clean up, though. A consulting firm would have to be hired as a receiver. They would have to track down every investor then find out how much money each is owed. Claim forms would have to be sent out. It's usually a huge pain and takes years to complete. The best we can do at the moment is to alert the SEC and keep Stewart in your city lockup until he has a court appearance."

I added, "Let's not get sidetracked by him. The bigger problem is the murders. That has to be our first and foremost concern."

J.T. tipped his head. "Why don't you make the call to Spelling? I want to view that broadcast Stewart is whining about before we go back into the interrogation room."

"Sure, I'll catch up with you in a bit." I found a quiet

corner in the visitors' lounge to make that call to our boss. It was after eight o'clock, and we still had a while to go before we'd wrap things up for the night. I updated Spelling with the news Stewart had given us.

"I can understand why investors would be outraged. Still, depending on how many people got sucked into his scheme, it could take forever to figure out if one of them is committing these murders."

The call went silent. "Boss?"

"Yeah, I'm pondering. None of this feels right to me. It takes time before an investor would realize they've been had, and if Stewart is a smart guy, neither his personal name nor any other entities he owns would be attached to Wipast Holdings. I hate to say this, Jade, but we don't have the luxury of investigating every person who put money into his scam, especially while there are murders taking place right under our noses. Go back to the drawing board and use old-fashioned detective work and get plenty of feet on the ground. Stewart will be held accountable for his own crimes, but I really don't think the murders are connected to his Ponzi scheme. Email me the initial list he's putting together, and I'll get the ball rolling on this end with an alert to the SEC first thing Monday morning."

"Yes, sir, I'll get that over to you within the hour. Good night."

"Good night, Jade."

I clicked off the call and pocketed my phone. I joined J.T. and Hardy in the interrogation room, where Stewart sat with his hands folded on the table.

"Short list?" I looked down at the paper and saw ten names at most.

"I don't have a photographic memory. All of the paperwork for that investment is at home in my file cabinet."

I leaned over the table. "Let me enlighten you, Mr. Stewart. It's a scheme, not an investment. Don't delude yourself."

"Whatever."

Hardy spoke up. "Do you have a passport?"

"Of course I do. My family and I enjoy vacations."

Hardy cracked a smile. "I hate to burst your bubble, Mr. Stewart, but your family vacations are a thing of the past. You're spending some time here, at our modest facility, but soon enough you'll be enjoying Club Fed. Tomorrow, we're picking up your passport and all of those important papers. We wouldn't want anything to accidentally get shredded. I'll have the warrant in hand by morning."

"We need your phone, Mr. Stewart," J.T. said.

"I want my phone call now. I should have asked to do that at the beginning." William dropped his head to the table.

"But you didn't. You can make your call from the phone in the hallway. Decide wisely—you only get one call. Is it going to be to your lawyer or your wife?"

Stewart stared at the floor. "My lawyer."

Hardy asked several officers to escort Mr. Stewart to the phone. He was read his rights before he left the interrogation room.

"So, did you guys catch that news segment from this afternoon?" I asked.

J.T. responded. "Yeah, a memorial was set up in front of Sarah Cummings's house. They ran the broadcast from a few houses away so they could zoom in on the crowd and the fact that the For Sale sign had been taken down. In my opinion, the media is trying to instill fear in the community so every family tunes into their station to get the latest information. I'm sure part of it is because we haven't made a formal statement to the public yet."

"We didn't have anything to give them."

Hardy furrowed his brows at me. "And we still don't."

Chapter 29

Ed was pleased with his pick. Marilyn LaSota, a female name chosen out of a hat, was the next victim who would feel the burn of Ed's knife piercing her flesh. Ed studied the map and the best route in and out of her neighborhood. Her home, advertised as a newer private retreat, was the last one at the end of a cul-de-sac in a recently built subdivision. Vacant lots still dotted the neighborhood.

Easy pickins.

Ed would make the first round in the truck to drop off the sign, then exit her street, park several blocks away, and return on foot.

According to the PeopleSeeker website, Marilyn was a fifty-six-year-old divorcee who lived alone. He tapped the computer keys to pull up a mapped grid of all the houses in a three-block area of her home that were armed with alarm systems. Hers wasn't.

"Perfect." Ed checked the time and still had an hour to kill. He wanted to make sure it was late enough that most people had settled in for the night. No barking dogs or teenagers getting home at their ten o'clock curfew, just peace and quiet. He'd slip in and out, unseen and unheard.

He clicked the porch light, slid into his sneakers, and made his way to the shed. Inside, he felt for the string and pulled it. The single-car garage-sized room lit up.

"Aah, the sign turned out perfectly if I do say so myself." He admired his artistic skills and the colorfully painted board as he tugged on the eye bolts screwed into the top. They were lodged deep into the wood and secure. He wrapped the sign in a sheet, carried it out of the shed, and placed it in the bed of the truck.

Back inside the house, Ed clicked on the television set. A half hour more and he'd leave. The drive to Marilyn's home would take twenty minutes at that time of night. He thought about the news station that had run a segment in front of Sarah Cummings's house earlier that day.

What channel was that?

He remembered seeing the station's logo on the microphone as the reporter handed it back to her assistant.

Oh yeah, Channel 9.

Ed scrolled through the stations. The Channel 9 Evening News was already broadcasting and airing the weekend's weather update. He rose from the couch and grabbed two cheese sticks out of the refrigerator. They would hold him over until he returned from his task. Back on the couch, he waited through six commercials before the news resumed. He mindlessly bit into the cheese sticks as he stared at the screen.

"Whoa, there's the segment from this afternoon." Ed

turned up the volume and listened as the reporter talked. He mouthed her words as if he had memorized everything she said. Her piece ended, and the cameraman panned the house, the enormous array of flowers and cards, and finally the crowd. "Shit!" Ed stood and threw a sofa pillow across the room, knocking a glass off the kitchen counter. It exploded into shards that slid across the floor. "There I am, front and center on the damn screen." He paced back and forth and muttered. "I thought I walked away before the cameraman zoomed in on everything. What if that FBI woman watches this and recognizes me? So what. Plenty of other people were there too, showing their respects. There's no reason for her to be suspicious, and that's if she even sees it. She probably forgot what I look like, anyway." Ed dug his fingertips into his scalp and cursed his stupidity. "Damn women, damn women, damn women. It's all their fault, and they're going to pay."

He burst out the front door and climbed into the truck before slamming the door at his side. Everything he needed was next to him on the passenger seat. He set his phone's navigation to end at 1663 Fremont Court. Marilyn had less than an hour to live.

Chapter 30

"Let's call it a night, agents. My wife doesn't even wait up for me anymore. I'm surprised she still remembers my name. There isn't much we can do about Stewart until we get the warrant in the morning. All he did was open up an enormous secondary problem that doesn't solve the first."

I fisted my yawn. "Yeah, sounds good. I emailed that short list to Spelling already, so I guess we're done for the night. He's dumping Stewart's scheme on the SEC first thing Monday. It'll be their mess to figure out. Just so you know, Spelling doesn't think these cases are related."

"Great, I guess we're back to ground zero." J.T.'s stomach began to rumble, so he gave it a rub. "Apparently, we forgot to eat dinner tonight."

"We sure did. Let's hit a drive-through on our way back to the hotel."

The three of us walked the hallway toward the building's main entrance.

"Cap!"

We turned to the voice behind us. Sergeant Lyles was speed walking our way.

With his hand deep in his pocket, Hardy jiggled his keys and pulled them out. "What's up, Lyles?"

"Patrol just found Jackie Stern's car."

"Shit." Hardy raised his brows at us. "Can dinner wait?"

J.T. tipped his head toward the double glass doors. "Yeah, let's go."

Lyles climbed into the driver's seat of the nearest cruiser, and Hardy took the passenger side. Lyles stuck his head out the window and looked back as we climbed into the Explorer. "Follow me."

Fifteen minutes later, after we bore down the freeway behind the cruiser, its lights and siren engaged, we finally exited onto a surface street. We followed Lyles for five more blocks and into what looked to be an older, somewhat run-down neighborhood.

Brake lights flashed in front of us, and the cruiser turned in to a parking lot. I unlatched my seat belt as J.T. brought the Explorer to a stop. "Looks like we're here."

We joined Lyles and Hardy next to their car. Lyles pointed. "These buildings are tenements that were constructed in the late sixties. At the time, they were fine for newly married couples, guys returning from Vietnam, and people working at low-paying jobs. Now, the area is a heroine hot spot and riddled with criminals and prostitutes." He jerked his head to the right. "Anyway, that's enough of a jog down memory lane. Here's her car. Patrol noticed it when they did their nightly rounds."

"Anyone look inside yet?" Hardy asked.

"No, Cap. They were waiting for your go-ahead."

As we approached Jackie's orange Fiesta, Lyles illuminated the way with his flashlight. Hardy was the first to slip on gloves. He jerked on the door handle. "Locked." He walked around to the passenger side and pulled on the door. "Same over here. Lyles, grab your punch and pop the driver's side window."

"Yes, sir." Lyles walked back to his cruiser then returned moments later. With a tap of the emergency rescue tool, he shattered the window glass, reached inside, and unlocked the door.

Hardy pointed at the back of the car. "Pop the trunk."

Lyles pulled the lever along the footwell, and the trunk release engaged.

"Ready?" J.T. asked.

We nodded. Lyles shined the light, and Hardy lifted the trunk lid. I held my breath. We let out a simultaneous sigh. The trunk was empty.

"Let's get the crime lab's flatbed out here to pick up the car. May I?" I reached for the flashlight and shined it into the interior of the Fiesta. "At least it doesn't look like anything violent has taken place inside. How many units do you think this complex has?"

Lyles rubbed his chin then pointed. "These are projects, Agent Monroe, and they cover several blocks. I'm guessing there are over a hundred units in total. There are at least twenty buildings. That's a lot of interviews to conduct."

"I agree, and that means we're going to need help. We'll probably be here until sunup."

Chapter 31

Ed inhaled deeply through his nose to calm himself. He closed his eyes and slowly blew out the air through his mouth. The therapist he had been court-ordered to see during the divorce proceedings recommended those techniques to calm his outbursts of rage. Sometimes it helped and other times it didn't, but Ed couldn't work effectively if he went in half-cocked.

The male voice on his GPS told him to turn right at the next set of lights. Ed rolled to a stop at the red light, checked for oncoming cars, and continued on. A quick left and one more right took him to the intersection of Grange Street and Fremont Court. He made the last turn and followed Fremont to the end of the cul-de-sac, where he killed his headlights. There, standing alone, was the home of Marilyn LaSota. Her nearest neighbor was four lots away.

Yeah, I can work around that. Now I just have to find the For Sale sign.

Ed coasted along the curb at a snail's pace as he looked for the sign. He squinted at every shape, trying to make out its form. Shadows from low-hanging limbs fooled him while others blew slightly in the breeze. He tapped the brakes lightly and slowed to a stop. Ed shifted into Park then rolled down the passenger side window. A familiar noise caught his attention.

That's the sound of the sign swaying.

Ed scooted across the bench seat and climbed out the passenger side. That door, with less cancerous rust, didn't creak as badly as the driver's door. He stretched his arms and reached into the truck bed to catch the end of the sheet that the sign was wrapped in. Ed pulled it toward him and lifted it out. With the sign in his arms, he followed the sound. There, along her flower garden and hidden slightly from above by limbs, stood the For Sale sign. Ed dipped his hand in his pocket and pulled out the flashlight. He made a circle with the beam and checked his surroundings. It was time to get to work.

With the sign eased off the hooks, Ed set it on the ground and replaced it with his own. He carried the original sign to the truck and wrapped it in the sheet. With that sign lying flat in the truck bed, Ed climbed in the passenger door, scooted across to the driver's seat, and quietly slipped away. Back at Grange, he switched on the headlights and continued to the next intersection where he turned right. At the end of that street, he killed the engine and stepped out before locking the truck.

Walking parallel to Fremont Street on Vine would prove safer for Ed. Even if innocent eyes took the time to peer out of their windows, not a soul would be seen on Marilyn's cul-de-sac. He cut through vacant lots that hadn't been excavated yet and finally arrived at Marilyn's backyard. Ed was only fifty feet from the side door that opened into her garage. He slipped on his gloves. Short bursts of the flashlight gave Ed just enough illumination to see the door. He pulled a tension wrench and a paper clip from his pocket and slid them into the knob's locking mechanism. He used an up-and-down scrubbing motion, and it took only a minute for the door's lock to release. The flashlight guided Ed around Marilyn's car as he slunk through the garage to the interior door. He gave it a slow turn. It was open. Ed slipped off his shoes before entering the laundry room and tucked them under his arm. Standard new houses had floor plans that usually led from the laundry room to the kitchen. Beyond the kitchen would be a family room, dining room, and a hallway. He'd find Marilyn in one of those bedrooms. Ed thought about Sarah's house, where the layout was almost identical.

With a quick burst of light, Ed checked the kitchen floor. No dog dishes—a plus that would make his job much easier. He tiptoed into the living room and placed his shoes next to the front door then continued down the carpeted hallway. Behind the first open door was a full bath. Farther down were two empty bedrooms. The final bedroom, located on the right side of the hall, was partially open. That one had to be hers. He had just enough space to squeeze through sideways without disturbing the door. Ed took a deep breath, let it out slowly, and inched forward. She was only twenty feet away.

He could hear her constant, even breaths—in and out, in and out. Soon she would be silenced for good. Ed patted the sheath and lifted the Taser out of his pocket. The partially open blinds let in enough of the crescent moon that Ed could see the shape of a body under the blankets. He slowly crept toward her then froze in place when she rolled over and rearranged herself. He waited, barely breathing, before continuing. Ed rounded the bed and stared down at her, only two feet away. He needed to find skin that wasn't covered by the blanket, and the only exposed area was her head.

Guess you're getting it in the face, lady. Sorry about that, but it won't matter much in a few minutes, anyway.

Ed pressed the Taser against her head and pulled the trigger. The ticking sound on her skin sent shivers up his spine. She grunted and twitched violently then went limp. He didn't have a lot of time. She'd come to in less than a minute. Ed ran to the wall and hit the lights. Then he jammed the Taser back into his pocket. She was regaining consciousness and began to moan. With his fist cocked, Ed delivered a hard punch to her face and knocked her out cold. With several hard jerks, he ripped the blanket off the bed and wrapped her in it. Heaving, he picked up her body, slung her over his shoulder, and carried her out into the night.

Ed thought about the statement the sign would send, especially with a dead body perched against it.

If this doesn't do the trick, nothing will.

He dropped the blanket to the ground and unwrapped

Marilyn. Then he dragged her to the post. With her back propped against the sign, Ed slid out his knife from the sheath and plunged it into her throat. She jerked, then her head slumped against her shoulder. The release of air was audible as he pulled the knife back. He listened until she went silent. After several swipes against the lawn to clean it, Ed put the knife away and draped the blanket over Marilyn's body. She reminded him of a Halloween prop, sitting in the yard as blood at her neckline seeped through the white blanket. With the help of his flashlight, he stared at his handiwork then pointed the beam at the sign. He whispered the words he had written and smiled. "Yep, that ought to do it." Ed retreated into the vacant lots. Minutes later, he drove away.

Chapter 32

The residents who actually opened their doors weren't happy. We were intruding on their Friday night, and it was late—well past three o'clock in the morning. We had been at it for hours. Four officers from the nearest precinct joined us in the knock and talks. Doors opened only a crack, and sour faces peered out. We weren't invited in, and I understood why. From the angry, guilty, and tired looks on their faces, the residents probably felt imposed upon and more than likely had something to hide. I was certain police officers were the last people they wanted to see, and it was glaringly apparent we weren't welcome.

We took a break on the second-story landing in building seven. We needed to regroup.

I pulled out my cell phone from my pocket and checked the time. "We've only been to seven buildings, and it's three forty-five in the morning?" I groaned. So far nobody had anything helpful to tell us.

The crime lab had taken the car back to the evidence garage several hours earlier. Upon initial exam, they said nothing looked unnatural for a car belonging to a twenty-seven-year-old woman. Several fast-food wrappers were balled up on the floor, and a half-drunk bottle of water sat in the cup holder. A cell phone charging cord hung from the power port, and a romance novel—with a bookmark at chapter nine—lay on the back seat. Todd Mills from the crime lab also informed us that the driver's seat was positioned correctly for someone between five foot three and five foot seven. Their in-depth inspection would take several days to complete.

"Ready to continue?" J.T. asked.

I gave him a tired yawn and nodded. "Yeah, but I wish I had a hot cup of coffee in my hand."

"Let's push through another hour of this and then take a break. There has to be an all-night diner around here somewhere."

"Actually there is, Agent Harper, about three blocks away," Lyles said.

We agreed and continued down the block to the next group of buildings. Our results were the same at every door we knocked on. No one had seen the car being parked or noticed a suspicious looking person in the area. I had to chuckle at the thought. Everyone in that area looked suspicious, including the tenants.

We decided to break before entering building twelve.

"Which is faster, Lyles, walking to the diner or back to our cars?"

He looked up the street then back at the area we had come from. "Honestly, Agent Monroe, I think we should walk. By now, most of the shady characters in this neighborhood have gone to bed."

"Fine with me." I grinned. "I think we look intimidating enough to scare anyone off, anyway."

Hardy piped up. "I'm too tired to intimidate anyone, and I wouldn't have the energy right now to bother. I just need a doughnut and a large coffee. Talk to me about intimidation afterward."

J.T. patted Hardy's back. "We'll be done in a few hours, Cap. Maybe we can take turns catching a short nap at the station."

My mind flashed back to the days we'd searched for J.T. and his sister Julie. I'd be surprised if anybody on our team got eight hours of sleep during that entire week.

"Here we are," Lyles said. "It looks like we have the place all to ourselves."

I groaned my relief. "I just hope the coffee is fresh and strong."

The all-night diner was quiet at that time of morning. We entered and seated ourselves at the long lunch counter. Four tables, lined against the glass wall that looked out over the sidewalk, were empty. A man who'd probably been dozing in the back came out when the bell above the door dinged.

"Morning, officers." He passed out a handful of menus as we turned over our coffee cups.

I spoke for the group. "Coffee for starters would be great."

"Sure thing, ma'am. I'll make a fresh pot."

"How old are those doughnuts?" Hardy pointed at the glass case behind the man.

"The bakery delivers them every morning at three o'clock. We get our morning rush of customers"—he looked at his wristwatch—"in about forty-five minutes."

"Then I'll take two chocolate-filled eclairs." Hardy rubbed his stomach. "I don't think I've eaten anything since yesterday's lunch."

"None of us have. I'll take two apple fritters," J.T. said.

We took turns ordering our sugary breakfasts, knowing we'd be back at the interviews before the morning crowd entered the diner. With the carafe of hot coffee and plenty of doughnuts in front of us, we'd be set for the next few hours.

"Maybe we should pass the interviews off to the local beat cops and busy ourselves with something more productive," Hardy said. "This actually isn't our jurisdiction."

"It's your call, Cap," I said. "We're here to help with whatever we can." I poured another round of coffee for each of us and bit into my second French cruller.

Hardy's phone rang as he took a gulp of coffee. "Nothing good happens at this time of morning." He furrowed his brows and answered. "Captain Kip Hardy here." He paused while the person on the other end spoke. "What? Where? Who found her?" He slammed his open hand on the counter. "Son of a bitch. Thanks, Mike, we're on our way."

I jumped off my stool. "Somebody found Jackie?"

"No, another murder, except this time it was in

Bellevue. Let's go. The locals are already on-site."

I turned to the four officers. "Guys, please continue the interviews. Have your sergeant call me as soon as he can. I slid my card across the counter then handed the waiter a twenty. I grabbed my cruller and raced out the door behind Hardy, Lyles, and J.T.

We headed to our vehicles as Hardy explained what the caller had said.

"That was Chief Mike Gebhardt from the Bellevue PD. He's been following the sporadic news broadcasts and thought the crime scene was similar enough to alert us at the central station. The night desk sergeant patched him through to me."

"Who found the victim?" I asked.

"The newspaper delivery driver saw something odd in the yard when he stopped to toss the newspaper in the driveway."

"What the hell could be in the yard?"

"The body," Hardy said. "Mike told me the victim has a neck wound just like the others."

"So it's a female?" J.T. asked.

Hardy nodded. "The only difference is, she was placed outside and covered by a white blanket. The perp leaned her against the For Sale sign."

Lyles whistled. "Holy shit, that's brazen."

Stress covered Hardy's face. "Chief Gebhardt said the sign was replaced with a different one. The new one contained a message from the killer himself."

"He's getting bolder. Apparently, he isn't getting the

reaction he's looking for. How far is Bellevue?" J.T. asked when we reached the vehicles.

"It's about fifteen minutes to our south," Lyles said. "We'll lead the way."

Chapter 33

J.T. checked his mirrors and fell in line behind Lyles. We merged onto the freeway and headed south.

"This is getting out of control. Spelling thinks we should start over. We need to develop a profile of this killer and what his motivation is before we'll ever know who we're looking for. You caught that about the neck wound being the same as the others."

"Sure," J.T. said. "The victim is a woman."

"Then Spelling is on the right track. The killer isn't after Stewart. He's someone who's enraged by a particular woman. He's taking out that hate on other females, surrogates in a way."

"Then why kill Bob King?"

"Wrong place, wrong time, possibly?" I thought hard about my response since Bob King was indeed the only man killed so far. "J.T., I think I have it. The newspaper was lying open to the crossword puzzle, and Chad's name was written in the margins. We've established that was Gloria's chair since ladies' glasses were on the side table, along with the house phone. Somebody with a burner phone, probably the killer, was the last entry in the call log that night. Gloria had to be the one who answered the phone. Maybe the killer thought she lived alone and had no idea Bob was there. It was the perp who pretended to be Chad Nolan. That's why his name was penciled in on the edge of the newspaper."

"You know, Jade, that's the most logical thing I've heard since we got to Omaha. That has to be how it happened. So what is similar with all these women that he chose them?"

"I don't know. Their ages were totally different. They didn't live in the same neighborhoods or work in the same fields. They didn't have friends in common." I rubbed my temples and hoped it would help me think. "Hair color, maybe? Each woman's hair was a shade of brown, but none were exactly the same."

"Let's revisit that theory and others when we get back to the station. It looks like Lyles is slowing down."

We exited the freeway at the ramp and turned right at the lights. Traveling several more blocks down Grange Street took us to Fremont Court.

"I guess we're here," J.T. said as we made a right turn behind Lyles and were immediately stopped by a patrol unit blocking the street. We waited as Lyles spoke to the officer and handed over his badge. The officer clicked his radio and spoke to somebody farther down the street before giving the badge back to Lyles. He moved the barricade aside and waved us through. The sun, peeking over the horizon, was lighting the sky. I was thankful for the daylight. We'd be able to check out the crime scene and evaluate it much better.

We couldn't make it to the end of the cul-de-sac, so we exited our vehicles and walked the final hundred feet.

"Looks like everyone is here," I said as we got closer. "I hope they're keeping this off the scanners."

The ME and crime lab vehicles filled the driveway, and three squad cars and several cruisers took up the curb space in front of the victim's house. The yellow tape that wrapped the perimeter of the property flapped in the breeze. A privacy barrier had been erected in front of the body to hide the gruesome scene from curious neighbors. The officers on-site were instructed to keep them away and say nothing.

Hardy jerked his chin toward the foldout barrier. I had seen and used them plenty of times in my career. Nothing good ever lay beyond those curtains.

A man who looked like the one in charge at the moment turned toward us and reached for Hardy's hand. "Captain Hardy."

"Mike. Hate to meet up under these circumstances."

The man nodded and shook Hardy's hand. Cap introduced the chief to J.T. and me.

Joe Torres, the ME, looked up over his shoulder. "Cap."

"Joe."

We moved in closer and knelt at Joe's side. "What have we got?" J.T. asked.

"Dead middle-aged female. Her name is Marilyn LaSota, according to the newspaper delivery guy. All we have so far is that she lived here alone."

"What's your initial assessment?" I asked.

"Rigor has begun. I'd say she's been dead at least three

hours but not more than seven. Manner of death is the same as the other women—multiple stab wounds to the throat. Strangely enough, she's been hit in the face with the Taser."

The blanket had been pulled down to the woman's waist, and her nightgown was exposed.

J.T. spoke up. "She was obviously in bed when he attacked her, hence the sleepwear and blanket. Her face could have been the only area exposed as she slept. What's with the mark on her cheek?"

"At the moment it's only a guess, but I'd say he punched her." Joe carefully cupped her face and nodded. "Feels like her left cheekbone is broken."

I pushed off my knees and stared at the sign in front of me. "J.T., what do you make of that?"

"He wants to get in people's heads." J.T. mumbled a few curse words before reading the sign in a whisper.

Hatred fills your heart and arrogance spills from your mouth. Innocent blood stains my hands because of it, and in the end, you'll be forced to swallow your pride.

J.T. pulled out his cell phone and snapped several pictures. "These words could mean a hundred different things depending on how they're interpreted. This sign is one more riddle we need to decipher, just like everything else with this case." He turned to everyone in the yard. "Listen up, people. I don't want the media to see this sign. They'd have a field day with it, and that's what the perp wants. He needs to feel in control, to run the show, and that's why he wrote it. He wants to see his work on TV. We aren't going to play along. If this sign or any information that didn't come directly from me or Agent Monroe gets leaked to the media, everyone standing here will answer to the FBI. Got it?"

A dozen people looked at J.T., nodded, then went about their business.

I patted J.T.'s shoulder and gave him an eyebrow raise. "All good, partner?"

"Yeah, sorry, that sounded too threatening."

"Nah—cops are tough. Harsh words roll off them like water off a duck. No worries." I approached Stan Fleet. "How far have you guys gotten?"

"We've photographed everything out here, primarily the victim. Now we're ready to go into the house. My guys will print all of the doorknobs, windows, and check for forced entry. I'm guessing the perp spent most of his time in the master bedroom. We'll go over that room thoroughly." He pointed at the vacant lots in the neighborhood. "Gebhardt's officers already cleared the yard, and now they're expanding their search out there."

"Okay, I'd like to join you in the house."

"Sure thing, Agent Monroe."

I jerked my head to get J.T.'s attention. He pocketed his cell phone and crossed the lawn.

"What's up?"

"I'm going inside. Just wondering what officer took that newspaper delivery driver's statement and if the driver is still around."

"I'll check that out. Go ahead with Stan and his team."

I walked to the house with Stan, Todd Mills, and Tony Myers. "Which door do you think he used to get inside?"

Stan stood back and took in the length of the house. He pointed at the side door that led into the garage. "Let's start with that one. Normally the bedrooms are the farthest distance from the garage. If I were an intruder, common sense would say to gain entry a good distance from the sleeping homeowner's bedroom."

"And the exit point?"

"He knew where and how he wanted to stage her, so likely the closest door to the sign in the yard."

"Makes sense, so that would be the front door."

"Correct."

We reached the side door, and Stan turned the knob. It popped open.

"Just as I thought. Either the victim forgot to lock the door or this is how the killer went in. He wouldn't care about locking the door at his back." Stan flipped on the interior garage light. "That door should be unlocked too."

It was, and we entered the laundry room.

"Watch your every step. There could be evidence anywhere."

"Understood." I glanced at the floor before I stepped in. "Stan, what's your take on those tiny pieces of dirt?"

"Check it out, Todd."

"It's real dirt, boss, like from outside."

"Okay, bag it. He could have crossed those vacant lots after all. Good eye, Jade."

We passed small pieces of similar looking dirt as we entered the kitchen. The trail, like little bread crumbs, ended before the hallway. "Give me a second. I want to see something." I crossed the living room to the front door and knelt. "Check it out, Stan. This is where he left his shoes." Crumbled pieces of dirt lay next to the doormat. "He must have carried them over here so he wouldn't wake her up. If he had them on, there would be more dirt on the floor."

Stan smirked. "You've never studied forensic science, huh?"

"Nah. Common sense, remember?" I gave him a quick smile.

"Let's check the master bedroom. We'll give the house a thorough going-over later, but since the homeowner lived alone, she likely slept in there."

I followed the forensic team down the hallway to the last door on the right, which stood wide open.

Stan gave me a questioning look. "Tell me this, Agent Monroe. Are you someone who sleeps with your bedroom door wide open, halfway closed, or fully closed?"

"I close my door completely, but we do have a cat and two birds in the house. Without pets, maybe halfway but never fully open."

"Most people don't sleep with the door open. He sneaked in here without waking her, so maybe it was partially open, but he'd have to swing it all the way open if he was carrying her out. We'll print the entire bedroom door, not just the knob."

We stepped into the room and looked around. The only

noticeable disturbance was at the bed, where the sheets lay partially on the floor.

"It doesn't look like there was any kind of a struggle," I said.

"I'm sure there wasn't. He zapped her then cold-cocked her as soon as he reached the bed. She didn't have a chance. I just hope the poor woman never woke up before he killed her."

"Me too." I took in a deep breath. "I'll let you guys get on with your work. I'm going back outside."

Stan nodded and began snapping photos.

Chapter 34

"Learn anything new since I was out here last?" I approached J.T., Lyles, Gebhardt, and Hardy, who had gathered a few feet from the body.

Gebhardt spoke up. "We called our tech department and gave them the plate number off her car. Her full name is Marilyn Jane LaSota, age fifty-six. She's a divorcee and has lived at this house for just over two years."

"Hoping to sell after the two-year capital gains time frame?"

"Maybe. We don't know who her next of kin is yet. I'm sure there's a cell phone in the house somewhere, but we'll get to that soon enough. I don't want foot traffic in there while Forensics is working."

"What about the statement from the newspaper delivery guy?"

"We took that as soon as the first officers arrived on the scene. He's going to come into the station and give us his formal written statement once he finishes his route. He was pretty shaken at the time, and I'm actually surprised he could work at all with her image in his mind."

Joe Torres joined us. "I'm about to load her up, guys."

"Yeah, go ahead. How soon before you have something for us?" Gebhardt asked.

"I'll email all of you my findings before five o'clock. I should have enough basic information by then." Joe called out to the assistant ME. "Let's get her on the gurney."

Stan and his team met up with us in the yard. "I'll take that blanket and sign back to the lab and go over them with a fine-toothed comb. If I was a lucky man, the paint on the sign would be something unique and easily traced, but in reality, it's likely just an acrylic base found in any store across the country. Todd and Tony are processing all the doors in the house along with the master bedroom. The dirt Jade noticed is probably from those vacant lots." Stan pointed beyond the house. "There look to be five or more empty lots on this cul-de-sac. I'd suggest having your officers walk all of them. There could be footprints leading back to where he came from."

Gebhardt called several of his men over. "Have you walked every vacant lot?"

"Only the one on the left side of the house, sir."

"Clear all of them. Make sure you're watching for footprints leading in and out."

"We need to get back to the station and figure out this maniac," J.T. said. "He's spreading his wings to different cities, which means nobody is safe."

We said goodbye to Chief Gebhardt and exchanged cards with him. I was certain we'd be in close communication with the Bellevue PD until this case was solved.

Back in the vehicles, we followed Lyles north to the central Omaha police station.

"Kind of quiet, Jade. What's on your mind?"

I shrugged. "Just trying to put the pieces together. We need to decipher that sign and figure out who this man hates so much and why his actions seem to revolve around Scenic View Realty."

J.T. gave me a surprised look. "Do you think they're actually related, or is it only because Scenic View is the largest real estate company in the area?"

"Who the hell knows? Every murder took place at a house with their For Sale sign in the yard. That can't be completely coincidental. Like Spelling said, we need to pound the pavement and talk to everyone these victims knew."

"Hardy's guys are already on that. We'll get their updates once we get back to the station."

"What about the news coverage and the tip line? Anything there?"

"Only what has come in, which isn't much, and what has aired, which is very broad. Don't forget, we haven't given the media a lot of information, only that several murders have taken place, and of course, they know the addresses. They're loose cannons, Jade, and have already given the killer a moniker. I'm sure he's totally on board with that. I had an idea I was about to share with you yesterday that got interrupted when Hardy had Tara on Skype."

"And that was?"

"Well, it's actually something you told me you and the team did when you were trying to find Julie and me."

"Go crazy?" I gave J.T. a thoughtful smile. "I don't ever want to relive that week again."

J.T. smirked his response. "Neither do I. Anyway, you said you guys watched street camera footage for days looking for the same vehicle to pass my condo."

"Right, the gold Mercedes. There were a lot of repetitive cars, though. People use the same routes to and from work every day. The Mercedes only stood out because it was going suspiciously slow and had limousine-tinted windows."

"True, but going with that idea, we can find the closest street cameras in the proximity of the victims' homes and watch for the same vehicle to drive by. That would definitely be more telling since none of the victims lived near each other."

"You're absolutely right. Now we may have something valid to work with. I want to see that news video from yesterday at Sarah's house too. We'll catch up on everything the officers have done so far, try to figure out what that sign means, then track down every camera the perp would have to pass to get to the homes. I think we finally have something to keep us busy other than chasing our tails. For now, as a precaution, we need to make sure every listing from Scenic View has been taken off the MLS database and every yard sign comes down."

"That's hundreds of homes throughout the state, Jade."

"And hundreds of lives."

Chapter 35

Once again we gathered in the conference room, and every chair had an occupant. Half the people in attendance were closing in on forty hours without sleep. Before the meeting began, Hardy asked Dana to bring in two carafes of coffee and a stack of cups.

"Okay, people, we're going around the table. I want to know everything that's been done so far and the outcome up to this point." Hardy pointed at Andrews. "What do you have, Fred?"

Fred rubbed his forehead as he studied his notes. "I can speak for Tyler, myself, and at least three of the officers in here, sir. We've interviewed personnel at the salons used by Sarah Cummings and Gloria King. Nothing stood out after speaking with the stylist that each of these women used. They only spoke of the weather, the monthly gossip magazines, and their latest activities. We couldn't find hardware store receipts or gym membership contracts at either home. The Kings seem to frequent Sammy's Steakhouse several times a month, but again, only the typical waiter-and-customer conversations were exchanged."

"Did we hear anything from the precinct where Jackie's vehicle was found?"

"We did, sir," Dixon said. "They didn't come up with any witnesses."

"And where is Forensics with the vehicle?" I asked.

"Not far enough, ma'am," Dixon said. "Half of the team is still at the latest victim's house in Bellevue."

I nodded solemnly. "That's true."

J.T. spoke up. "Is it feasible to pull Scenic View's listings from the MLS database?"

Hardy looked at Andrews. "I hate to ask, but can you call Lisa and find out how that's handled?"

"I'm on it, boss." Andrews stood and left the room.

"J.T., did you send those pictures to the printer?"

"I did, Cap, and they should be ready to pick up."

Hardy tipped his head at Franklin since he was closest to the door. "Paul, would you mind grabbing them?"

"Not at all."

I bumped J.T. with my knee to get his attention. I wanted him to mention his idea while we waited for the photos of the sign.

He cleared his throat. "I have an idea that we should implement immediately. It could prove useful, and I know this tactic has worked in the past."

"The floor is yours," Hardy said.

"We'll need to locate cameras nearest each of the victims' homes. It could be street cameras, retail space cameras, or cameras mounted on the sides of banks or office buildings. It doesn't matter, but it should be the last camera at an intersection the killer would have to drive through to get to each victim's house. We need to view those tapes starting on the day Sarah was killed and through the day Jackie went missing. If the same vehicle passes by each camera, we can be almost one hundred percent sure it's our guy."

"That'll work. What do we need, J.T.?"

"A satellite view of the streets that lead into the neighborhoods of Sarah Cummings, Mr. and Mrs. King, and Jackie Stern. From there, we'll establish where the closest commercial cameras are for the properties that the killer had to drive past. We have to bottleneck him in each neighborhood.

"Tyler, call Leon in Tech. Relay everything to him that J.T. just told us. Have him pull up the satellite images of every store and intersection that leads into the neighborhood of each house. Print them out and get them back here as soon as you can."

Tyler pushed back his chair and left the room just as Andrews returned.

"Lisa said she'd see what she could do about minimizing those homes on the MLS website. No matter what, she doesn't think the listings can be canceled without Mr. Stewart and the homeowner signing off. They are legal, binding contracts, and the homeowner couldn't relist with another Realtor unless the first contract was legally canceled."

Hardy groaned. "This is an atypical case, though, and it involves risk to every homeowner."

"I'm just listening to the voice of experience, sir. Lisa is checking into the legalities and will call back as soon as she knows something."

"Okay, fine. Sorry, but patience isn't my strong suit."

I nodded.

"Here we go. Got enough copies for everyone?" Hardy asked as Paul entered the room with a stack of printed photos of the sign.

"Sure do, sir." Paul passed them around the table then took his seat.

"Jade, you want to take charge?"

"Thanks, Cap, I'd be glad to." I stood to address the group. "I'm sure everyone here is aware of the murder that took place in Bellevue overnight. The image in front of you is of a sign the killer hung on the post that originally held the For Sale sign. He wants our attention and expects us to give the media carte blanche to run with this case. That isn't happening. The media will only get the information that we, the FBI, offer them. I hope each and every one of you takes that to heart. Now, I'm not a profiler in any sense of the word, but I do know this man is trying to instill fear throughout the community but also to the person who has him so enraged. Our job is to remain levelheaded, keep the community safe, and find this killer before he strikes again. I want everyone to read that message on the sign and throw out your ideas of its meaning. During the meeting we recently had with Dr. Collins, a forensic psychiatrist, she offered her opinion. I'd like to see if any of your thoughts match hers. Please, take a few minutes to write down your ideas, and then we'll open up the table for discussion."

I sat down and poured myself a cup of coffee. I stared at

the photo lying on the table in front of me and began jotting down my own thoughts.

Minutes later, most of the pens had been placed next to the photo, and the group had finished writing. I stood and walked to the head of the table, where the whiteboard rested on an easel. I picked up a marker.

"Anyone care to start?"

Dixon began by mentioning that the note didn't imply a gender, yet most of the victims were women.

"That's absolutely true, Officer Dixon, and that's why we're leaning in the direction of him being angry at a woman. Does anyone feel differently?"

Andrews spoke up. "What's the issue with Scenic View Realty, then? That corporation is owned by a man."

Hardy agreed. "Write both of those points down, Jade. If anyone is arrogant, it's William Stewart. Now that he's been busted for running a Ponzi scheme, he's definitely going to have to swallow his pride."

I added Stewart's name to the whiteboard.

"The note sounds like the perp isn't taking any responsibility for the murders. He's putting all of the blame on the person he's addressing. He's a psychopath for sure," Lyles said.

I wrote that down too. "What else?"

J.T. set down his coffee cup and shook his head. "I have to agree with Spelling on this one. Read the first four words written on the sign. The killer wrote, 'Hatred fills your heart.' During the taped interview Brad had with him earlier in the week, Stewart said he didn't have any enemies and that everyone loved him. That doesn't sound like the words of one who had hate in his own heart. I think Stewart is an arrogant blowhard who got in over his head, but I don't picture him as a hateful person."

"Does Stewart have a business partner?" I asked.

"Nope," Andrews said. "Not in his real estate holdings, anyway."

"Okay, what do you guys make of the part where he writes 'in the end.' What constitutes the end?"

"He kills the person that this rant is aimed at," Lyles suggested.

Tyler spoke up. "No, otherwise they couldn't swallow their pride."

"He means when justice is served," Hardy said.

"Now we're getting somewhere. Okay, let's take a look." I turned to the board. "We have a psychopath who's really pissed at someone. He feels wronged somehow and is taking it out on innocent people. He has a misguided idea that the person he's angry with is hateful, although they may not be. He's killed primarily women, and he went out of his way to create this elaborate sign in hopes that the person it's aimed at will see it on the news. He wants to instill fear in them and in the citizens of Omaha and now Bellevue. How about physical attributes?"

I looked around the table. I could almost see the wheels turning.

J.T. offered his opinion. "He has to be strong enough to carry Marilyn LaSota from the bedroom to the middle of the yard. I can't tell you her weight, especially since she was posed in a sitting position, but"—he looked at me—"help me out, Jade."

"Sure thing. I'd say she weighed about one hundred thirty pounds. Since I was in the house, I'd say the distance from the master bedroom to the middle of the yard was well over one hundred fifty feet. The guy is big and strong, or he flung her over his shoulder to carry her, which is somewhat easier."

Lyles added his two cents. "I wouldn't put him over sixty years old, then. I doubt if someone that age has enough stamina or desire to hunt down people and plan ways to kill them."

I wrote *under sixty* on the board. "What about the fact that he stabbed every woman in the throat, but he didn't do it to Bob King?"

"That's hard to ignore," Hardy said. "I'd go along with the doc on that one. She says it could represent the act of silencing someone. One could take that several ways too. Maybe a particular person's voice grates on his nerves, or somebody could have lied to him or fabricated a story about him."

Dixon added, "Or they just never shut up."

I nodded. "According to the doctor, if it's a female he's trying to silence, the two major women who come into play would be the mother and the wife. What do you guys think?"

"Definitely the wife. They constantly yammer about nothing." Dixon's face went red when he caught me smiling at him.

"Are we still profiling the killer, Kyle?"

The room broke out into a much-needed round of laughter.

Hardy brought the group back into the moment. "Why do you think he used garrotes on the Kings but nobody else, Jade?"

"Good question, Cap. In my opinion, the perp carries the tools of his trade, so to speak, in his vehicle. He's smart enough to have a backup plan with him at all times. If he truly wasn't expecting Mr. King to be at the house, a theory J.T. and I discussed, then the garrotes may have been used to subdue the couple. If he wasn't aware that a man was present, then killing two people that night wasn't in his playbook. By having those garrotes with him, his job just got easier. I don't think they were implemented with any kind of message in mind, just used out of necessity."

Fred's phone buzzed on the table. He gave the screen a quick look. "It's Lisa." Hardy nodded an okay for him to answer it right there. "Hi, honey, I have you on speakerphone in our conference room. What did you find out?"

"Hello, everyone. I hate to say it, but my hands are tied. I checked into the legalities of canceling listing contracts, and they do have to be agreed upon by both parties. If not, nasty lawsuits can come into play."

"What about pulling Scenic View's listings off the MLS database?" Hardy asked.

"That opens another can of worms. Every real estate company has the right to show and sell those houses, even when listed with a different Realtor. This is going to have to be addressed one house at a time and signed off on by the homeowner and Mr. Stewart. The homeowner can't even legally pull the sign out of their yard. It's another form of advertising, yet I doubt if your killer is trolling neighborhoods and looking for houses that might be for sale with a particular real estate company. That would be way too time consuming. He's definitely checking the MLS listings."

I piped in. "I didn't think the public had access to MLS listings."

"They normally don't, but he found a way to get in. Sorry I couldn't help out."

"Thanks, honey, you did what you could." Andrews clicked off the call. "So now what?"

J.T. sighed. "Now we need to go downstairs and talk to Stewart."

Chapter 36

Leon Tripp, the tech department lead, said he'd have the satellite images of the intersections and businesses ready for us in thirty minutes. We broke so everyone could catch up with their duties and grab a quick lunch. Hardy told his men to be back at one o'clock.

"You sure you don't want to join us?" J.T. asked as the group dispersed and the conference room emptied out.

I grabbed my briefcase containing my laptop and rode the elevator down with them. "I need to update Spelling and my to-do list. I also want to view the footage that has Stewart so pissed off. He may have a legal right to go after the media for slander."

"That's what his attorney says, but right now we have to convince him to pull his listings for the sake of the community."

"Good luck with that. His Ponzi scheme is a different business entity called Wipast Holdings, so it doesn't fall under the Scenic View Corporation. I'm pretty sure Scenic View can legally continue to bring in revenue. If his intentions are really to pay back investors, he's going to need the real estate company to keep operating."

"He might want that, but what sane person is going to list their home with him?" Hardy asked.

"I don't know, Cap, but currently he has hundreds of properties listed across the state on the MLS database. I hope you can talk some sense into him."

We parted ways outside the elevator doors, and I turned left. I needed to feel the sun against my skin and take a few breaths of fresh air that weren't spent looking over the body of a dead woman. I stepped outside and leaned against the brick column that faced the sun while I made a quick update call to Spelling. I told him J.T.'s idea about watching for the same vehicle leading into the neighborhoods where the victims' houses were located.

"That worked for us a few months back, but we were only surveilling one location. It sounds like a daunting task, Jade."

"It does, but the ME gave us his estimated TOD for each victim. We'll narrow down the time line on the camera tapes to an hour in each direction of when the victim died."

"So far it sounds like the only thing to do. Are there any reliable leads coming in?"

"Unfortunately not, and nothing has come in on Jackie Stern, either. She's disappeared into thin air. The longer she's missing—"

"I know, Jade. It doesn't look good. Keep me posted."

"Will do, boss." I clicked off and sent a text to Amber, letting her know we'd probably be here into early next week.

I sent my love and pocketed my phone. Back indoors, I headed to the visitors' lounge to find a quiet corner where I could watch that news footage.

I pulled out the laptop from my briefcase and settled in at a table near the back of the room.

What station did J.T. say that was?

I Googled the reporter's name, which I remembered was Tammy Hawn.

There it is, Channel 9. Now I just need to watch their footage on the murders from yesterday.

I typed the station's name into the search bar, and their website popped up.

Wow, they really are sensationalizing this case, and now with the Marilyn LaSota murder, they're going to have a field day.

The home page hadn't been updated yet beyond the news of Jackie Stern going missing, but I was sure it would be in no time. The media depended on the police scanners for their latest information. Every bit of news they could glean about the Scenic View Serial Killer was spread across their website. In Mr. Stewart's defense, I couldn't blame him for his anger toward the media. I clicked on the video that was taped yesterday outside Sarah Cummings's house. I hit the full screen icon and lowered the volume.

The segment, only a few minutes long, was mostly about the brutal and senseless murders and how the local police were stumped and had no suspect in custody and no motive to work with.

Gee, thanks for the boost of confidence in law enforcement you're putting out there for the city to see. We're doing the best we can with nothing to go on.

The camera zoomed in on the memorial in front of Sarah's house. Hundreds of flower bouquets were placed on the grassy median between the sidewalk and street. Beneath the yellow crime scene tape that wrapped her yard lay even more flowers and cards. Before she closed the segment, Tammy Hawn spoke of the For Sale sign being taken down by police, yet the public wouldn't forget where the crime took place.

No kidding, Tammy. You just gave the TV viewers the street and house address.

As a final closing, Tammy signed off, and the camera panned the crowd of mourners gathered at Sarah's home.

My finger was on the icon to close the video when a face flashed across the screen.

Wait a minute.

I paused the footage and backed up the scrubber bar a few seconds.

Why does that guy look familiar? It's something about his eyes.

I hit Play. The camera panned the crowd one more time, and my finger hovered over the pause button. I leaned in close and watched for the face then stopped the tape again.

There he is. I recognize that face even if he is wearing a baseball cap. I know I've seen him somewhere before.

I rubbed my forehead and closed my eyes. I was overtired, and thinking logically came hard. I looked again at the paused footage and stared at the screen.

That's it. You're Ed Tanner, the guy who dropped his license at the gas station. Why are you there, or are you just paying your respects like everyone else?

The hair rose on my arms, and a strange chill tingled my spine.

I need to run this by J.T.

I powered down my laptop, slid it into my briefcase, and zipped it closed. Chances were, J.T. and Hardy were still talking to Mr. Stewart. I headed in the direction of the city jail, which was downstairs and on the far side of the building. I checked in at the counter and asked where to find J.T. and Hardy. They hadn't signed out yet, so they were still in one of the interview rooms.

"They're with Mr. Stewart in box three, Agent Monroe."

"Thanks." I took the left hallway to the end of the corridor and entered the observation room. Through the glass, I saw Hardy and J.T. talking to Stewart and his attorney.

Crap. I need to talk to J.T.

I checked the time. The meeting couldn't go on much longer since everyone was expected in the conference room in fifteen minutes. I turned on the intercom and leaned back in the chair. I'd wait it out.

The slamming door in the adjoining room startled me out of my sleep. I had dozed off, and luckily the sound woke me. I did my best to seem alert as I opened the observation room door and stepped out.

"Jade, what were you doing in there?" J.T. eyed me suspiciously.

"Fine, you busted me. I was waiting to talk to you and fell asleep."

He patted my shoulder. "Who could blame you? I'd love to sleep for a couple of days. Did you catch any of the interview?"

"Um—"

"Yeah, the short version is Stewart refused to break the contracts. He's already complaining that no new sellers are calling his office to book with Scenic View."

"How would he know that? He's locked up."

"From his attorney. He's the mouthpiece for the company, and all conversations back and forth go through him. Stewart says if he gets a deal, he might work with us. His attorney wanted to talk to him privately."

"What a jerk. Anyway, I have something that may or may not be something."

Hardy raised his brows. "Are you still asleep?"

"Sorry, guys, my mind is fuzzy. Give me a second to get my words to match my thoughts. Okay, I watched that Channel 9 news footage from yesterday at Sarah's house."

"Yeah, we did too. What about it?" J.T. asked.

"The cameraman panned the crowd at the memorial, and I saw Ed Tanner."

"Who the hell is Ed Tanner?" Hardy asked.

"A guy Jade is crushing on."

"Knock it off, I'm serious. Why didn't you tell me he was in that video?"

"Jade, I never saw the guy. I only saw you approach someone who was pumping gas into a rust bucket truck. He was completely hidden from my view."

"Sorry, I didn't realize, but what do you make of that?"

J.T. shrugged as we boarded the elevator. "I don't know if I make anything of it. There were a lot of people in that footage paying their respects. He could have just been another person in the crowd."

"Or the killer coming back to bask in all of the attention he's getting."

"That means everyone there could be doing the same. Ed was filling his truck with gas at a downtown gas station. Chances are he lives somewhere in the area. If he hadn't dropped his license or if you hadn't been the person to pick it up, he would have just been another face on TV."

"I don't know. He seemed edgy when he was paying for his gas. That's probably why he dropped his license."

"Which makes that your lucky day. Have Leon pull his name later and see where he lives. It'll probably explain everything."

"Yeah, maybe."

Hardy tipped his wrist and checked the time. "Right now we need to check out those satellite images."

We returned to the conference room, where Leon had an overhead projector set up on the table.

"Wow, I wasn't expecting this," Hardy said.

"It's better than printer-sized sheets of paper. I've outlined onto these transparencies the satellite images that go out several miles in each direction around all three houses. I've noted each business that has CCTV cameras or a different type of private security camera. The red circle on the transparency indicates the location of the victim's house."

"This is perfect, Leon. Thanks." J.T. approached the wall screen that had been pulled down. "This first transparency is from Sarah Cummings's neighborhood. It appears that once you get into her master-planned community, all the streets are residential and exit to that main intersection with the traffic lights. That location should be easy enough. We'll need to use the closest business that has video storage capabilities and reliable equipment." He pointed at several rooftops on the screen. "We'll have to contact these three businesses and see how long the footage is stored."

Hardy jerked his head at Lyles. "That's Creek Crossing and Trenton Street. Contact those three businesses nearest that intersection and start asking questions."

"You got it."

I nodded at Leon. "Okay, let's see the next transparency."

We continued with the neighborhoods around the King home and Jackie's too. After we'd chosen the best locations that the killer would have to pass by, it was time to give each business a visit.

Hardy's phone buzzed as we were about to leave. He raised his hand for us to wait. The call was short, but the look on his face when he clicked off told us he had something important to say. "Everyone, hold up."

Andrews, Tyler, Lyles, and Franklin stopped in the hallway and turned back.

"That was Gebhardt. He said his guys found fresh

footprints that led right to Marilyn LaSota's house from one of the vacant lots. His officers originally missed them because they were at the edge near the tree line. Luckily, they were noticed on a second round."

"Anything they can cast?"

"He didn't think so since the lots are made up mostly of large dirt clods. What *is* helpful is where the trail led."

"And where was that?" I asked.

"At the next street parallel to Marilyn's house."

J.T. nodded. "We've run into that before. It's the best way to stay out of sight if going in from yard to yard or, in this case, through vacant lots."

"We need to find out what kind of cameras are in that area."

"It's Bellevue's jurisdiction, Jade," Hardy said.

"Sorry, Cap, but as FBI agents, we have the entire Midwest as our jurisdiction. J.T. and I will head over there, meet up with Chief Gebhardt, and go over our plan. We don't intend to step on anybody's toes. Everyone else can go ahead with the local locations."

J.T. reached in his pocket for the Explorer keys. "Let's head out."

Chapter 37

Our drive to Bellevue wouldn't take long. The city to our south was only ten miles away. I pulled out the card Gebhardt had given me and entered the address for the Bellevue, Nebraska Police Department into the search bar on my phone. We needed directions.

"I remember the way to Bellevue, but we've never been to the police department," J.T. said.

"I'm pulling it up as we speak. Okay, stay on I-75 south until we see Cornhusker Road." I smiled at the name. "We'll exit the freeway there and go east. Cornhusker turns into Harvell Drive. Stay on that until we reach Galvin Road South. That will take us right to Wall Street, where the police department is located. That sounds easy enough."

We reached the police department without getting lost. I was becoming an expert copilot. J.T. parked, and we walked to the building's main entrance. We showed our credentials to the desk sergeant and asked for Chief Mike Gebhardt.

We waited as the sergeant made a call. Several minutes later we were escorted to the chief's office.

He stood and shook our hands when we entered. "Agents, I didn't think I'd see you again so soon." He gestured at the guest chairs. "Have a seat."

"We heard about your latest findings."

"The footpath in the vacant lot?"

"That's right," J.T. said. "We were actually on that same wavelength with checking camera footage on neighboring streets in the Omaha cases. That will take some time and manpower since we'd have to compare vehicles in three locations. Hardy's men are starting that process now."

"How can we help?"

I spoke up. "We appreciate your offer, and if you can spare a minute, we'd like to see a satellite view of the area around Marilyn's house and what the neighboring businesses are, especially the ones near that parallel street. We can take it from there unless you, or someone from your team, would like to assist."

"Sure, follow me."

We walked down several hallways with Gebhardt and ended at their tech department. Inside the large room filled with computers and oversized wall-mounted monitors, the chief introduced us to the person in charge.

"Agents Monroe and Harper, this is Camille Sills, our lead in this department."

I was pleasantly surprised when she welcomed us with firm handshakes.

"What can I do for you, agents?"

J.T. took over. "We need a satellite view, spread out a mile around the neighborhood of Fremont Court."

"Aah, of course, this morning's murder victim. Sorry to hear about that."

We leaned in behind her and watched as she tapped the computer keys to pull up the image.

"Please, scoot some stools around." She tipped her head toward the wall. "It's a strain on your back leaning in that way."

Gebhardt and J.T. rolled the stools forward and placed them alongside her chair in the cubicle.

"Okay, here's the satellite imagery. Unfortunately it was shot during the summer months, and the streets and buildings are hidden under tree cover. How about going with street mode instead? Once we pinpoint the best locations, I'll pull up Street View so we can actually see the storefronts."

"That should work." With my elbow resting on the tabletop of her cubicle, I propped my head in my palm and stared at the monitor. J.T. wrote down the names of the businesses nearest Vine Street as Camille moved the street view from store to store.

"That should do it," I said. The entire process took less than a half hour. J.T. and I thanked her and left the tech department. We had four businesses to visit. "You're welcome to pound the pavement with us, Chief," I said.

"Nah, but I would appreciate being kept abreast of your findings. I have plenty on my plate with contacting Ms. LaSota's next of kin. We still have to interview her ex-husband and go through her contact list. Each one of those people will have to be interviewed too."

I stopped in the hallway before we had gotten too far.

"Forget something, Jade?"

"Chief, as long as we're still here, would it be all right if Camille does one more quick favor for me?"

"Of course."

We turned back and entered the tech department again.

"Camille, Agent Monroe has a request."

"Sure, what do you need?"

"Thanks, and I promise it will only take a minute. Can you pull up the name Edward or Ed Tanner and see what pops?"

"No problem. Is he a Nebraska resident?"

"Yes, as far as I know."

With a few taps on the keyboard, Camille entered Ed's name and waited. The next screen opened. It showed zero results.

Camille shrugged. "If he's a recent transplant and hasn't changed his driver's license yet to Nebraska, it isn't going to come up."

"Shoot."

"If he's a known felon, then—"

J.T. gave me the eyeballs.

"No, I'm not going to invade anyone's privacy. I don't have anything on the guy to warrant that, just curiosity, that's all. Okay, thanks."

We walked out to the lobby with Chief Gebhardt and said our goodbyes. J.T. and I had businesses to reach out to at the intersections of Grange and Vine.

Marilyn LaSota's house was on the west side of Bellevue,

a ten-minute drive from the police station.

"Can I have your notepad? I want to call those businesses and find out what their security systems are like. They need ones that don't tape over themselves every day."

J.T. stopped at the red light and pulled out the notepad from his inner jacket pocket. "Sounds like a good idea. Maybe they can even get things set up for us. But before you do that, call the ME's office and see if they can give you a tighter time line of Marilyn's death. We don't want to watch hours and hours of video footage if we don't have to."

I placed the call, pressed the numbers called out by the automated attendant, and waited on hold for several minutes. Finally a real human picked up.

"Medical Examiner's Office. How can I help you?"

"Hello, this is FBI Agent Jade Monroe calling for ME Torres. Is he available?"

"One moment, please."

I groaned my impatience.

"On hold again?"

I nodded and studied my cuticles.

"Agent Monroe?"

I sat up and paid attention. "Yes, this is she."

"This is Dr. Torres's assistant, Myron Goran. How may I help you?"

"Hello, Myron. I'm wondering if the doctor has a tighter time line on Marilyn LaSota's TOD."

"I'll see what he says. Give me just a moment, please."

"Damn it, I'm on hold again. No music, only dead silence." I rolled my eyes.

J.T. grinned. "Fitting, isn't it?"

Myron returned to the phone several minutes later. "Okay, the best he can commit to is that Ms. LaSota expired between eleven p.m. and three a.m."

"Okay, that helps. Thank you, Myron." I clicked off and sighed. "No help there."

"Didn't you just say—"

"I was being nice. The TOD is no different than what he said this morning. Guess we're going to be sitting in front of video cameras for a while."

J.T. agreed. "We'll split up. It's the only way to expedite things."

I called several of the stores at the mall and got their voicemails. Maybe we'd have better luck in person. J.T. pulled into the strip mall that had two of the businesses we hoped would have camera surveillance, along with modern technology. We exited the Explorer and looked to our left and right. Vine Street was two blocks to our west.

"Damn it. We aren't going to see anything this far away. Where are those other businesses that came up on street view?"

"That's probably them." J.T. pointed at the intersection kitty-corner to Vine. Heavy equipment was hard at work leveling buildings at that corner.

"This strip mall isn't close enough, J.T."

He tipped his head. "It's all we have to work with. Come on. Let's walk down to the stores at the end and see what they have. Hopefully, if they do have cameras, they're equipped with wide-angle lenses.

J.T. and I had hoped that the check-cashing business

would be perfect, but seeing the location in person gave us a different viewpoint. That store, along with Pelmar Financial Services next door, was too far from Vine to make out any vehicle turning down that street, especially at night.

The strip mall held nine storefronts, and the few at the end could work if they had cameras. They were only a block from Vine Street.

"We've run out of pavement," J.T. said as he kicked a final rock. "Let's see what we have."

We turned to the store in front of us—a dry cleaner. My hopes deflated quickly.

"This is our last chance," I said as I walked ten feet ahead of J.T. I looked at the sign in front of the last store. "Hey, it's a liquor store, and there's a roof-mounted camera."

We entered the building and approached a young man who was busy stocking the coolers with cases of beer.

"Excuse us," J.T. said. "Do you work here, or are you the vendor?"

"Nah, it's my dad's store. What do you need?"

I pulled out my badge to cut to the chase. "We're FBI agents. Is your father here?"

"Whoa, for real?"

I smiled. "Yes, for real."

A man appeared from the back room. "Did I hear someone say FBI agents?"

"Dad, she showed me her badge. It's the real deal."

The father shushed his son and told him to get back to work. "Kids these days. Anyway, what can I help you with, agents?"

I noticed several customers in the store and realized the son probably wasn't old enough to ring up a liquor purchase. We needed to make it quick. "Do you have camera equipment with good clarity and modern technology?"

J.T. grinned at me.

"Um, sure I do. This store, being on the end of the strip mall like this, has been robbed several times. I'm tired of fuzzy images that nobody can identify on the tapes."

"Dad, somebody needs to check out."

"Excuse me for just a minute, agents."

"Not a problem." I peered into the chilled refrigerator as we waited. "Awesome."

"What's that?"

"They have Scottish Ale. I'm leaving here with a six-pack to take back to my hotel room."

"So you're assuming you'll have time to drink it?"

"I'll make time, and I'll even share."

The storeowner returned. "Okay, sorry about the interruption. I think I have enough time to show you what we have in the back. Billy, holler if you need me."

"Okay, Dad."

"I'm sorry. We didn't get your name, sir," J.T. said.

"Alan Caldwell." He turned and shook our hands. "Pleasure to meet you."

"And you as well. I'm Agent Jade Monroe, and my partner is Agent J.T. Harper."

"Here we are. After you."

We found ourselves in a back office typical of any mom-and-pop store. The room, with dark paneling, was about the size of an average bedroom. Two four-drawer file cabinets stood side by side, and the fluorescent light above our heads flickered and made a ticking sound. Alan's desk was in disarray. He looked to have been working on his books.

"Sorry about the mess. My wife is our secretary"—he grinned—"but she's out of town at the moment. I guess I'm no good at keeping order. Grab a chair. You can toss those magazines on the floor."

We did, and Alan turned his computer to face J.T. and me. He stood alongside us and clicked a few keys then hovered the cursor over the thumbnail image of his security system.

"Here we go. I have a pretty sophisticated system now. Had it installed six months ago, and I'm glad I did. The images are crystal clear."

I glanced at J.T. with a hopeful smile.

"So, what are you agents looking for, anyway?"

"Images that can show up in the dark at the intersection of Grange and Vine."

He raised his brows. "That's a block away. I've never paid attention to anything in the distance, only outside in the parking lot and at the cash register. There's one way to find out, though." He typed *two a.m.* into the parameters and clicked Enter. A widescreen image of the parking lot popped up with perfect clarity. The farther away from the center of the camera, the dimmer the image became.

"I guess the fact that it's right outside with the store's light on helps. There used to be more ambient light until those buildings down the street came down."

"How about straight out on Grange?" J.T. asked.

"There aren't any vehicles passing by at that time of night. Let's try eight p.m. The traffic is still pretty active then." Alan typed in the earlier time, and the footage started at eight o'clock.

"That isn't bad," I said. "You can't make out the vehicle's colors, but you can tell if it's a light or dark car, and the clarity is good enough to identify if it's a two-door, four-door, sports car, compact, full-sized, or hatchback. So, unless a vehicle passes right in front of your store, either coming from or going to Vine, we're probably out of luck."

"Unfortunately, that seems to be true, Agent Monroe. Do you have a time and date in mind?"

"We sure do," J.T. said. "Can you set it to run from eleven thirty last night until five a.m. this morning?"

"Sure. If there aren't any cars passing in front of the store, you can fast-forward it by tapping the right arrow key."

"Perfect. Thank you, Alan."

"I'll leave you to it, then. Just holler if you need anything."

Chapter 38

Ed stomped in front of the television as he held the remote and surfed every news channel. He had watched the local news at noon, and there wasn't a thing about the murder of Marilyn LaSota or his sign. Even at that hour—three o'clock—the news had no updates on the Scenic View Serial Killer.

What the hell is going on? I'm not about to go unnoticed. I want them to fear me, to look over their shoulders, to have sleepless nights. They have to pay in the end.

The drive north to that secluded fishing spot wouldn't take long, a short thirty minutes, and Ed had plenty of time on his hands. He was curious and needed a distraction, something to squelch the anger building inside. He'd check on Jackie to see what remained of her body. Ed climbed into his truck and sped away.

He reached his destination just off Yocum Street at three thirty and turned the truck around at the widened area near the lake. Being able to drive away quickly if necessary was always the smart thing to do, and of course having the truck registered in Arkansas helped—no front plate was needed.

Ed killed the engine and climbed out. He pocketed the keys and took in his surroundings during the daylight hours. His childhood memories returned—the good memories of fishing with his dad. Ed trudged into the brush. The deeper he got, the stronger the stench became. He was definitely going in the right direction, and the odor would lead him to Jackie's side. Ed pinched his nose and pushed on while trying to ignore his gag reflexes that were kicking in. Jackie had been dead for several days and out in the elements—she was getting ripe.

He reached her body and stared down at it, then cocked his head to the left. The last time he saw a rotting corpse was thirty years prior. He knelt down and studied every inch of her exposed skin. The deep throat wounds, which he last saw with dried blood around them, were now black goo filled with bugs, flies, and maggots. Her eyes, ears, nose, and mouth had insects swarming in and out, busying themselves with what insects do best—ingesting remains. Her arms and legs wore visible signs that a larger animal had been by. Skin and muscle had been torn into and pulled away from the bone.

Ed pushed off his knees and stood then kicked dried leaves over her body. The bugs would take care of the rest. Soon Jackie would be nothing more than a distant memory, and her corpse would dissolve into the earth as if it had never been there. Ed would return before the first frost and dispose of any bones that remained.

He muttered a few words over her body and turned

back. He'd go home and check the evening news. Something would show up by then, he was sure of it.

With his foot lifted to take that last step out of the brush, Ed heard voices near the truck. He peered through an opening between young saplings. Two boys with fishing poles in hand had climbed off their bicycles and stared into the brush toward the sound.

Ed exited the woods and walked toward them. Evil intentions filled his mind. "Hello, boys. What's up?"

Chapter 39

Watching cars driving by in each direction was as hypnotic as staring at a pendant suspended on a swinging chain. I was ready to fall asleep. An hour had passed, and we still had no idea what we were looking for. Even if the killer drove by, would we know? I sighed.

"The only thing that's going to work is if the killer rolls down his window and yells out to us." I rubbed my tired eyes and looked at J.T. "This technique seemed effortless when we were searching for clues in front of your condo."

"But they were daylight images in front of one residence, and you guys searched through a week's worth of tapes."

"Yeah, I know." I fisted my yawn and rolled my aching neck. "I wonder if the guys are having any luck at the other locations. At least their tapes are during daytime hours."

"Not at the King house."

"True. Hey, I have an idea that might help."

J.T. gave me two raised brows. "Yeah, what's that?"

"Even from here, we can see if a vehicle turns down Vine Street. We may not be able to identify it initially, but we can take note of the times they were there and then have Tech see what they can do to enhance the footage later. For now, let's just watch cars that turn on Vine. What's the point in staring at every vehicle that passes in front of us if they don't turn down the street the killer was on?"

"Excellent idea, and that should speed up this entire process."

J.T. and I got through five and a half hours of taped footage by six o'clock.

"So how many vehicles do we have?" I asked.

"We don't have an exact count because some could be the same car going in then coming out later. We have forty-six sightings, though. Too bad Vine isn't a cul-de-sac. There would only be one way in and one way out."

"Right, but forty-six sightings is a hell of a lot better than hundreds." I tipped my head toward the door. "Let's let Alan know we're done. I'm sure we've worn out our welcome by now."

"Nah, he seems cool. We need to have him separate this footage from the rest of the week then email it to us."

I stood. "Yeah, I'll go get him."

Alan gladly took care of the technical help we needed and emailed the most recent recordings to J.T.'s address. I grabbed a six-pack of Scottish Ale and paid for it. With firm handshakes for Alan and his son, Billy, we expressed our thanks and left.

"That wasn't so bad," I said as I grabbed the handgrip and pulled myself into the Explorer. "Now we just need to see if Leon or his guys can work any magic with it."

We headed back in the direction of downtown Omaha but made a quick stop for dinner first. Forty-five minutes later, we checked in at the station's counter and headed for the tech department. Inside, we found Hardy, Lyles, Franklin, and Andrews gathered at a corner table.

"Look who's here, J.T." I pulled up a chair and took a seat next to them. "Get anything useful today?"

Lyles rubbed his brow. "It's tough, Jade. Too bad there isn't a system in place that can pick out a repeat vehicle from hours of footage at three different locations."

"Yeah, but maybe Leon can impress us with his technical expertise."

"Did somebody mention my name?"

J.T. waved him over. "Sure did. We need your help, Leon."

"I'm listening."

"We have a tape from the Bellevue murder neighborhood. Evidence tells us that the perp drove in on Vine Street, parked, and cut through a vacant lot to arrive at Marilyn's house unseen by any neighbor on Fremont Court."

"Smart approach."

"I agree, but the surveillance tape we have is grainy at best because of the distance of the mounted camera to the entrance of Vine Street. We watched Vine because the traffic coming in and out of that street would be less congested than on Grange, a much busier street."

"So you want to know if we can improve the clarity of the cars on Vine so they're identifiable."

"Is it possible?" I asked.

"Depends on the distance from the camera."

J.T. grinned. "How does a block sound?"

"Yeah, that should work. Got the footage with you?"

"In an attachment on my email. Can you also eliminate the same car coming in and out numerous times so we have an accurate count?"

"Sure, no sweat. The license plate should be visible. Let's head over to my desk."

J.T. opened his email and dropped the file onto Leon's desktop.

"Okay, here we go." Leon hovered the cursor over a program on the screen and clicked. "Watch closely, folks. The magic is about to begin."

A buzz made all of us turn and look toward Andrews. Fred pulled out his cell phone. "Sorry for the interruption, but it's Lisa. She might have something on the Stewart situation."

Hardy waved him on, and Andrews stepped out into the hallway. We continued to watch Leon work with the footage in front of him. Every adjustment he made improved the quality of the tape a tiny bit.

Moments later, Andrews burst through the door. "Lisa said there was breaking news on TV."

My heart sank as if a weight had pulled it to the floor. "Please don't say there was another murder."

"I won't, but Lisa said two boys were just interviewed at the northwest police department on Wiesman Drive. They told police that they rode their bikes to a small fishing lake they frequent weekly. Out of nowhere a man emerged from the woods and began chasing them. Knowing the area as well as they did, they knew where to hide in the dense thicket. They stayed put until the man climbed into his vehicle and drove away. One boy swore he saw a knife in his hand. They also said the area smelled bad."

"Let's go!" Hardy stood and headed for the door. J.T. and I were on his heels. "Get somebody from that station on the phone for me. We need to know where this location is now!"

Cap charged down the hallway toward the building's exit. Andrews took up the rear and waved his cell phone. He called out to the captain, "I have a Lieutenant Jackson on the phone, sir."

Hardy grabbed the phone. "Captain Kip Hardy here from central headquarters. What have you got, and where is this location where those boys saw the man? Yes, I know the general area. Cypress Creek Drive for two miles then turn right on Yocum? We'll find it. Are you en route? Good, then have a squad car sitting on the road to lead us in." Hardy gave his watch a quick glance. "We'll be there in twenty-five minutes." He clicked off the call and handed the cell back to Andrews. "Round up the posse and follow us. I want everyone out there searching. It's almost dark."

J.T. and I jumped into the cruiser with Hardy. I barely had the back door closed before he hit the lights and siren and stepped on the gas. The tires squealed as the car barreled out of the police department's parking lot and headed north.

Lyles, Franklin, Andrews, and Tyler were on our

bumper in two squad cars, their lights and sirens engaged too.

"We should be there in twenty minutes at this rate," Hardy said.

"What do you expect to find, Cap?"

"I don't know, Jade, but if a strange man came out of the woods, he may have a camp set up back there. He could be living off the land for all we know, and there might be evidence lying around. The kids said the area stank, possibly of an animal he killed to eat."

I leaned forward between the seats. "Or worse."

"I don't want to think that way, but we have to be prepared for anything and everything. The boys said the man drove away, so I'm assuming he went to look for them, not to leave the area. He could still be there and hiding in the woods. No matter what, we'll be interviewing those boys tonight. We don't have a choice."

J.T looked over the seatback at me. "This could be our lucky break. If those kids can give us a rough idea of the vehicle the man drove and then it shows up on any of the tapes, his fate is damn near sealed."

I glanced through the side window and looked up at the sign for the street we had just turned on—Cypress Creek Drive. I remembered hearing Hardy repeat that name over the phone. I knew we were close. We continued on for several miles, then he made a right on Yocum. Up ahead I saw the early evening sky glow with the reflection of flashing lights. We had arrived. An officer stepped out of his squad car as we slowed to a stop. Hardy opened the window.

"Evening, Captain. I'm Officer Jenkins. I've been asked to escort you and your group in. There isn't enough room back there"—he gestured over his shoulder—"for this many vehicles. Why don't you three join me, and the others can follow in one car?"

"Yeah, good enough."

We climbed out of the cruiser, and Hardy walked back to tell Andrews the plan. He returned, and we joined Jenkins in his car.

Nighttime was closing in quickly and evidence could be missed, especially in the dense woods that engulfed our vehicles on both sides. We drove down the lane for what seemed like a half mile.

"There's a lake at the end of this trail?" I asked.

"More like a big pond, ma'am, but there are plenty of fish in it. People have come here for years, and because it's a well-kept secret among the locals, it hasn't been fished out."

"So how would a stranger or someone who lives in Omaha know about it?" J.T. asked.

"That's a good question, Agent Harper. I'd think you'd have to live right in this area to know of its existence. It's hidden back here, that's for sure."

We reached the widened area at the end of the trail. One cruiser and a squad car sat tucked back as far as possible to make room for our vehicles. Jenkins parked, and Andrews pulled in alongside us. Three people with flashlights were checking the perimeter of the woods. They approached us as we exited the vehicles.

Cap extended his hand. "Who's in charge here?"

"That's me, Lieutenant Jackson. Captain Hardy, I presume?"

"That's correct. I have Agents Harper and Monroe here too from the FBI. I'm sure you're well aware of the murder investigation we're conducting. This man could very well be our murderer. Have you gone into the woods yet?"

"No, Captain Hardy. We've only checked the edges of the pond and the tree line. We were waiting for you and your team to arrive. You've noticed that odor, haven't you?"

Hardy turned back. "There's something dead in the woods. How many flashlights do we have?"

Andrews spoke up. "There are two in my squad car, and Lyles pulled the other ones out of their car."

"Good thinking. Jenkins, how many in your vehicle?"

"I have two as well, Captain."

"Okay, that will have to do. A couple of you buddy up. Let's start on the side the smell is coming from and go in several hundred feet. Spread out so we cover the widest area. We aren't sure what we're looking for yet, but if it isn't native to the landscape, call out to the rest of us."

I partnered with J.T., and Cap was twenty-five feet to our right. The three of us were nearest the water, and the rest of the group was spread out to our left. We trudged through tangles of wild grapevines, branches, twigs, and underbrush. It was a slow process, which was fine. We had no intention of missing anything that could possibly be out there. We had to find whatever was giving off that death odor, even if it was only to eliminate the chance of it being human.

I asked Lieutenant Jackson how far away the boys lived and if they were brothers.

"They aren't brothers but best friends. Terry Mitchell is nine, and Sam Cooper is ten. Same grade in school, though. They came into the station together with both sets of parents. Sounds like they only live a few miles east of here."

"First and foremost, we have to find what died back here. After that, we'll leave the rest of the search to the others. If that man is still in the area, he's farther back and has hidden his vehicle at a different location. It's imperative that we interview those boys tonight before it gets too late."

"You're right, Jade. I want their recollection of the man to be clear."

We were only fifteen minutes into the search when Tyler yelled out. "Over here, everyone. We just found a body."

We headed toward the flicker of flashlights deeper in the woods. Cursing and gagging sounded in the distance.

I was nearly out of breath when we reached Tyler and Andrews. Tripping over downed branches made getting to them quickly nearly impossible.

"What do you have?" J.T. yelled.

We were twenty feet away when the stench of death hit us right in the face. I raised the back of my hand to cover my nose. I had come across bodies decaying in the elements numerous times, and I recognized the smell of human remains.

Tyler shined the light on the raised mound that was partially covered with leaves. A left arm, scratched and chewed on, torn jeans, and a clump of brown hair were exposed on the side that faced us. "We've got what's likely a female under these leaves. I can't see much more than that without disturbing the scene. We should stand back a bit and get the ME and Forensics out here right away. Looks like the bugs and elements are making short work of her and any evidence that may be in the proximity of the body."

I kicked the tree nearest me. "Son of a bitch. How much do you want to bet that's Jackie Stern?"

Hardy jerked his chin at Lieutenant Jackson. "Go ahead and make the call. We'll need the addresses and phone numbers for the parents of those boys too. Tyler and Andrews, stay here at the scene until Forensics and the ME arrive, but stay back twenty feet. Lyles and Franklin, back out of this area and start searching a fifty-foot perimeter of this spot for anything that doesn't belong. I want an update by ten o'clock."

"Sure thing, Cap."

Hardy nodded at J.T. and me. "Come on. We need to talk to those kids."

Lieutenant Jackson spoke up. "Have Officer Jenkins get you the phone numbers and addresses of the families. I'll update you later tonight, Captain Hardy."

"Thanks, Lieutenant."

Hardy, J.T., and I headed back to the car with Jenkins so he could drive us out to our cruiser.

Once inside the car, he called his precinct and got the information we needed from his desk sergeant. I wrote the addresses and phone numbers down. Several minutes later we were back at our cruiser, where J.T. made the calls to the parents of Terry Mitchell and Sam Cooper.

From the sound of the conversation on J.T.'s end, we would have the opportunity to interview the boys together. He hung up moments later.

"Okay, we're going to the Mitchell house. Sam Cooper and his mom and dad are on their way. Apparently the folks are close friends too and only live four blocks from each other."

With the address programmed in my GPS and only a short distance from the pond, we arrived at the Mitchell house in less than ten minutes. We pulled in behind one of the two cars that sat in the driveway.

"Looks like the Coopers may already be here," Hardy said with a chin jerk at the other car.

"I hope those boys have plenty to say. As of now, they're the only eyewitnesses we have."

J.T. gave me a look of concern. "You better hope that's Jackie in the woods, otherwise there's two killers roaming around."

We followed the sidewalk to the front door, and Hardy rang the bell. Seconds later, the door swung open, and a man who looked to be around forty greeted us and welcomed us in.

"This way, folks." He motioned us toward the living room. "I'll make the introductions."

We entered a large, welcoming room with plenty of seating. Two boys sat on the fireplace hearth and whispered back and forth.

"My wife, Sheila, is right here." He pointed at the pretty

blonde sitting on an upholstered chair to his right. "Tom and Linda Cooper are Sam's parents. Everyone, this is Captain Hardy from the central station downtown, and Agent Monroe and Harper from the FBI."

Sam's eyes nearly doubled in size. "Wow, FBI!"

I gave him a grin and took off my badge. "Here, check it out."

We shook hands with both families and took our seats on the couch opposite them. The three of us naturally pulled out our notepads.

Sheila Mitchell stood. "Can I get coffee for any of you?"

I was dying for coffee, but we needed to get down to business. We gratefully declined, then I asked the boys to come closer and take a seat next to us.

I leaned to my left, where J.T. took up the center, and Hardy sat beyond him. "You want to lead the questioning?"

J.T. turned to Hardy. "Any problem with that?"

"Nope, go ahead."

"Okay, boys, we need your attention because the questions I'm about to ask you are really important."

"We answered the officers' questions earlier. Didn't they tell you what we said?"

"Terry, that's enough! Agent Harper may have other questions to ask that are different than what you were asked before."

"Sorry."

J.T. smiled. "No problem. Are you guys ready?"

They both nodded as Sam handed my badge back to me. I gave him a wink.

"Okay, let's pretend it was earlier today when you boys decided to go fishing. You grabbed your poles, jumped on your bicycles, and took off, right?"

They both nodded.

"Okay, Terry, why don't you take it from there, and Sam, go ahead and add anything you can remember."

"We always ride our bikes down the old deer path, because it's faster than the road."

"And that's what you did today, Terry?" I asked.

"Uh-huh."

J.T. continued. "Then what happened?"

"Then we rode down the long trail that goes to the pond and—"

Sam interrupted. "And I even said it looked like somebody drove back there."

"Why did you think that, Sam?" Hardy asked.

"Because all of the tall weeds were bent down."

"Great observation," I said. "Maybe you'll grow up to be an investigator."

Sam elbowed Terry and grinned.

"Go ahead, Terry." J.T. flipped the page of his notepad.

"When we got to the pond, we saw a truck. We got off of our bikes to see if anyone was fishing, but nobody was by the water."

"You didn't see anyone right away?"

"Nope."

"So what did this truck look like?"

"I remember," Sam yelled out.

"Okay, go ahead, Sam. It's your turn."

"It was rusty."

"Do you remember what color it was?"

"It was the color of rust."

"So it was rusty *and* the color of rust, or just a rusty color, like orangish brown?"

Sam wrinkled his forehead. "It was both."

"Good job, boys, and then what happened?"

Terry's eyes began to water. "Then that man from the woods came toward us. We were scared."

"Did he say anything?"

"Yeah." Terry put his face in his hands. Mrs. Mitchell took a seat on the floor and comforted him.

Sam continued. "He said, 'Hi, boys, what's up?' He said it scary, though."

"So you were afraid of him?" J.T. asked. "You don't think he was there to fish?"

"We didn't see any fishing poles, and he looked mad. He started walking fast at us. That's when we ran into the woods. He chased us, but we knew where to hide."

"Did he say anything when he was chasing you?" I asked.

"He said, 'I'm gonna get you.'"

Sam's expression told me he was on the verge of tears too. "Okay, let's take five minutes."

The mothers gave us an appreciative look. They offered us coffee once more, and this time we accepted. The boys needed a break.

Hardy tipped his wrist to check the time. Ten minutes had passed, and it was closing in on nine o'clock. We needed to wrap up the interview. He whispered to me to call the station. We needed to get a BOLO out for any truck matching that description.

"Okay, if everyone is ready, I think we'll be done in about fifteen minutes. You boys okay to continue?" J.T. asked.

They each took a deep breath and nodded.

"How long did you stay hidden?"

"Until he drove away," Sam said.

"Do you think that was five minutes or longer than that?"

"Longer, like ten minutes. We ran back to our bikes and grabbed our fishing poles. Then we took off for home."

Hardy gave them a thumbs-up. "That was a very smart thing to do."

"Do you boys think you can describe this man?"

"We didn't stare at his face," Terry said. "We just wanted to hide."

"I know, but how about a general description like if he was tall or short, heavy or thin, old or young, bald or not?"

"He was the size of my dad," Terry said.

I turned to Mr. Mitchell and asked him to stand. "So he was a little bit tall and sort of strong looking?"

"Uh-huh."

"Did he look older or younger than your dad?" J.T. asked.

"About the same. He was a regular man except mean looking."

We wrote that down.

J.T. closed his notepad and slipped it back into his inner

pocket. "And finally, did you notice his hair?"

Sam spoke up. "It was brown, like yours."

"And the same length too?"

Sam nodded. "I think so."

We stood to leave. "Okay, boys, that's it for tonight," I said. "You both did great, and we really appreciate your help." I pulled the parents aside. "Do you remember any more from their initial interview, or even when they were alone with you, that may help?"

"Only the part about the knife," Mrs. Mitchell said. "I appreciate you not bringing that up. Mentioning it to the police set both of them off into a crying frenzy."

I patted her shoulder. "Understood. Were they able to describe that knife?"

"Only that he pulled it out of his belt, I'm assuming a sheath, and it was big," Mr. Cooper said.

Hardy shook his head. "That had to be terrifying for them."

We passed out our cards and told the parents to feel free to call us anytime. They escorted us to the door, and we left.

Chapter 40

Hardy received an update call from Lieutenant Jackson as we drove back to the precinct. The ME had just loaded up the body, and Forensics was still on the scene. At that point, nothing more had been found in the woods. According to Joe's initial assessment, Jackson said, the damage from bugs and animals told him the body had been in that spot for a good twenty-four hours or more. He was pretty certain the body was Jackie's—her throat was riddled with stab wounds, but he still had to get a positive ID on her before confirming that.

"I had a gut feeling. So that sick bastard went back to the scene where he dumped her out of curiosity? He needed to see the damage outdoor conditions and animals could do?" I rubbed my brow. "That guy is unbelievable."

"But now we have something to work with," Hardy said.

"Yeah, the truck. All we have to do is identify it on the tapes."

"The daylight videos are going to help the most. We'll focus our attention on the tapes near Sarah's and Jackie's houses tomorrow. Right now, we're calling it a night. None of us has slept for nearly two days."

"But—"

J.T. interrupted. "Jade, this isn't open for discussion. I'm exhausted, and I'm sure everyone else is too. We all need sleep."

Hardy's phone rang again. This time it was Lyles. He explained to the captain everything Jackson had just told him. Hardy said to call it a night and tell the rest of the officers to go home. We'd reconvene at nine a.m.

We said good night to Hardy at the station and climbed into the Explorer.

"When was the last time we ate anything?" J.T. asked when he heard my stomach growl.

"To be honest, I don't remember."

"Want to grab a bite at an all-night diner?"

"I'd love to. If I go to bed hungry, I won't be able to sleep, anyway. This damn stomach noise will keep me awake. We can discuss our ideas as we eat."

J.T. found a well-lit restaurant three blocks from the police station. "How's this?"

"It looks like a place that would serve bacon. I'm all in."

He smiled as he pulled into the parking lot and killed the engine. "Did you ever check your lottery ticket from yesterday's drawing?" J.T. held the door open for me.

"No, did you?"

"Yeah, I'm a loser."

The visit to that gas station on Thursday popped into my mind. I had stood in line to buy our tickets, and that was when I saw Ed Tanner's driver's license on the floor. I took it out to him at pump seven, where he had just finished putting gas in his rusty clunker.

I grabbed J.T.'s forearm and squeezed it.

"What the hell are you doing?"

I held my tongue until the hostess had seated us and walked away. "J.T., don't you remember?"

"What?"

"Ed Tanner's truck? It was a faded red rust bucket."

"Son of a bitch, you're right, but we can't go after him because of the color of his truck. There are probably plenty of men with junkers like that."

I put my finger to my lips. The waitress was coming toward our booth with two pots of coffee. She had noticed our upturned cups.

"Regular or decaf, folks?"

"This time of night? Better make it decaf or I'll never get to sleep."

"You too, sir?"

"Please."

"Do you need a few minutes?"

"No, we're ready," I said. I wanted to get back to our conversation without another pause. "I'll have the short stack with an order of crispy bacon."

"And you, sir?"

"I'll have the same except make mine a large stack."

"Sounds good. Would you like me to leave the coffee with you?"

I smiled. "That would be great, thanks." I waited until she

was out of earshot before continuing. I leaned across the booth and talked quietly. "Okay, but the tapes should confirm a reddish rusty truck driving by if the body in the woods is indeed Jackie. We have to find out in the morning whose neighborhood had better videotapes, Jackie's or Sarah's."

"I hate to suggest this but—" J.T. paused.

"Don't leave me hanging. But what?"

"We could have the boys watch the news footage in front of Sarah's house without telling them why."

"Because Ed's face shows up?"

J.T. nodded as he blew on his coffee.

"I don't want to traumatize them again, J.T. I'm a trained law enforcement officer. It's my job to notice things like that. They're kids who probably don't have very good recall, plus he was wearing a cap in that footage. Don't you think it's too coincidental that he'd be at the scene of Sarah's murder and then show up where Jackie was dumped? We have him dead to rights."

"Nice choice of words, and no we don't. We have to prove, without a shadow of a doubt, that Ed Tanner is the Scenic View Serial Killer or he'll walk scot-free."

"We still don't know why his residence doesn't come up in the Nebraska DMV database."

"If we can establish a positive identity, whether it comes from you or the boys, then we can pull up everything on Ed Tanner in the national database, including a credit check, background check, bank statements, and IRS reports. If Ed is the killer, we'll find out where he lives, one way or another."

"Damn it. I could have made this easy by studying his driver's license."

"That would have been a tad invasive, don't you think?"

I shrugged. "Not in hindsight."

"Don't beat yourself up. Be content. You're going to eat and sleep tonight. What could be better than that at the moment?"

"Real maple syrup for my pancakes."

J.T. chuckled.

An hour later, we were back at our hotel and saying good night after stepping out of the elevator.

"See you in the morning, partner. Seven thirtyish?"

"Yep. Good night, Jade. Sleep well."

J.T. watched until I was safely in my room. I liked that about him. He was a caring friend and a damn good agent.

I slipped on one of my dad's old T-shirts and my sleep pants. I felt close to my dad every time I put one of those T-shirts over my head. No matter how many times they were washed, I could still smell him. The scent would take me back to my youth, when he'd squeeze me so tight before bed, I thought I would burst. If only I could give him one more hug.

With a deep sigh, I washed my face, brushed my teeth, and crawled into bed for the second time since we hit the ground in Omaha.

Chapter 41

Ed slipped on his sneakers and went outside before dawn to steal the Sunday newspaper from a driveway four doors down. He was still in a foul mood. Those boys from yesterday got away. They saw his face and truck for a minute, but that could have been long enough to give law enforcement a good description. He'd have to either scale back his activities or stick to his nighttime plan and carry out his deeds in a different city.

Back in the house, he poured a cup of coffee and sat at the table with the paper in hand.

Let's see if the "Homes for sale" section has gotten any thinner.

Ed opened the newspaper and let each page that he had no interest in drop to the floor. He finally came to the home section and pulled it from the rest of the paper. "Aah, here we go. It actually does seem a bit lighter." Ed spread the pages and found what he was looking for. Scenic View was front and center, taking up both sides of the newspaper as always. He sighed.

I'm not sure if my actions are making an impact. There are so many listings, yet I don't see any that say "New listing." I think I'm off to a good start.

Ed tossed the paper in the trash can then gave the refrigerator handle a jerk. He pulled out the blue Styrofoam carton and removed two eggs. He cracked them over the thick pat of butter that had been sizzling in the cast-iron skillet, placed two slices of bread into the toaster, and pressed the lever. Ed pulled out a plate from the upper cabinet and set it next to the stove.

This person-by-person process could take forever, and I don't have that much patience.

He sat at the table with his breakfast and stewed. He wanted immediate results. He reached for the TV remote and clicked On.

There has to be something about the woman in Bellevue by now, and what about those kids? Did they go to the cops?

He flipped from news channel to news channel, and nothing came up.

What the hell happened to the coverage on me? People are supposed to hear about the Scenic View Serial Killer. That business has to tank, to go under, to fail. I have to ruin them. There's no other way!

He exploded. With a swing of his arm, the breakfast plate flew across the room, hit the TV, and shattered. Ed pushed back his chair and kicked it when it toppled over. Then he stomped down the hall. The rays from the rising sun sparkled through the slats of the bedroom blinds and created images on the opposite wall. Ed turned the wand

and peered through the blinds. He knew what he had to do. He'd wait several hours before wandering out—the streets would be busier. He'd lock the truck in the shed and call a cab. With no updates on TV, Ed would have to get answers any way he could.

Chapter 42

I woke at six forty-five and forced myself out of bed. I could easily have slept for another day. My feet unwillingly led me to the bathroom, where I turned on the shower. Back at the bed, I grabbed my phone off the nightstand and checked for messages. I was thankful there weren't any. With the four-cup coffeemaker started, I headed to the shower.

By seven fifteen, dressed and on my second cup of coffee, I finger tossed my damp hair, applied a small amount of mascara and blush, pocketed my lip balm, and gathered my supplies. I would surprise J.T. for the first time since I'd known him and bang on his door instead of him banging on mine.

I closed the door behind me. With a confirmation jiggle of the handle, I slipped my key card into the side pocket of my briefcase and walked two doors down to J.T.'s room. I banged on it then stuck my finger over the peephole. Chuckling came from the other side of the door, then it swung open.

"Bang, you're dead." I pointed my index finger at him

as if I had just shot him. "What the hell did you learn in the FBI 101 safety course?"

"Not to open doors without asking who's on the other side?"

"That's correct."

"Get in here. Everyone down the hallway is probably staring at us through their own peepholes." J.T. closed the door behind me. "Why are you so jacked up? Have too much coffee this morning?"

"Nope, there's never enough coffee. I'm just anxious to get started on those tapes now that we know what kind of vehicle to watch for. Are you ready to go?"

"Yeah, give me a sec to grab my stuff. Want to do the Continental breakfast downstairs?"

"Sure since we aren't meeting with the rest of the group until nine o'clock, anyway."

We sat down to a filling breakfast, which hopefully would hold us over for most of the day. I had no idea when we'd eat again once we dug our feet in.

We arrived at the station at eight forty-six. Hardy had just parked and was waiting for us next to the Fallen Officers Memorial.

"Cap." I gave him a nod as we approached.

"I hope you two slept well. It looks like we've got a busy day ahead of us."

J.T. raised his brows. "Has some new information come in?"

"Joe called as I was driving here. He said the body in the woods was positively Jackie Stern. The picture of her and

Tara together that the officers took out of the house, along with the butterfly tattoo on her wrist and the knife wounds to her throat, confirmed it. Unfortunately, Tara agreed to be the one to give the positive ID."

I shook my head. "It's just not right. Even if she was estranged from her folks, she was their daughter, and they should have stepped up."

"If they can't be found, what's a person to do? We have enough on our hands trying to track down this killer. We don't have time to track down Jackie's parents too," J.T. said.

"I know."

"Shall we?" Hardy led the way into the building.

Dana greeted us as we passed the front counter. She tipped her head toward the group of chairs in the lobby. "There's someone waiting for you, Cap."

We turned to see Tammy Hawn, the reporter from Channel 9, heading in our direction.

Hardy let out a deep, long moan. "I don't have time for this," he whispered under his breath.

"I'll handle her, Cap. Why don't you two go ahead and get the meeting started?"

"You sure, Jade?"

"Absolutely, I got this."

The clip-clop of her heels on the marble floor echoed throughout the entryway. "Excuse me, Captain Hardy, I'd like to have a word with you."

I stepped in front of her, blocking her access as Cap and J.T. disappeared around the corner.

"Who are you, and what are you doing? I need to speak to the police captain."

"No you don't. You can speak to me or I can show you the door."

"How dare you. I'm a well-known news reporter."

"And I'm a well-known FBI agent." I pulled out my badge from under my collar. "Shall we have a seat?" I pointed at the area behind her. She wasn't going to get any farther into the building than that.

She stammered her objections as she followed me to a private grouping in the corner, two chairs with a table between them.

"This should do just fine. Now what can I help you with?"

"I want to know why the police department is withholding information about the Scenic View Serial Killer from the public and the media. We have a right to know what's going on, and it's your civic duty to serve and protect."

I smiled. "You're absolutely right."

She sat up a bit straighter and smoothed her blouse. She seemed pleased with herself.

"But"—I watched as her shoulders deflated before I continued—"it isn't our civic duty to get the news channels higher ratings by instilling fear in the citizens of Omaha and the surrounding communities. That said, the only thing I'll tell you until this perpetrator is apprehended is that you should watch what moniker you tag the killer with. Rumor has it there's a lawsuit in the works as we speak, against you personally and Channel 9. That could be the end of your reporting career, Ms. Hawn. Have a good day." I stood, smoothed my pants, and walked away.

The meeting was in full swing when I entered the conference room. Hardy paused what he was saying until I was seated and had my notepad on the table.

He gave me a quick grin. "Everything under control downstairs, Agent Monroe?"

"Absolutely, and Tammy Hawn and I have a newfound understanding of each other."

J.T. chuckled. "I bet you do."

Hardy continued where he left off. "Anyway, Jade, I was updating the guys about the phone call I got earlier from Joe. J.T. briefed us on the theory you came up with and the name of the man you talked to at the gas station on Thursday. All we need to do now is find that truck on the surveillance tapes."

"Lyles, you viewed the tapes around Sarah's neighborhood, correct?"

"Yeah, I used Community Bank's parking lot footage. It was the most sophisticated of the choices I had. I'll admit, not knowing what you're looking for kind of feels like a waste of time."

"Same here," Franklin said.

"Whose house were you assigned to?" J.T. asked.

"The King home."

"We're ruling that out since the coverage was at night. Let's stick with Sarah and Jackie's neighborhoods."

"I had Jackie's," Andrews said.

"Okay, do both of you have that footage on your

computers, or do we need to go back to the locations to view them?"

"The bank emailed me their file from last Monday. I watched it on my own computer," Lyles said.

"And you, Andrews?" I asked.

"I had to sit in the back room of the gas station on Hillside Street. They were the closest establishment with a camera. I'll admit, their equipment sucks. Everything is on VHS tape, so they have two for every day. They've probably had the same VCR since 1995."

"But they did have tapes from Thursday, correct?" I asked.

"Yeah, they change the tapes twice daily, mark them Monday through Sunday, then start again by taping over them."

"At least we can fast-forward the footage as we're looking for a rusty, reddish-orange truck. I'll head over there myself."

"You sure, Jade?" J.T. asked.

"Yeah, not a problem. I just need the keys to the Explorer."

"Okay, I'll review the Bellevue tape again," J.T. said.

Lyles added, "And I'll watch the tape from Sarah's neighborhood."

Hardy rapped his fingertips on the tabletop. "Okay, everyone, let's get started. We'll need to see that same truck on every tape to make something stick. Hopefully we get a good image of the driver and the license plate number."

J.T. walked to the elevator with me and handed over the

keys. "Text me if you see the truck, and make sure to bring the tape back with you if you do."

"Sure thing, Mom."

"Wiseass. Stay safe."

"Meaning what? Don't eat gas station pizza for lunch?"

He jerked his chin at the elevator. "Get going and no, don't eat gas station pizza for lunch."

I boarded the elevator, turned around, and knew J.T. would still be standing there. He was, so I blew him a kiss, and he flipped me the bird. I laughed as the doors closed and the elevator took me to the first floor.

Chapter 43

Andrews texted the address of the gas station to me, and I programmed it into my GPS before taking off in the Explorer. I messaged Amber just to say hi and that I missed her and the gang. I told her to send my love to everyone in the sheriff's office bull pen on Monday.

With my phone in the cup holder and the GPS set, I drove out of the parking lot and followed the directions that the navigation called out. It would be only a fifteen-minute drive.

I thought about J.T. as I drove. He seemed to be his old self again. I'd call Spelling before returning to the station and update him on J.T., who was back to form and a partner I could depend on. I hoped Julie was doing as well. Several times in the past few days, J.T. had stepped away from the group and made private calls. I didn't want to pry, but I assumed he was checking on his sister. Our assignment to Omaha was the first time he was away from home at night since their kidnapping nearly two months ago.

The voice on the GPS said my destination was two

hundred feet ahead. I looked down the street and saw the gas station on my right. It looked old, greasy, and more like an auto repair shop than a gas station, which I'd envisioned being clean, modern, and having a quick mart inside. I wouldn't be eating anything there and had concerns that even a bag of chips would be beyond its expiration date.

Me and my big mouth. No wonder Andrews didn't object to me taking the gas station this time around. He didn't even offer to go back.

I parked the Explorer on the side of the building and reluctantly climbed out. The place looked like a grease monkey, good-ol'-boys type of establishment. I'd have to suck it up and make the best of it. I hoped I'd be in and out quickly. Three gas pumps told me what to expect—a small, no-frills corner gas station that had probably seen better days.

I pulled open the finger-smudged glass door and entered. A man standing alone behind the counter smoked a cigarette and grinned at me.

"How ya doing today, sweetheart? Didn't see you out there pumping gas. If I did, I'd have come out there and given you a hand."

"Thanks, but I'm quite capable. You can smoke in here?" He looked me up and down, which made my skin crawl.

"I can do whatever I want, missy. I own the place."

I was sure it was a sense of pride I heard in his voice. "Great, let's cut to the chase, then. Your name is?"

"I'm Elvin Freed. And what's your name, pretty lady?"

I pulled out my badge and held it a foot from his face. "My name is FBI, but you can call me Agent Monroe. I'm here to review your videotapes from Thursday."

His expression soured quickly. "I've already shown that tape to a police officer yesterday. What's so damn important about it that the FBI sent you to look at it too?"

"Well, Mr. Freed, the FBI didn't send me to look at it, I offered, which is my bad. Either way, would you please show me where it's located so I can get this done and be out of your hair as soon as possible?"

"Whatever. Follow me."

I always made sure to carry wet wipes in my purse, and that day I was thankful I still had some left. Andrews was probably having a good laugh at my expense.

I entered a closet-sized room with calendar pages of seminude women taped to the walls. I groaned.

"Have a seat. I'll load up the VCR. You said Thursday, right, sugar?"

"Thursday is correct, Mr. Freed, and I'll need the second tape too."

"It's right here, and you don't need to be so formal. You can call me Elvin." He gave me a tooth-stained grin.

"Right. Is the first tape ready to play, and where's the remote?"

"One minute now. Don't be in such a hurry. Okay, missy, here you go."

Elvin handed me the grimy remote then stood back against the doorframe.

"What?"

"I have to make sure you're doing it right, don't I?"

I got up and walked toward him. "Thank you, Elvin, but I can handle it. Now, if you'll excuse me." I stood my ground until he walked away, then I closed the door behind him. "Gross." I pulled out the wet wipes from my purse and scrubbed the chair and the remote.

The footage, having been taped over dozens of times, was grainy at best. I scooted the chair closer to the VCR and leaned forward as I watched. Since that older technology wasn't time-stamped, I had no idea what time of day I was viewing. All I could hope for was that Elvin started them in the proper order. I had to watch the entire tape but tried to fast-forward through every stoplight after checking the vehicles in line.

I was on my second hour of staring at the footage. So far, I hadn't seen the rusty, reddish truck pass by. I rubbed my eyes and continued watching. The sound of men cackling on the other side of the wall was distracting but so was the fact that I had to use the ladies' room. I was certain that the station Elvin was so proud of didn't have separate restrooms, and the thought of what it likely did have sent shivers up my spine. There weren't enough wet wipes in my purse for that. I remembered seeing a fast-food restaurant about a half mile back. I needed coffee, anyway, and a light snack couldn't hurt. I ejected the tape, turned off the VCR, and peeked out the door. Four men, standing elbow deep against the counter, were telling each other off-color jokes. I sucked in a deep breath, grabbed my purse, and headed out.

"Done already, FBI lady?" Elvin cracked a wide smile at me.

"Actually, I'm not, so please don't mess with the VCR or tape. I'll be back in fifteen minutes."

"Anything you say, sugar."

Laughter resonated at my back as I walked out and headed to the SUV.

Five minutes later, I entered a civilized business, found the ladies' room, and scrubbed my hands thoroughly. At the counter, I ordered coffee and a fruit cup with yogurt. I paid, shoved a stack of napkins into my purse, and climbed into the Explorer.

A text came in from J.T. just before I headed back to Elvin's establishment from hell. J.T. said that the tech department was working on the footage from Bellevue. A truck had turned on Vine Street shortly before eleven o'clock that Friday night. Tech was trying to enhance the image the best they could. He asked how it was going on my end. After writing that I didn't have anything yet, I added several emojis depicting my displeasure and told him to let Andrews know we'd have a conversation later. He replied with his own emoji—a laughing face.

I sipped my coffee as I headed back to the gas station. Jackie's house was just a few miles farther down the road. I'd make a quick stop to check that the doors were secure and the crime scene tape still stretched around the property. Now that we had confirmation of her death, the house would have to be gone through once more to search for information on the whereabouts of her parents or brother.

Somebody in her family needed to take possession of her house and make arrangements for her funeral.

I passed the gas station and continued through the intersection toward Jackie's home. I had several miles to go.

The neighborhood leading into Jackie's street appeared as normal as any other street in the area. The news of Jackie's death hadn't been released. Nobody, other than law enforcement, knew that the young lady who lived at the house wrapped in yellow crime scene tape had been found murdered in the woods a half hour north of there.

I pulled along the curb and parked. I studied the area—quiet, safe, neighborly. This was a street where people sat on the porch with their morning coffee, walked their dogs at ten p.m., and watched out for each other, yet nobody saw a thing that day.

I killed the engine and climbed out. I'd make a quick sweep of the property, check the doors, and head back to the gas station, hopefully to spot that truck on the video footage. I dipped under the police tape and checked the front door—secure. As I turned at the garage, a flash of movement rounding the house and entering the backyard caught my eye.

Who the hell was that?

I reached inside my jacket for my service weapon. As I turned the corner behind the house, a gut-wrenching pain nailed me like a lightning bolt. Blue eyes stared me in the face, then I hit the ground.

Seconds later and with a deep gasp, I caught my breath and rubbed my midsection. I saw the contact burns from a

Taser and realized what had happened. I did a quick scan of the yard. Nobody was there, and luckily my gun was still in my shoulder holster. I reached for my phone then remembered it was in the Explorer. With the back wall as a brace, I stood slowly and lifted my blouse. Two eraser-sized marks were burned into my abdomen.

That son of a bitch was here, but why?

I pulled out my weapon and hugged the wall as I peeked around the corner. All was clear. I headed back to the Explorer to call J.T. I hadn't seen the truck as I drove into the neighborhood. Could he have stolen a different vehicle? Did he take public transportation? How the hell did he get there? One thing I knew to be a fact—Ed Tanner was the Scenic View Serial Killer. Now we needed to find out why and apprehend him.

Chapter 44

"Are you sure you're okay?"

"Yeah, just sore. I don't know if he's on foot or drove in with a different vehicle, J.T. I can't place that truck here at the scene."

"Seeing blue eyes won't stand up in court, Jade. We need that truck on tape. I'm on my way. Did you get a look at what he was wearing?"

"Nah, it happened too fast. I'm going to drive around this area and see if I can find him."

"Just stay put. I'll get Patrol to take care of that. I have to let Hardy know, and I'll have someone else finish up at the gas station. We have to identify that truck on the tapes today before Ed goes off the deep end again and kills another person, especially now that he knows you saw his face. You're lucky to have only gotten zapped."

"J.T., I was only doing what any officer would have done. I didn't come here looking for trouble, and I sure as hell wasn't expecting to literally run into him."

"I know that, and I'll be there in fifteen minutes. Keep

your eyes peeled but stay in the Explorer and lock the doors. Hang on."

I listened to silence for several minutes.

"Okay, I'm back. Hardy has Patrol on their way. They should be arriving in the area in the next few minutes. They'll search the neighborhood for any man on foot. Give me a rough idea of his height and weight. I'd take your description as fact over what the boys said."

"Yeah, he has your hair color, and it was about the same length but not groomed, more of a scrappy cut like he does it himself. I'd put him at six foot and one hundred ninety pounds. He's probably around forty years old. The only thing striking about him were those deep blue eyes, otherwise he could easily blend in with the crowd."

"Got it, and I'll relay that to Patrol. Hardy and I are heading out."

With my head on a swivel, I watched out every window, the rearview mirror, and the side mirrors. I never got a second look at Ed Tanner before he was in the wind. Minutes later, several patrol units pulled up alongside me. I stepped out of the Explorer and led them to the backyard, where Ed had been lurking.

"Here's the spot where I came around the corner and he zapped me. I never caught a glimpse of which direction he went after that."

A car door slammed, and I looked around the corner toward the street. J.T. was charging toward me with Hardy right behind him.

J.T. squeezed my shoulder. "You sure you're okay?"

"Yes, I'm fine. This is the spot where I saw him turn the corner. At that point I didn't know it was him, only that somebody had just gone into the backyard. When I rounded the back of the house, he nailed me with the Taser. The problem is, these yards aren't fenced in. He could have gone anywhere from here. Why do you think he came to the house, J.T.?"

"I don't have the slightest idea. He went back to where he dumped Jackie too. Maybe there's something about her in particular. Either way, we have four units patrolling the neighborhood, five blocks in each direction. They arrived minutes after your initial call, Jade. If he's still in the area, they'll spot him, but so far nobody has reported seeing anyone."

"Damn it. We need solid evidence against him. Maybe he has a second car. What ever happened with the cars we photographed around the neighborhood?" I asked.

"They were checked out, and every one of them belonged to people who lived on the block," Hardy said.

"Then we have no choice except to finish looking at those tapes."

"Lyles, Franklin, Tyler, and Andrews are working diligently on that. Andrews picked up where you left off, Jade."

I smirked. "Good, that place was disgusting, and so was Elvin Freed."

"Who?" Hardy asked.

"Never mind. Maybe we should spread out and look for Ed first."

"That isn't happening. Patrol is doing fine. I'm not letting you out of my sight, especially now since he probably recognized you. You could be his next target. Let's go."

I frowned at J.T. "Where?"

"Back to the station. We need to figure out who Ed Tanner really is."

J.T., Hardy, and I walked back to the vehicles. I had my doubts that anyone would spot Ed wandering through the neighborhood.

"We'll follow you, Cap," J.T. said as we climbed into the Explorer.

Hardy waved in acknowledgment and led the way.

Chapter 45

I stared out the side window as J.T. drove. "There's a missing link, and I can't put my finger on it."

"About what?"

"If Ed is our guy and he's angry at a woman, like Dr. Collins believes, then how does anyone in real estate, particularly Scenic View, come into play?"

J.T. shrugged. "That's the million-dollar question, isn't it? The second his truck is confirmed on video in at least two of the four neighborhoods, we'll pull all known records relating to Ed Tanner. It won't be considered invasion of privacy since we'll be looking at him as a murder suspect. We'll have a very strong case. If only we knew where he was staying and had a picture to post on the news."

"You want the news involved?"

"Not yet, but as soon as we have confirmation of his truck, we'll hold a press conference and list everything we know about him on the news channels. Having help from the public will be the fastest way to flush him out, especially since we don't have a known address for him locally. He could literally be anywhere and sleeping in the woods, his truck, or people's backyards."

"The second we know positively that Ed's our guy, I'm going in and interrogating William Stewart. There has to be something he isn't telling us."

"Do you think you remember Ed's face well enough for a composite to be drawn up? It's something since we have no actual photographs of him."

"Let's wait on that. Once we figure out where he's from, we can pull up his driver's license photo. A picture is always better than a drawing of somebody I've had a twenty-second conversation with on one occasion."

J.T. agreed to wait. He pulled into the station behind Hardy, and we entered the building together.

I headed to the elevator. "I'm going upstairs to start a list."

"Of what?" J.T. asked.

"Of everything we need to find out about Ed like where he lives, who his known associates are, where he grew up, and if he has a job."

Hardy scratched his cheek. "A job seems doubtful. He was out prowling neighborhoods during the daylight hours and at night. When would he have had time to work?"

"Okay, that would be another thing to find out, then. How does he support himself? We need to pull bank statements and his tax returns."

"Take a breath, Jade. Let's see if Tech has anything on the nighttime images going in on Vine Street."

I sighed. "Yeah, okay."

We entered the tech department at the end of the hall and almost slammed into Lyles coming out.

"I was just going to see if you were back. You aren't going to believe what Leon and I just saw on the tape near Sarah's house."

"Please, let it be a piece-of-shit, rusty red truck."

Lyles grinned. "In the flesh, so to speak."

"Finally." I fist pumped the air. "Show us."

Leon turned in his chair. "Grab a stool and roll on over here. I'm trying to get in closer and still maintain a crisp image. It would help to know the make and model."

"Can you get a number off the front plate?" J.T. asked.

"Nope, there isn't one."

"I wonder if that's an accident or by design. Some states don't require front plates, and if he isn't listed with Nebraska's DMV, that could be why." Hardy pushed a few roller stools toward us.

"Anything on the nighttime images in Bellevue?" J.T. asked. "Can you confirm that the truck turning on Vine is the same one?"

Dave Lawrence spoke up. "I took over that duty when Lyles needed Leon. I'm seventy-five percent sure. Give me a few more minutes to do some tweaking, Agent Harper."

I picked at my cuticles while we waited. J.T. gave me a disapproving frown.

Leon leaned back and stretched. "This is as good as it gets, agents. I can't get any emblems off the footage. That truck is too old and faded to see much of a contrast. I'm betting either the emblems have fallen off or they're so corroded the chrome is gone."

I stared at the tape from Sarah's neighborhood. "From what I recall, it sure looks like Ed Tanner's truck. Don't you agree, J.T.?"

"I'd say so."

Hardy's cell rang seconds later. "Cap here. What have you got, Andrews? No kidding? Get that tape back here immediately." He hung up and grinned. "Andrews just saw a rust bucket red truck turn at the intersection in front of the gas station."

I punched J.T. in the shoulder.

"What the—"

I interrupted enthusiastically. "All we need to do now is compare the footage to see if it's the same truck in both tapes. The best part is, they're the two tapes we needed most, the ones during daylight hours."

Hardy tipped his head at Tyler. "Busy?"

"Not at the moment, sir. What do you need?"

"Get started on tracking down Jackie Stern's next of kin. I'd say her brother may be the easiest to find. He's in the service and deployed overseas right now, but he can certainly get a bereavement leave. As soon as Andrews gets here, I want both of you to head back over to Jackie's house and start looking for an address book. Maybe we can find her folks too since her cell phone was never recovered. Call Tara Lamar if you need more information."

Five minutes later we heard footsteps approaching. The door swung open, and Andrews appeared wearing a wide grin. "Here you go. I stopped the tape right at the moment

I saw the truck." He handed the VHS tape to Leon. "You only need to rewind it a few seconds."

Leon stared at the tape as if it were an alien object. "Do we even have a VCR?"

Hardy smirked. "You better hope you do."

"Just joking, Cap. You never know who you'll come across that still lives in 1990. Okay, let's line up the images side by side and see how they look." Leon handed the tape to J.T. and tipped his head. "Turn on that TV and pop the tape in the VCR."

"Got it."

"Okay, go ahead, but pause it the second the truck comes into the frame. I'll do the same with the image on Sarah's footage."

Leon nodded, and J.T. clicked Play. The tape progressed.

"Any second now," Andrews said. "There, stop!"

I squinted at the image. "No shit, it looks like Ed's truck. You can't identify the driver, but I can tell in both views there's only one person inside."

Leon inched his footage forward with the scrubber bar then paused it. He looked from the TV screen to his computer monitor. "It's too bad I can't do anything to enhance a VHS tape, but the shape of the truck looks the same on both images, and the color does too—faded reddish orange. I'm leaning toward them being the same vehicle, and what are the odds of it being near both crime scenes?"

"I think our odds just improved one hundred percent." I pointed at the videotaped image. "Look. That truck doesn't have a front plate, either."

"Bingo!" Hardy said as he slapped the desk. "Let's start pulling everything we can on Ed Tanner. Meanwhile"—he turned to Franklin— "take a picture of that truck and head over to the homes of those young boys. I want to know if it's the same truck they saw."

"Right away, Cap."

"All right, let's get busy. Grab something to tide you over, and let's meet in the conference room in ten minutes."

Chapter 46

Ed exited the city bus and walked two blocks to a small community park. He sat at the picnic table in the shade of a large evergreen where he was well hidden from view. He needed a minute and had to think. He had gone to Jackie's house, the only one he hadn't visited yet. Without TV coverage, he had no idea if a memorial had been set up for her or even if the police had found her body.

Maybe those boys were too scared to tell anyone about me. If they went to the police, the area surely would have been searched. The cops would have found her, and there would have been a memorial set up by now. Of course, I had to check things out for myself, but that damn FBI bitch showed up and saw me. As usual, women screw things up, and they're the reason my life is in shambles.

Ed was giving that FBI agent more thought as the day went on. He added her to his list of maybes. If she didn't stay out of his way, she might have to be eliminated too.

The beeping phone disrupted his train of thought. The timer had gone off.

Aah…it's time to call the main bitch.

He didn't store her name or number in his contact list. He wasn't that stupid. The number was engrained in his memory, and if she changed it, he'd find the new number with his PeopleSeeker software, anyway. She couldn't hide from him.

Ed picked up his phone, blocked the number, and dialed. She answered on the second ring.

"Hello."

"I want to see my kids."

"Leave me the hell alone, Ed, or I swear I'll call the cops. I have enough going on in my life right now without your crap too. If you don't leave us alone, I'll have a restraining order filed against you."

"For wanting to speak to my kids? I can call them whenever I feel like it."

"You're harassing me, and they aren't home, anyway."

"I think it's time for a visit."

"That's not happening. We've been over this a million times. You're unstable, and I have full custody."

"You're really pissing me off, P—" Ed heard the familiar click on the other end. She had hung up on him again. "You're going to be sorry you did that."

Ed made another call, this time to a car service. He needed to be driven only a few miles, and he'd walk the rest of the way. Nobody needed to know the whereabouts of that tucked-away cottage he rented by the week. The three-month advance payment from his last disability check kept the elderly owner happy, and no questions were ever asked.

Chapter 47

With a soda and sandwich in hand, I entered the conference room and took a seat. J.T., with his own hands full, was right behind me. I grabbed my briefcase that I had tucked away in the corner of the room earlier that morning. My laptop, along with the list I had started yesterday, lay inside.

J.T. leaned toward me and checked out what was written on the sheet of paper. "Looks like Ed was your main suspect all along."

"Nah, he's the only suspect, we just don't know the reasoning behind his actions. I need to jot down a few things so I don't forget, then we can start checking databases."

Hardy, Andrews, and Lyles entered the room, each carrying a laptop, and took their seats.

"Good news, agents."

I looked up and actually saw a smile on Hardy's face.

"Dave finished cleaning up the Bellevue tape. He's certain that truck matches the others. It's time to find Ed Tanner."

J.T. spoke up. "And that's exactly what we're starting to do. Let's begin with a national background check on his name and see if he's in the database. If he has a record, we'll know what state he's from, then we can pull his driver's license information."

Hardy tapped computer keys while I Googled Ed Tanner's name.

I groaned at the results. "No help there. I have a doctor from Boca Raton, an ex-football player, and an obituary for an eighty-eight-year-old man who died in 2002." I crossed that entry off my list.

"If we had his Social Security number and a middle name, we'd have everything we needed to know in five minutes," Andrews said.

"But we don't, and believe it or not, there isn't a criminal history for anyone named Ed Tanner in the age parameters we've established," J.T. said.

Hardy looked hopeful. "IRS records?"

"Yeah, but not without pulling teeth and certainly not on a Sunday afternoon. That would have to be a request from higher up and with a phone call. It could still take days, especially without the Social Security number to go along with the name," I said.

"We have to rely on the public, then. Ed's face has to be put on the news along with his general description. The BOLO is out on the truck, right?" J.T. asked.

Lyles nodded. "Already taken care of, Agent Harper."

"I hate to contact Channel 9 and ask them to air that footage in front of Sarah's house, but it may be our only option. Ed's face does show up on that tape," J.T. said. "We haven't been very forthright with the media or given them anything of value to air. They're fearmongers, and now we want their help?"

I looked at Leon. "Is there any way to take his face out of that footage and make it a still shot? I doubt if Channel 9 asked everyone's permission to have their cameraman pan the crowd."

"True, but they own the rights to that footage."

"Just pull Ed's face out of the crowd. Nobody has to know where it came from. People post things on YouTube all the time without permission. If you take a picture of his face without any of the background showing, nobody will know the difference. We'll offer it up to Channel 4."

J.T. agreed. "It's a bit shady, Jade, but let's do it. We don't have time for anything else."

Leon entered the website address for Channel 9 and pulled up the video footage filmed in front of Sarah's house. "Just tell me when you see him. I can lock in on his face and separate it from the background. I'll drop it on my desktop, make sure nobody else is in the image, and save it."

I flipped over my sheet of paper and grabbed a pen. "Meanwhile, I'll put a description together. We can't state his name to the public yet, only that the man in the screen shot is a person of interest. We'll include his description and his vehicle information. Everything we have on Ed is circumstantial. We don't have prints, a weapon, or a motive. He doesn't even have a record that we can find, so we have to be careful how we involve the public. There's no way we can afford to have this go sideways. All we need is one person who recognizes him and knows where he's hunkered down. Let's put up a new tip line number so we know that if and when information comes in, it's from the most recent broadcast."

J.T. checked the time. "We can get this up on the evening news if we hurry."

"Check out what I have," Leon said. "Do you think this will work?"

J.T., Hardy, and I stared at Ed's image over Leon's shoulder.

"Too bad he's wearing that damn hat, but go ahead. It's all we have."

Footsteps sounded in the hallway, and Franklin entered the conference room. "The kids confirmed that it's the same truck. They said the truck was parked facing them when they rode in on their bikes. They noticed there wasn't a front plate."

Hardy slapped his hands together. "The rope is tightening around your neck, Ed Tanner, you just don't know it yet."

"I'm going downstairs to pay William Stewart a visit." I pushed back my chair and stood. "Where is that picture of Jackie and Tara together?"

"Andrews spoke up. "It's in my desk drawer in the bull pen."

I tipped my chin toward the door. "I'll walk with you."

"Jade."

I turned to see what J.T. wanted.

"Stewart won't talk to anyone without his attorney present."

I shrugged. "I can still try."

I joined Andrews in the bull pen momentarily while he retrieved the framed picture from his desk. He handed it to me.

"Thanks, Fred. Tell the others I won't be long." I turned and headed for the elevator.

Downstairs, I signed in and asked to see William Stewart. The officer behind the counter made a call and told me it would be about ten minutes. I texted Amber while I waited and told her we were making progress on the case and hoped to be home in a few days.

"Agent Monroe?"

"Yes, that's me." I looked up to see a guard standing ten feet away. "You can see Mr. Stewart now. He's agreed to give you only five minutes since his attorney isn't present."

"Great, thanks."

"What's that in your hand?"

"A framed picture. I need to ask him something about it."

"The photograph needs to come out of the glass."

"Oh, of course. Sorry," I pulled off the back of the frame and slid the photograph out. "Here you go." I handed the frame to him.

"Right this way."

I followed the guard to interrogation room two, where he opened the door and allowed me through. Mr. Stewart sat at the table on the side that faced me.

"I'll be watching through the window, ma'am."

"That's fine, and I won't be long." I took a seat across from Mr. Stewart.

He huffed at the sight of me. "I thought you'd be that other FBI agent. You do realize he's nicer than you, right?"

"So I've been told, but I have tough skin. Harsh comments roll right off my back."

"What do you want? I have better things to do."

"Really, like what? Have you been staring out your two-inch-by-eight-inch slot of a window or dreading tomorrow when the SEC comes to pay you a visit?"

"See what I mean? You're a bitch."

I chuckled. "I've been called worse. Actually, I do have a serious reason to be here, William, and I hope we can put our sarcasm aside for a few minutes."

"Whatever. I'm not talking about my case without my attorney."

"I'm not here about that." I pulled out the photograph from my pocket. "Do you know the woman with the dark hair? Were you having an affair with her?"

"Affair? I've only had one af—"

"You caught yourself, didn't you? So you have had an affair? Only one?"

"That was several years ago, and it's none of your business."

"Please, look at the picture." I handed the photograph to William and watched his expression.

"That's strange. She's a dead ringer for my wife, Pam, but no, I've never met her."

"Her name is Jackie Stern. Does that name ring a bell with you?"

"Can't say that it does."

"Have you ever been to 4830 Crenshaw Lane on the southeast side of town?"

"Is that where she lives?"

"Please answer my question."

"Nope, never have."

"How about some other woman, then? Is there an angry husband who found out you were messing around with their wife and now they're coming after your real estate company?"

"We're done. I said I wasn't going to talk about my businesses unless my attorney was present. Now you're crossing the line. Guard!"

The guard entered and asked me to leave. I snatched the picture off the table but turned before walking out. I looked back at Mr. Stewart and smiled. "Good luck with the SEC tomorrow."

"Fu—"

The door slammed at my back.

I had been gone for only a half hour and returned to the conference room, where everyone was still hard at work.

Hardy furrowed his forehead when I entered. "Care to share your findings?"

"It was a bust. I wanted to know if William Stewart knew Jackie. I thought about the cheating aspect. Maybe Jackie had a boyfriend nobody knew about or Mr. Stewart's wife found out that he was cheating and went after Jackie.

He started to say he's never cheated but caught himself. He finally admitted he had, but he said it was a few years ago. I did find something peculiar, though, and I'm not sure how we can connect it to this case."

J.T. scratched his cheek then gave me a nod. "What's that?"

"He said Jackie is a dead ringer for his wife."

"Nice play on words," Hardy said. "Hmm, maybe we have something and we don't even know it. So Ed kidnaps Jackie instead of killing her right away like the others, then he kills her anyway but goes back to where he dumped her to have a second look and, finally, ends up at her house earlier today just in time to zap you in the stomach."

I instinctively touched the spot just above my bellybutton. It still hurt.

"But Ed did go back to Sarah's house too," Andrews said.

"Speaking of that, did you guys get everything set up with Channel 4?" I asked.

J.T. shuffled his papers. "Yep, and it airs in a half hour. Let's think more about the connection with Stewart's wife looking just like Jackie. What could that possibly mean to Ed?"

"Maybe Ed was having an affair with Stewart's wife."

"That makes no sense at all, Franklin," Hardy said. "It wouldn't connect Jackie to anyone."

"Oh yeah."

"Not so fast. Franklin might be on the right track. Maybe Ed is *infatuated* with Stewart's wife, and Jackie reminded him of her. There's a reason he chose Jackie, and the fact that her house was for sale with Scenic View sealed the deal for him. He may have been stalking her because he couldn't get close to Stewart's wife. I need to see what she looks like." I woke up my laptop and typed the words *Pamela Stewart, Omaha, Nebraska*, into the search bar. The guys crowded around my computer and waited. I clicked on Images, and dozens of photographs came up of her and William at fund-raisers, galas, dinner parties, and so on. "Wow." I pulled out the picture of Jackie and placed it on the table next to my computer. "I can't believe the similarities."

"You need to talk to Stewart again."

I smirked. "I don't think so. As I left the interrogation room, he told me what I could do with myself." I smiled at J.T. "He said he likes you much better, anyway."

"Okay, forget him. Let's go pay Mrs. Stewart a visit. Make sure to tape the Channel 4 news while we're gone. Grab that photograph, Jade."

J.T. got the home address from the interview notes that were filed, and we left while the rest of the group continued their efforts to track down Ed Tanner.

Chapter 48

The GPS system called out the directions that led us to the northwest lake community of Newport Landing near Bennington. We arrived at a beautiful home nestled against a large lake and tucked among tall pines. The home, primarily brick, was a two-story traditional with white columns and a wide welcoming porch.

"What do you think?" I shielded my eyes as J.T. parked the Explorer, and we got out.

He pointed toward the rear of the home. "There's a car back there by the garage. Let's see if anyone answers the door."

We followed the brick sidewalk to the front door, and J.T. pressed the bell. We waited for what seemed to be a few minutes. The fluttering curtain at the bay window on my right caught my eye. I tipped my head to get a better look then elbowed J.T. The setting sun lit up the young girl's golden-blond hair. She peered out at us with a curious smile. I waved, and she disappeared.

Moments later, the door opened only slightly, and a strangely familiar face stared out at us. It was uncanny how much Pam Stewart resembled Jackie. They could have been sisters.

"Mrs. Stewart?"

"Yes, how may I help you?"

I pulled out my badge, and J.T. did the same. "We're from the FBI, and we need a few minutes of your time."

"What is this in reference to? William said not to speak to anyone about the predicament he's in."

I led the conversation in hopes that as one woman speaking to another, I would make her more comfortable and willing to talk. "This isn't actually about William's side business. May we come in?"

"I suppose." She looked over her shoulder. "My kids are home, and I don't want to upset them."

"Can we find a spot to speak privately, then?"

"Give me a minute." She turned the corner and left J.T. and me standing in the foyer. Moments later, she returned and ushered us through the house and into the library. "This has been a difficult time for our family. I'm sure you understand. My kids have been wondering where William went."

I thought it odd how she worded that statement. "How old are your children?"

"Missy is four, and Lucas is six. They don't understand any of this. I'm sorry, so why are you here?"

"How long have you and William been married?" J.T. asked.

She gave us a bewildered look. "Two and a half years. Why?"

I was sure my own face now wore a bewildered expression. "So you were married before?"

"Yes. Is there a reason my personal life is important to the FBI?"

"Do you recognize this woman, Mrs. Stewart?" I pulled out the picture of Jackie and passed it across the coffee table to her.

She held it to the light. "Wow."

"Ma'am?"

"Um, oh, I'm just stunned, that's all. It's almost like looking in the mirror, but they do say that everyone has a twin out there somewhere. So what did you ask me?"

"If you recognized her. Her name is Jackie Stern."

"No I don't. Should I? Does William?"

"We haven't put the connection together yet, ma'am. Have you always lived in this area?"

"William and I?"

"No, Mrs. Stewart, just you," I said.

"I'm originally from Little Rock, and that's where I met my first husband. He was native to Omaha, so we eventually moved back here."

"And that's when William came into the picture?"

She began to fidget, and I knew I'd hit a nerve. "Where are you going with this questioning?"

"Has anyone ever stalked you or had an obsession with you that you're aware of?"

She snickered. "Is mental instability and harassment considered an obsession? We keep our dirty laundry out of the public eye as much as possible, agents. William has an enormous reputation to uphold."

I turned my head and gave J.T. an eye roll. "Ma'am, you do realize his arrest is going to become public as early as tomorrow, don't you? The SEC will be taking over his case."

"It's all a misunderstanding. I'm sure it will get swept under the rug."

I sighed. That woman was in serious denial. "Okay, back to the person who's mentally unstable. You said they've been harassing you?"

"Yes, and it's escalating."

J.T. raised his brows. "And you haven't called the police?"

"Like I said, William doesn't need that kind of publicity. I married a very wealthy, well-respected man in the Omaha area." She looked over her shoulder then continued in a whisper. "It's my problem, not his. The person who's been harassing me is my ex-husband. It's only been by telephone, though. We had a very contentious divorce, and I was awarded full custody of our children. He's been severely depressed and unstable for years, but he always took his meds. Frankly, I think he's dangerous. Anyway, after the divorce, he moved back to Little Rock, where he still had a few friends. He doesn't have family living in Omaha anymore."

"How long has it been since you've seen your ex?" I asked.

"Three years. The only communication we have is when he calls me. He's malicious and threatens to kill me if I won't let him see the kids. He insults me with demeaning names and tells me to shut up every time I try to speak. He snarls about hating my voice. That's usually when I hang up on him. Thank God he doesn't live here anymore. I'd always be looking over my shoulder."

I gave J.T. a concerned glance.

"I've changed my phone number dozens of times, but somehow he always finds out what it is. Ed is definitely psychotic and getting worse. I'm sure he's stopped his medication."

My head almost spun off my shoulders. "Did you say Ed?"

"Yes, my ex-husband. He despises me and hates William even more. He considers William his archenemy and would do anything to ruin his reputation. It's all about jealousy."

I looked her straight in the eyes. "Because you and William were having an affair, weren't you?"

She nodded and dropped her head to her chest. "Ed had nothing going for him, and William had everything. I was sick of our ho-hum life together, and I knew William could raise the kids in the lifestyle they deserved. That's why I shoulder the brunt of Ed's hatred and try to shelter William from all of it."

I felt my stomach lurch. "What is your ex-husband's last name, Pam?"

"Tanner. His name is Ed Tanner."

I told Pam to stay put as J.T. and I went outside to call the precinct. I swatted a branch out of my way as we stepped around to the side of the house to talk. "Son of a bitch, I didn't see that coming. It's obvious that Ed isn't in Little

Rock and Pam is as dense as a doorknob. Doesn't she own a TV?"

"Jade, we haven't given the news anything for days."

I felt like ripping out my hair. "You're right, but why did William say he didn't have any enemies? If he would have told us about Ed right away, chances are Jackie and Marilyn wouldn't have died. Killing people was how Ed wanted to ruin William's reputation? Why not just kill William?"

"First off, it could be true that William didn't know how dangerous Ed was, and as far as killing William instead? Maybe ruining him financially and taking down his oversized ego, along with destroying his company, was more satisfying to Ed. It's obvious he didn't know the real estate business was just one of William's many corporations. The irony of it all is that William is about to ruin his own reputation without Ed's help." J.T. pulled out his cell phone and made the call to Hardy. "Cap, I have you on speakerphone. Jade and I just had an interesting conversation with Pam Stewart. You aren't going to believe this."

"At this point, I'll believe anything."

"Ed Tanner is her ex-husband." J.T.'s eyes bulged at the choice words flowing from the other end of the phone call.

Hardy cursed into his phone. "Can this case get any more convoluted? What the hell? And William said he had no enemies, that lying son of—"

"Cap, apparently the wife knew how dangerous Ed was, but she was under the assumption he was in Little Rock. He moved back there after their divorce. She said he calls, screams at her, and makes threats. She hangs up on him, changes her phone number, but he still finds a way to reach her. She's been keeping all of that to herself."

"What the hell for? She could have gotten law enforcement involved."

I took my turn. "That's exactly what she didn't want. No police, no television coverage, and no newspaper articles. She didn't want to tarnish William's sterling reputation and his over-the-top ego. Sounds like she thought he'd regret his decision to marry her if the entire town got wind of her dirty laundry and crazy ex-husband."

"Right, and that's all at the cost of five lives that we know of for sure."

"Anything come in on the tip line? We have to get Ed in custody as soon as possible since he may be ready to strike again. I'm sure he's pissed that there was no coverage of Marilyn or Jackie's deaths. And his sign never got on the air, either. He could be a ticking time bomb by now," J.T. said.

"And if he sees his face on TV instead of only being known as the Scenic View Serial Killer, he may feel like a caged rat," Hardy added. "I have four officers answering calls on the tip line. Finish up at the Stewart house and head back. I have an idea that might help."

Chapter 49

I'm sure I'm not the only one who saw my face on the news coverage.

Ed was livid, and he knew it was just a matter of time. He paced back and forth and peered out the window every few minutes.

That stupid FBI bitch put this together. She's the only person who could have. I'll have to show her a thing or two. I'm not about to let her ruin my plans, I've come too far.

Ed gathered what he needed, stepped out to the porch, and locked the door behind him. It was time to get creative. He was sure his truck would be spotted now that everything about him had been aired on the local evening news.

That old widow lives at the end of the street. I bet she wouldn't mind if I borrowed her car.

Ed walked the quarter mile to her house and peered through the windowpanes of the only illuminated room. Night had fallen, and the narrow lane that led back to the cottages was as dark as ink. Ed stared at her as she lay snuggled up on her recliner with a throw over her legs. Her eyelids appeared closed from his angle, and her partially open mouth led him to believe she was asleep. Ed backed away from the window and crossed the yard to the front porch. He stepped carefully to avoid causing the old wooden boards to creak. He turned the doorknob slowly. To his surprise, the door was unlocked.

Stupid old hag, don't you know there are prowlers everywhere?

He slipped off his shoes and crossed the threshold.

Now where would an old woman keep her car keys? Purse, key rack, kitchen table?

The purse hanging from the back of the kitchen chair caught Ed's eye. He tiptoed to it and pulled the zipper. With his hand inside, he felt for the set of keys. A smile crossed his face when he touched that familiar ring with several keys attached. He pulled them out then dipped his hand back inside, removed her wallet, and emptied it of cash. Ed zipped the purse and exited the house. With his shoes back on, he headed to the driveway, unlocked the car, and shifted it into neutral. Ed steered with his left hand as he pushed the car out onto the street. He climbed in, slipped the key into the ignition, and sped away. It was time to silence that FBI agent for good, and he knew exactly how to draw her in.

Chapter 50

"What are you searching for?" J.T. glanced at me while I tapped the phone keys.

"Seeing if Arkansas requires a front license plate."

"What's the answer?"

"Nope, it sure doesn't."

J.T. pulled into the station's parking lot by eight o'clock. We entered the building and headed to the third floor. In the conference room, Hardy was leading the discussion with the rest of the group. We took our seats and pulled out our notepads.

"We've already begun, agents, but I'll give you the quick version of my thoughts."

I stared at the back wall. A transparency of an enlarged area of Omaha filled the drop-down roller screen. Leon must have been hard at work again while we were gone.

"What I've circled in red is the homes of each victim except Marilyn. I'm sure she was used primarily as a message to law enforcement that nobody is safe from his reach. Anyway, I have the homes of Sarah, the Kings, and Jackie

Stern circled. Most criminals don't venture too far away from the areas they know well. They have to be aware of escape routes, nearest freeways, etcetera. The blue circles indicate the intersections we've seen his truck pass through, and the arrows show which direction it came from."

I nodded as I took notes. "Great work, Cap, and I see where you're going with this. You want to narrow down his stomping grounds."

"That's right, and assuming he came from wherever he's hunkered down each time he attacked someone, the direction he came from may lead us back to where he lives."

J.T. spoke up. "Go ahead and draw a circle around the outer perimeter of the home locations, just to lock everything in. We'll check areas within that circle to see if something looks promising."

"Sure thing." Hardy removed the transparency, drew a border around the homes' locations, then placed it back on the lens. "Weird. The Kings' home dips way in, yet Jackie and Sarah's homes are spaced about the same distance apart."

Andrews spoke up. "And Mr. and Mrs. King were killed at night. We're assuming it was under the false impression that Chad Nolan was stopping by. Ed probably didn't wander too far from home, considering the time that last phone call came in to the King house and the time we got the 9-1-1 call from Beth Sloane."

"And on Sarah and Jackie's tapes, both areas where Ed's truck entered the footage lead back toward the direction of the Kings' house," J.T. said.

The conference room phone rang, and Hardy picked it up. "Captain Hardy here. Uh-huh." He grabbed a pen and paper and began writing. "Okay, get Patrol out there right away and keep me posted."

"What's going on?" I asked.

"Somebody type in this address on their phone and see where it is. An elderly lady just reported that her car has been stolen."

My fingers were a blur as I tapped my phone keys. The location came up immediately on my Google Maps. "Crap."

Everyone turned to me. "You have the location already?"

I nodded. "And it's dead center in the area we want to check out."

Hardy tipped his head at my laptop. "Wake that thing up, and let's get a satellite view of that area. I want to see if it's a practical location where Ed could hide."

Once I had the satellite view of the neighborhood where the call about the stolen car came from, we gathered around my computer.

J.T. leaned in closer. "It looks like a private enclave nestled at the edge of the city limits." He pointed near the top of the screen. "We've got a lake there, a narrow road, and by the size of these rooftops, they must all be cottages. This could have been a resort type of area back in the day when Omaha was much smaller."

I mentally counted the rooftops. "Twelve homes in all. It wouldn't take long to do a knock and talk. We'll print out a handful of those still shots of Ed and see if anyone recognizes him. If we get a positive ID, that means he lives within walking distance of that lady's house. He knew she was elderly and that she lives alone. She was an easy target. Stealing her vehicle means Ed saw the news coverage and has his truck tucked away."

"Find out from dispatch which patrol officers were sent to her house. Text them the image of Ed, have them show it to the woman, and see if she recognizes him." J.T. slapped the table. "Meanwhile, let's get a dozen pictures printed of Ed and head out."

Chapter 51

Ed knew the kids were in bed. Pam always made sure they were tucked in by eight o'clock. He pulled into the kiddie park several blocks from her house and slipped the dark sedan into a parking space. He'd walk the rest of the way.

Bordered by pines, the Stewart driveway offered him plenty of cover as he inched closer to the house. His anger at his ex-wife and her rich husband escalated each time he drove by. They had everything—a beautiful home, prestige in the community, lots of money, and his kids. Ed was invisible, but that night, that was exactly how he wanted to be.

He followed the driveway to the garage and peered through the window, his hands cupping the sides of his face. He squinted, trying to get a focus on the darkened room. Cars were parked inside. He moved on and rounded the rear of the house, staying in the shadows of the shrubbery and ancient trees. The kitchen, with a large set of French doors that led out to the two-tiered deck, faced the backyard and lake. Interior lights were on, and Ed made himself comfortable near the trees. He needed to see who was up and wandering about. He could easily subdue Pam, but the husband was a large man, and taking him down would definitely have to be a blitz attack. Once the husband was incapacitated, Ed could take his time with Pam. He had things for her to do.

He leaned back against the large oak and watched for movement. The rear of the house, since it faced the lake, was mostly windows and decks. When he heard a sound coming from above him, Ed ducked behind the tree. The slider to a second-story deck had just opened. He listened as Pam's voice echoed through the backyard.

"Yes, William will be home tomorrow, Mom. There was a slight business misunderstanding that caused him to be away for a few days. No, there isn't a problem. His attorney is taking care of everything. Okay, I'll talk to you soon, and plan on dinner here next weekend. Good night, Mom."

Ed peeked around the tree trunk and saw Pam go inside the house. The sound of the slider closing confirmed it, and the deck light went off.

So, she's alone. He chuckled at his good fortune. *I guess it's time to get busy.*

Back at the garage, Ed jimmied the lock, just as he had at Marilyn's house. He crept through the garage toward the next door, but before entering the home, he noticed off to the side some stairs that led down.

Perfect, there's a basement entry too. She'll never hear me come in if I use that.

Ed took the staircase to the basement level and turned

the knob. The door popped open.

Oops, big mistake, Pammy. Somebody forgot to lock the basement door. Guess it's my lucky day.

Ed pulled out the flashlight from his pocket and gave the room a few short bursts of light. A bar, pool table, and large-screen TV filled the space. Plenty of toys lay scattered about. He'd have to watch his step.

Across the room was the open staircase that led to the main floor. An ambient glow from the rooms above gave just enough light for him to see where he was going. Ed inched up each step slowly and deliberately. As he neared the final steps, he saw the kitchen directly ahead and the dining room beyond that. He looked from left to right as he took that last step. The house was quiet, yet the lights were still on. He peeked around the corner into the family room—nobody there, either. He continued on through the butler's pantry and past the formal living room. Another staircase lay ahead. He stopped and listened—a shower was running upstairs. The right side of his mouth curled up into a grin. He slicked back his hair and continued on.

This is going to be as easy as pie.

Ed reached the landing and looked both ways. He turned right and followed the hallway to the end where the master suite was situated. The shower was still running. Ed entered the room, closed the door behind him, and took a seat on the chair to the left of the bathroom door. Pam wouldn't see him until it was too late to react. Ed would pounce quickly and subdue her. The last thing he wanted to do was wake his kids.

The shower stopped, and Ed sat upright on the edge of the chair, ready to spring into action. He'd finally see the bitch again, up close and personal. He'd smell her damp hair, fresh with the scent of shampoo. The fragrance of lavender soap would linger on her body and bring back memories of what they once had, but that was then, long before she turned into a cheating, money-hungry skank.

He saw the knob turn, and the bathroom door opened. Pam stepped into the bedroom, wearing her white chenille robe and towel drying her hair. Ed leapt forward and zapped her hard and deep in the back then covered her mouth with his hand to keep her quiet as she dropped to the floor. He didn't have much time. He had to act quickly while she was stunned. With two lengths of rope ready in his pocket, Ed tied her hands behind her back and her ankles together. He grabbed a pair of socks from the dresser drawer and stuffed one in her mouth.

Pam moaned and opened her eyes.

Ed sat a foot away, grinning at her. "Well, aren't you in quite a predicament?"

Thrashing against her restraints got her nowhere. Ed pulled out his knife from the sheath and held it against her cheek.

"Don't make a sound, understand? Do you really want to wake the kids and have them witness this?"

She shook her head with wild, fearful eyes.

"You need to listen to me closely, Pam, because I'm only saying this once. If you do anything off script, I'll slit your throat and gut you on the spot. Are we clear?"

She nodded.

"Good. First, have the police been in contact with you? Do they know my name?"

She nodded again.

"You stupid bitch." Ed punched her in the eye, sending her head backward, where it hit the bed frame. "I bet that hurt, didn't it?"

Her groan confirmed it.

"Have you spoken with the FBI? And don't lie to me. I know they're in Omaha, and as a matter of fact"—Ed opened his wallet and pulled out Jade's card—"have you spoken to Agent Jade Monroe?" His fist was curled in a tight ball, ready to strike.

She mumbled a yes through the sock.

Ed punched her again then stared at her. "That eye is swelling closed, but at least you still have one that works. I'm going to pull that sock out of your mouth so you can talk. If you scream or do anything other than what I tell you to"—he slid the tip of the knife under his fingernails and cleaned them—"well, you get the picture, right?"

She nodded.

"Where's your cell phone?"

She tipped her head toward the bathroom. Ed got up and retrieved it.

"Now, here's what we're going to do."

Chapter 52

Six of us headed to the precinct's parking lot. According to Hardy, two patrol officers were on-site and interviewing the woman whose car was stolen. A BOLO was issued for her car.

"Did they show Ed's picture to her?" I asked as we crossed the lot to our vehicles.

Hardy nodded. "Yeah, but Dixon said she didn't recognize him."

My phone rang right as we reached the Explorer. I dipped my hand in my pocket and pulled it out. "Hang on, guys. It's Pam Stewart." I clicked Talk and answered. "Agent Monroe here, how can I help you? Yes, I suppose I could. Uh-huh. Sure, give me a half hour." I clicked off.

"What did she want?" J.T. asked.

"She said Ed called again and unnerved her. She has some new information that may help, and she'd like me to come back to discuss it."

"Okay, let's go," J.T. said.

"She asked if I would come alone."

"Why alone?" Hardy wrinkled his brow as he looked at me.

"It's got to be that woman-to-woman thing, don't you agree, J.T.? I mean, she opened up more when I took over the conversation this afternoon."

"Yeah, that's true. Okay, you take the Explorer, and I'll hop in with Cap. Keep us posted, and we'll do the same."

"Absolutely." J.T. handed me the keys, and I left. I had a half-hour drive to Newport Landing.

It was still early enough to make that call to Spelling in Milwaukee. Our time zone was the same, and the digital clock on the dashboard showed it was nine thirty. I made the call and put my cell on speakerphone then set it in the cup holder.

"Hey, boss, it's Jade. I hope this isn't too late to call."

"Not a problem. How's the case going?"

"It's very complicated. Turns out the wife of William Stewart, the owner of Scenic View Realty, used to be married to our suspect."

Spelling groaned through the phone line. "Wow, I didn't see that coming."

"None of us did, boss. It was a real shocker. J.T. and I interviewed her earlier today, and this all came out. She just called, and I'm heading back over there now. I guess she has more to say."

"Is the case progressing?"

I clicked my blinker and merged onto the highway. "Yes, it is. Actually the team is checking out a promising neighborhood right now. I wanted to talk to you while I was alone."

"About J.T.?"

"That's right, sir. In my opinion, he's as good as he's always been. He's bounced back from that trauma, at least in the FBI agent sense of the word. How his personal feelings are and what he's going through with Julie, I couldn't say. I have seen him wander off and make phone calls."

"Can you blame him?"

"No, sir, I sure can't. I just wanted you to be aware that he seems his old self as far as his job. He's one hundred percent."

"That's good to know. Thanks for the information, Jade. Stay safe and keep me posted."

"Will do, boss. Good night."

Fifteen minutes later, I entered the upscale neighborhood where the Stewart house was located. As I made a left turn, my headlights bounced off the side of a vehicle parked toward the back of the kiddie playground. It was late, and the playground had been closed for hours according to the sign posted at the entrance. Checking it out would take only a minute. I imagined seeing underage kids drinking or making out inside the car. I parked, leaving my headlights pointed at the vehicle, and approached it from the back. I called out, got no response, then shined my flashlight through the rear window.

Hmm, it's empty.

I circled the vehicle and panned my light through the playground. I saw nobody. From the looks of that neighborhood, a deserted ten-year-old Chrysler didn't fit in.

I pressed the phone number for J.T.

"Hey, Jade. We got here about ten minutes ago. We're planning our knock and talks around the neighborhood. Are you at Pam's house yet?"

"I'm a few blocks away. I made an unplanned stop at the kiddie park in her neighborhood."

I heard J.T. chuckle. "Feel like playing on the monkey bars for a bit?"

"Cute. Actually there's a deserted car that caught my attention. It doesn't fit in with this neighborhood. Could you have one of the officers pull up the plate number on their car's computer?"

"Sure thing. Go ahead."

"It's Nebraska A17-9H6."

"What? Repeat that please."

"It's A17-9H6. Is my phone cutting out?"

"Shit! That's the old lady's car. I have her information staring me in the face on the police report. It's a 2006 dark blue Chrysler sedan."

"Oh my God, J.T. You know what that means?"

"Yeah, it's a setup to draw you in, and Ed is holding Pam hostage."

"What the hell am I supposed to do? He's going to get suspicious if I don't show up in the next few minutes."

"We're on our way."

"J.T., it'll take you a half hour. I have to come up with an excuse now."

"Call Pam back and tell her something he can't check himself. Say you had a flat tire and had to change it. You'll be there in twenty minutes. With our lights and sirens, we can get there that fast."

"Okay, but you have to go silent a few miles out. We don't want to tip him off. I'll be waiting at the kiddie park. Please hurry. I don't want him to lose his patience and take it out on her."

"We're on our way. Jade, stay put."

"I will, I promise."

I sucked in a deep breath to calm my nerves. I had to sound believable when I made the call. I was sure Ed would be listening. I wanted so badly to go in and put an end to the madness Ed had created, but I couldn't put Pam's life in jeopardy. I pressed the recent calls button next to her name, and the phone rang on her end. It was time for me to lie through my teeth. She picked up on the third ring.

"Agent Monroe, are you here?"

Now that I was listening intently, I heard the fear in her voice. "Sorry, I had a little hiccup on the way, but I should arrive in about twenty minutes. Wouldn't you know, I ran over some construction debris a few miles back, and my tire went flat." I chuckled, trying to sound lighthearted. "I just finished changing it, so I'm heading out again. I'll be there soon."

"Oh, okay. Please hurry."

The phone abruptly went dead, and I feared for Pam's life.

Chapter 53

I paced the parking lot to get rid of my increasing tension. My patience was being tested to its limit. I visualized the layout of the house. We had seen the foyer and caught a quick glance of the family room, kitchen, and dining room as we passed by on our way to the library.

I imagined the probable scenario. Pam would have to be free and appear normal as she answered the door. It was the only way Ed would be guaranteed that I'd enter. He'd be hiding somewhere, likely at my back so he could attack me from behind. I was sure I'd get the Taser again, and Pam probably would too. It was how he'd disable both of us until we were restrained. That would be the worst-case scenario, and with a quick flick of his knife, he could slit our throats before anyone had time to reach us. I had an idea that might work and would share it with the guys as soon as they arrived.

I pulled out my cell phone and checked the time—ten minutes had passed since I spoke with Pam. I was going crazy with worry. At the fifteen-minute mark, I called J.T.

"What's your ETA?"

"We're exiting the highway right now and going dark—no sirens or lights. We'll be at your location in three minutes. Hold tight, Jade."

I hung up and looked east. Soon I'd see headlights from several vehicles heading in my direction. When a car passed by as it left the neighborhood, I ducked behind the Explorer. I couldn't take any chances with curious neighbors. Finally, I saw headlights in the distance. I inhaled deeply and shook off my fears. We had a job to do, and a woman's life was at risk. It was time to get serious. Three vehicles screeched to a stop in the parking lot across from the Explorer. Hardy, J.T., Lyles, Franklin, Andrews, and Tyler jumped out of their cars and headed toward me.

"You okay, Jade?" J.T. asked.

"I'm fine. We need to plan our approach and fast. Here's what I was thinking. Pam will appear as normal as possible when she answers the door. Ed wouldn't want her to do anything to raise my suspicion. He expects me to walk in casually, and that's likely when he'll try to zap me from behind."

"So we have to blitz attack him before he nails you," J.T. said.

"I'll take the hit if I have to as long as you guys get to him quickly. Don't forget about that knife he carries. He's probably going to be watching from a window that illuminates the porch."

"Is there another way in where he won't see us?" Hardy asked.

"Nothing that would be close enough to him. That's why I think my plan will work."

J.T. raked his hair and shook his head. "I don't like this already."

I gave him a frown. "Just listen before you rule it out. I'll put on a vest under my blazer. He'll zap me when I walk in, and I'll fall to the ground. It's the only way to get him close enough to take him out. A few elbow slams to the face will knock him for a loop, and then you guys can rush him. You have to be hiding in the bushes near the door. He'll see anyone on the porch."

"You're assuming it's going to go like you've planned. What if the porch light is off?"

"So much the better."

"What if he isn't behind the door but hiding somewhere else in the house?"

I shrugged. "He won't be far from Pam, I'm sure of that, and we don't have other options at the moment. My gun has more reach than his knife." I jerked my chin. "I need a vest."

Hardy opened his trunk and grabbed one. "Be careful, Jade."

I pulled the vest over my shoulders and tightened it around my torso then situated my shoulder holster. "I will, Cap. This isn't the first time I've done this."

Hardy gave J.T. an eyebrow raise.

"Okay, I have to drive in so everything looks normal. Go ahead and start out. Once you reach the driveway, stay behind the trees. Remember, he could be watching from any window. You need to be in position when I reach the door. If the porch light is on, go with my plan to hide in the shrubbery. If it's off, you can stay out of sight on the porch."

The men took off on foot and ran until I couldn't see them any longer. I climbed into the Explorer a minute later. As I passed them at the bottom of the driveway, I gave them a thumbs-up and glanced back through the rearview mirror. They cautiously approached the house while staying in the shadows of the trees bordering the driveway.

The porch was illuminated by six brass coach lamps. I knew the plan and parked strategically to block any chance of the guys being seen as they crossed the driveway. They needed that extra barrier between the driveway and the porch in case he was watching. I approached the house slowly as I nonchalantly glanced at every window that faced the front. I remembered seeing the curtains flutter earlier that day when Missy peeked out, and they'd just fluttered again. Instinctively, I reached to my waist to activate my radio and realized I wasn't wearing one.

The guys knew what to do. I had to have faith that everyone would come out of this okay, especially Pam. I stepped up to the porch, glanced at both sidelights, and rang the doorbell. I listened closely. Did I hear two sets of footsteps, or had he already taken his place, waiting to pounce? The clip-clop of shoes approached the front door. I peered through the right sidelight, but with thick gauzelike material covering the glass, I found it difficult to see anything clearly. I quickly looked to my right as the doorknob turned. Movement in the shrubbery told me the guys were in place.

The door opened, and Pam stood on the other side. She wore a deep black mark under her right eye. "Agent Monroe, thank you for coming back." Pam looked to be forcing a smile, and her eyes darted to my left.

I took that as my clue that Ed was hiding somewhere on that side of the door. She held the door open, and I passed through. I hadn't anticipated her slamming it at my back and turning the dead bolt.

"What the—"

"I'm so sorry, Agent Monroe."

Within seconds I felt a thick arm around my neck and hot breath against my ear. "You think I was born yesterday, Agent Bitch?"

He blindsided me and came from the right. Then he pulled my service weapon out from under my blazer. He began a wicked round of laughter. "Wearing a vest, are ya? You came prepared for the Taser but not for anything else."

"Don't give me so much credit, Ed. It has nothing to do with you. I always wear a vest." I couldn't let him think I came prepared and that the team was right outside.

He pushed me out of the foyer and jerked his head at Pam. I didn't have a clue where we were going, and the guys would have to guess what to do next.

Pam cried out. "Ed, please, the kids are in the house."

"Then keep your damn mouth shut and you won't wake them up. Get in the dining room and take a seat."

I tried to remember the home's layout. Did the dining

room have windows or not? With my gun jammed against my back, Ed shoved me through the doorway. I took a quick glance at the right side of the room and breathed a quiet sigh of relief. Three windows lined that wall.

I quickly pulled out the two chairs that faced the window. "Here, Pam, sit next to me."

I watched as Ed toyed with my gun and paced. He was a ticking time bomb. The knife sheath, strapped to his belt on his right hip, was exposed. He had to be carrying a bowie knife, just as Dr. Torres told us days ago, and from handle to blade tip, I'd guess it to be a foot long. If only I could find a way to grab it.

Ed yelled out, "This isn't how I wanted things to go down!"

"Tell me what you want, Ed, and maybe I can help."

"Shut up! You don't have a say in this. It's between me and that bitch."

He waved my gun erratically at Pam. I had to calm him before something terrible happened.

"Ed, I know you're angry. Pam left you for that piece of shit, which was more than wrong. You're a much better man than William. You were jealous of him because he was rich, but he's a horrible person. William is an arrogant, boastful, lying jerk, and you want to take him down along with his business."

"Damn straight I do."

I continued on and tried to distract him from focusing on Pam. "He needs to feel that humiliation, to lose all his money, and to have the entire city scoff at him. He deserves it, but that's already taking place."

"Agent Monroe, please." Tears sprang from Pam's eyes. I knew she didn't understand what I was doing.

Ed got dangerously close to Pam. I needed him to focus on me instead. "Ed!"

"What do you want, bitch?"

"Listen to me. You don't need to do anything. William is in jail, and he'll be exposed tomorrow. Everyone will know what a lying phony he is. His career will be ruined without you doing anything to anybody. He'll be in prison for years."

"Wrong. Don't try to play me." Ed held the barrel of my gun against Pam's neck. "I heard her talking to her mom earlier, and she said William was out of town because of a business problem. Nice try, Agent Dumbshit. No matter what, this cheating bitch is going to pay too. I have nothing to lose whether I kill five people or fifty. I'll get the death sentence no matter what."

I saw movement beyond the glass. J.T., Hardy, and the rest of the team, hidden under the windowsills, had their guns aimed at Ed.

Ed's anger was escalating, and in seconds he would attack. I had to do something now.

He tucked my gun in his waistband and slid the knife out of the sheath. "I've dreamed of this day when I could finally silence you forever." He reached for Pam's throat.

I looked at J.T., gave him a nod, then lunged at Pam and knocked her to the ground. Gunfire exploded through the windows, sending shards of glass in every direction, like hundreds of knives. We dove under the table, and I held Pam close to my chest. I turned my head and saw Ed slide down the wall only feet away, his body riddled with bullet holes.

"Don't move, Pam, and keep your head down." I crawled across the floor and ripped out my gun from Ed's waistband. I removed the knife from his clenched hand then checked his pulse—he was dead. I stood, looked out the window, and gave the guys a nod.

"Pam, it's safe to come out." I knelt at the table's edge and called her toward me. She didn't need to look at her former husband's bloody body. She crawled to me and stood. I quickly got her out of that room and closed the door behind us. "Why don't you check on your kids? I have to let my colleagues in."

I inhaled a deep breath and walked to the front door. J.T., Hardy, and the guys were waiting on the porch. When they entered the foyer, I gave them a welcoming hug.

"Are you and Pam okay?" J.T. asked.

"Yeah, we're good. It looks like she got punched in the face before I arrived, though." I closed my eyes for a second to take in everything that had transpired over the last twenty minutes, then I tipped my chin toward the back of the house. "She went upstairs to check on her kids." I gave J.T. a long grateful look. "Thanks, partner. I knew I could depend on you."

He squeezed my shoulder and smiled. "No sweat. That's what partners do."

Hardy directed his men to get busy. "Get on the horn

and call the ME. We probably need a medic here too, and get Forensics out here even though the SEC will be rifling through this place tomorrow. We have to do everything by the book."

Pam joined us in the kitchen ten minutes later. "The kids were awake in their beds. I got them calmed down enough to fall back asleep."

"I'd suggest taking them out of here tonight. This house is a crime scene, and the SEC will seal it tomorrow, anyway. Do you have somewhere to go?" I asked.

Pam gently dabbed her swollen red eyes and nodded. "We'll go to my mom's house." She reached for me and held me tightly. "You saved my life, Agent Monroe. I can never thank you enough."

My own eyes welled up with emotion. "Everything will be okay in time. We need to sit down and talk, though, before this place is teeming with people."

Chapter 54

Pam and I escaped to the quiet solitude of a spare bedroom on the far side of the second story. We sat across from each other on the bed, and I pulled out my notepad from my purse.

"I know this seems unusually formal, but I have to know why Ed went off the deep end. There will be plenty of paperwork to fill out before my partner and I leave Omaha."

"I understand, Agent Monroe."

I gave her a thoughtful smile—she had been through a lot. "You can call me Jade."

"Like I told you this afternoon, Jade"—she gave me a quick glance—"Ed and I divorced a few years back. As long as I had known him, he was kind of off, but stupid me thought of it as edgy and sort of wild. I had no idea he was mentally sick. After years of marriage, I began seeking out something else."

"Or do you mean *someone* else?"

She nodded and wiped her battered eye. "Ed quit work, and we were barely getting by. His mood swings became more frequent. He was seeing a therapist who put him on strong meds for his behavioral problems. After seven years together, I was just tired of him. I thought a divorce would end our bitter relationship, but that only caused things to get worse. The courts ruled in my favor, and I got full custody of the kids. That's when Ed moved back to Little Rock. I had no idea he returned to Omaha."

I set my pen on my notepad. "Pam, Ed has been here for some time. It doesn't sound like you watch TV much, and to be honest, there hasn't been news coverage on this case. We squelched what we reported to the media because they would have turned this city into a panic zone. There was news of a serial killer in Omaha, and that's why my partner and I showed up last Thursday. That serial killer was Ed."

Pam sobbed into her hands. "It's all my fault. He should have been committed years ago."

"Why was Ed so angry? It sounds like it began before you met William."

"It did, but the cheating and divorce made everything worse. Ed grew up in an abusive home and not what you might think."

I nodded. "Go on."

"It was his mother who was abusive, and her violence was taken out on his dad. She swore at him constantly, punched him, and threw things at him—it was nonstop. The woman was psychotic, and the police were often at their house because of domestic abuse. Then one day the father up and disappeared. From that point on, Ed was alone with the mom, suffering her verbal and physical abuse. She told him his no-good father left them and all men were trash. Ed felt worthless, and I believe it was at that point that he actually became somewhat misogynistic. Two weeks later, as he was walking near the creek at the far side of their property, he noticed a foul smell."

I groaned, knowing full well where that story was going. "He found his dad?"

"Yes, and it was during the summer. Ed could tell it was a human body even though it had decayed beyond recognition. The one thing he never got over was seeing the knife protruding from the man's throat."

"Oh my God. So his hatred all these years was actually toward his mom, not you?"

"For most of his life it was her. His mom went to prison, and Ed grew up in foster care. He resented everyone from that point on, so I was surprised when he wanted to get married. I believe our eventual divorce, and the fact that I was awarded full custody of the children, sent him over the edge and rekindled his hatred toward women. Recently, his phone calls became even more threatening. I think the fact that William had just legally adopted the kids sent Ed into a full-blown tailspin. That could have been the final trigger."

I patted Pam's hand. "Ed was delusional. Maybe he thought by ruining William's reputation and bankrupting him, he would somehow regain custody of the children. Truth is, Ed could have sat back and watched William ruin himself."

"But—"

"But that's the way it is, Pam. I doubt if William, his high-powered attorney, and all the money in the world will get him out of this jam. Greed got the best of him. You and the kids will be on your own for quite some time." I tipped my head toward the door and put my notepad away. "Come on. You need to pack some things. I'll help you get the kids ready."

Chapter 55

We spent the next morning tying up loose ends. Hardy's team, along with J.T. and myself, filled out pages of paperwork that went back to the first murder we knew was related to the case—Sarah Cummings. I contacted the ME's office and told Joe that he could release the victims' bodies to their respective families. We canceled the tip line, and I drew up a statement that Hardy could give to the media.

I excused myself from the conference room and took a trip downstairs to the city jail before the SEC arrived. I signed in at the counter and asked to see William Stewart. I waited only a few minutes before the guard escorted me in.

I knew William had to be worried. Today was the day he'd have to confess his sins to the authorities. There wasn't enough bravado in the world that he could muster up to get him out of the predicament he alone had caused. The SEC would come down on him hard, and he probably wouldn't see the light of day for years.

I entered the room where he sat alone. He looked up when I walked in yet held his tongue.

"William." I took a seat across from him.

"Agent Monroe. And to what do I owe the pleasure?"

"I have to tell you a few things before the authorities arrive."

"So you aren't the authority?"

I smiled. "Not that particular kind. I don't know how soon you'll be allowed to speak with Pam, so I'm here to tell you about last night."

"Last night? What happened last night?"

"Ed broke into your house. He was the Scenic View Serial Killer."

"Jesus Christ. Is Pam okay? I have to see her."

"That isn't going to happen, William, and it's time for you to face reality. Pam is fine, and she's at her mom's house with the kids."

He let out a long sigh.

"Ed is gone, as in dead. He was taken down by law enforcement as he was about to kill Pam. She's a total wreck, though, and you know the SEC is going to freeze all of your assets. Does she have anything in her name alone?"

"I don't know, I can't think. Will the SEC seize my other holdings?"

I nodded. "It's likely they will. What does Wipast Holdings stand for?"

"It's a combination of my name and Pam's. Two letters from William, two letters from Pam, and two letters from Stewart. It's just an acronym, nothing sneaky about it."

"Understood." I wrote that down.

"Pam has a key on her key ring. It goes to a safe deposit

box at our local bank. She has no idea what it's for. Tell her the box number is 43. Please, that's all you have to do."

"If it isn't in her name, I doubt they'd let her gain access to it."

"It's in the kids' names. I was saving it until they were older, but they need it now. Pam just has to show Lucas and Missy's Social Security cards to access it. Please, Agent Monroe. You won't be doing anything illegal. They can't take things that belong to the children. My name isn't on it."

"I'll see what I can do." I pushed back my chair to leave.

"Agent Monroe?"

"Yes?"

"Thank you." William stood and stuck out his hand. "You really aren't a bitch. It was me all along being the typical jerk I am."

I smiled and shook his hand. "Good luck, Mr. Stewart." I walked out and returned to the conference room.

J.T. glanced up when I entered. "I think we're about done here, Jade. Our reports are complete, and everything is checked off our to-do list."

"Give me just a few minutes. I'll be right back."

"Sure thing, partner. Is everything okay?"

"Yep, no problems." I stepped out into the hallway and found a quiet area. I needed to make one more phone call.

A half hour later, J.T. and I were saying goodbye to Omaha's finest. Under different conditions, I could easily see these men being close friends. A few snickers and jabs got the group going. I offered to buy everyone a beer, but they refused since they were all on duty.

I chuckled. "Why do you think I offered?"

J.T. and I gave our usual round of hugs, shoulder punches, and handshakes then headed out to the parking lot. We'd check out of our barely used hotel rooms and drive to the airport. I made the call to Spelling and told him to expect us that afternoon.

"There is one thing I'll miss about Omaha." J.T. climbed in behind the steering wheel and turned the key in the ignition.

"Yeah, are you going to tell me or just sit there with a stupid grin on your face?"

He patted the dash. "I'll miss the Explorer. This beast was one fine ride, that's for sure."

"Yeah, I guess it was okay. Kind of a manly vehicle, wouldn't you say? Personally, I'm more of a speed freak."

"Right, like I didn't know that." He gave me a suspicious grin. "You've never gotten a speeding ticket?"

"Nope. I can outrun the cops."

We both laughed.

"You're nuts, Monroe."

"Yes I am, so remind me to get a Snickers bar after a while."

Forty-five minutes later we boarded the jet back to Milwaukee, and quickly took to the sky. I watched J.T. as he leaned back his seat and stared out the window.

"I'm sorry there wasn't time to visit Curt's brother."

"Yeah, me too, but maybe next time. I'm sure we'll be sent here again." J.T. turned his head toward me. "I'll call him when we get back and see how he's doing."

"That would be nice." I reclined my seat and closed my eyes. Hopefully, J.T. was respectful enough not to take pictures of me while I slept. Amber and I had entire albums in our cell phones dedicated to blackmail pictures of each other. Sometime when he wasn't watching, I'd check his cell phone to make sure.

"Jade."

I felt a push against my shoulder. "What? I was having a perfectly good dream, thanks."

"We're going to be in Milwaukee in ten minutes. I thought you might want to wake up and splash some water on your face before we land."

I smiled. "Thanks, dude. Good idea, especially since I'm the one driving us to the office."

We landed at two thirty and waited for the steps to be secured to the aircraft. I gathered my briefcase and purse, and J.T. slung our go bags over his shoulders. We exited the plane on the tarmac and walked to my Mustang.

J.T. groaned when he climbed in. "Damn, I didn't realize how comfortable that Explorer was until now."

"Get used to it, mister. Your Camaro isn't any better."

"Yeah, I know."

It took a half hour to get to our office in Glendale. I was glad to be back, and I hoped we'd be able to keep our feet on the ground for at least another week. I missed my sister and our pets. I pulled around to the back where our parking lot was.

"Aw, there's that beautiful hot rod Camaro of yours. Haven't you ever named her?"

"Yeah, but I shouldn't use those kind of words."

I laughed and killed the engine. We climbed out of my car, and I grabbed my briefcase from the trunk. J.T. grabbed his go bag. I tipped my head to the third vehicle beyond J.T.'s car. "Check it out. Somebody is about to piss you off."

J.T. popped his trunk and threw his go bag inside. He peered around the other cars. "Damn, I wonder who that belongs to. This car is killing me."

I shrugged. "Come on. Let's go inside."

J.T. swiped his card, and the door lock clicked. We walked through, and he headed to our shared office.

"I'll be right there." I stopped at the front counter and pocketed what Diane had just handed me. "No problems?"

"Nope. They said they'd call you tomorrow."

I gave her a wink and thanked her then headed to my office.

J.T. sat at his desk and went over the last four days with Spelling, who was leaning against the doorframe.

"Welcome back, Jade."

"Thanks, boss. That was quite an intense case. Unfortunately, nobody came out a winner."

J.T. interrupted. "Not to change the subject, but who does that new Explorer in the lot belong to?"

Spelling shrugged. Maria, Cam, and Val walked in and grinned. Diane peeked around the door.

"What the hell is going on?" J.T. looked at me, his face glowing red.

I dipped my hand in my pocket and pulled out a set of keys. "Here you go, partner. It's yours. You have forty-eight hours to decide if you want it. The dealership promised to give you top dollar on the Camaro as a trade-in."

"You can't be serious."

"I'm as serious as a heart attack, which I'll have if you aren't driving something that's comfortable for you. The Corolla is gone, the Camaro will be soon enough, and you, J.T. Harper, deserve to drive something you really want. I won't even give you shit about it."

"How? When? Is that why you mysteriously walked away to make a call this morning?"

I mimicked zipping my mouth closed. "My lips are sealed."

J.T. leapt from his desk. "Like I said earlier, you're nuts, Monroe. Come on. Let's check it out!"

I shook my head as I followed J.T. outside. "Men— they're just like kids."

THE END

Thank you for reading *Malice*, the last book in the Agent Jade Monroe FBI Thriller Series. I hope you enjoyed it! Keep your eyes open for my new series coming out soon!

Follow the complete Jade Monroe saga starting with the **Detective Jade Monroe Crime Thriller Series**. The books are listed in order below:

Maniacal
Captive
Fallacy
Premonition
Exposed

The Agent Jade Monroe FBI Thriller Series follows on the heels of *Exposed*, Book 5 in the Detective Jade Monroe Crime Thriller Series. Currently available books are listed in order below:

Snapped
Justified
Donors
Leverage

Stay abreast of my new releases by signing up for my VIP email list at: http://cmsutter.com/newsletter/

You'll be one of the first to get a glimpse of the cover reveals and release dates, and you'll have a chance at exciting raffles and freebies offered throughout the series.

Posting a review will help other readers find my books. I appreciate every review, whether positive or negative, and if you have a second to spare, a review is truly appreciated.

Again, thank you for reading!

Visit my author website at: http://cmsutter.com/

See all of my available titles at:
http://cmsutter.com/available-books/

Made in the USA
Monee, IL
05 May 2022

95933814R00194